SWEPT AWAY

Acclaim for Radclyffe's Fiction

"Medical drama, gossipy lesbian romance, and angsty backstory all get equal time in [***Unrivaled***,] Radclyffe's fifth PMC Hospital Romance…[F]ans of small community dynamics and workplace romance without ethical complications will find this hits the spot."—*Publishers Weekly*

"***Dangerous Waters*** is a bumpy ride through a devastating time with powerful events and resolute characters. Radclyffe gives us the strong, dedicated women we love to read in a story that keeps us turning pages until the end."—*Lambda Literary Review*

"Radclyffe's ***Dangerous Waters*** has the feel of a tense television drama, as the narrative interchanges between hurricane trackers and first responders. Sawyer and Dara butt heads in the beginning as each moves for some level of control during the storm's approach, and the interference of a lovely television reporter adds an engaging love triangle threat to the sexual tension brewing between them."—*RT Book Reviews*

"***Love After Hours***, the fourth in Radclyffe's Rivers Community series, evokes the sense of a continuing drama as Gina and Carrie's slow-burning romance intertwines with details of other Rivers residents. They become part of a greater picture where friends and family support each other in personal and recreational endeavors. Vivid settings and characters draw in the reader…"
—*RT Book Reviews*

Secret Hearts "delivers exactly what it says on the tin: poignant story, sweet romance, great characters, chemistry and hot sex scenes. Radclyffe knows how to pen a good lesbian romance."
—*LezReviewBooks Blog*

Wild Shores "will hook you early. Radclyffe weaves a chance encounter into all-out steamy romance. These strong, dynamic women have great conversations, and fantastic chemistry."
—*The Romantic Reader Blog*

In **2016 RWA/OCC Book Buyers Best award winner for suspense and mystery with romantic elements *Price of Honor*** "Radclyffe is master of the action-thriller series...The old familiar characters are there, but enough new blood is introduced to give it a fresh feel and open new avenues for intrigue."—*Curve Magazine*

In ***Prescription for Love*** "Radclyffe populates her small town with colorful characters, among the most memorable being Flann's little sister, Margie, and Abby's 15-year-old trans son, Blake...This romantic drama has plenty of heart and soul." —*Publishers Weekly*

2013 RWA/New England Bean Pot award winner for contemporary romance *Crossroads* "will draw the reader in and make her heart ache, willing the two main characters to find love and a life together. It's a story that lingers long after coming to 'the end.'"—*Lambda Literary*

In **2012 RWA/FTHRW Lories and RWA HODRW Aspen Gold award winner *Firestorm*** "Radclyffe brings another hot lesbian romance for her readers."—*The Lesbrary*

Foreword Review Book of the Year finalist and IPPY silver medalist *Trauma Alert* "is hard to put down and it will sizzle in the reader's hands. The characters are hot, the sex scenes explicit and explosive, and the book is moved along by an interesting plot with well drawn secondary characters. The real star of this show is the attraction between the two characters, both of whom resist and then fall head over heels."—*Lambda Literary Reviews*

Lambda Literary Award Finalist *Best Lesbian Romance 2010* features "stories [that] are diverse in tone, style, and subject, making for more variety than in many, similar anthologies... well written, each containing a satisfying, surprising twist. Best Lesbian Romance series editor Radclyffe has assembled a respectable crop of 17 authors for this year's offering."—*Curve Magazine*

2010 Prism award winner and ForeWord Review Book of the Year Award finalist *Secrets in the Stone* is "so powerfully [written] that the worlds of these three women shimmer between reality and dreams…A strong, must read novel that will linger in the minds of readers long after the last page is turned."—*Just About Write*

In **Benjamin Franklin Award finalist *Desire by Starlight*** "Radclyffe writes romance with such heart and her down-to-earth characters not only come to life but leap off the page until you feel like you know them. What Jenna and Gard feel for each other is not only a spark but an inferno and, as a reader, you will be washed away in this tumultuous romance until you can do nothing but succumb to it."—*Queer Magazine Online*

Lambda Literary Award winner *Distant Shores, Silent Thunder* "weaves an intricate tapestry about passion and commitment between lovers. The story explores the fragile nature of trust and the sanctuary provided by loving relationships." —*Sapphic Reader*

Lambda Literary Award winner *Stolen Moments* "is a collection of steamy stories about women who just couldn't wait. It's sex when desire overrides reason, and it's incredibly hot!" —*On Our Backs*

Lambda Literary Award Finalist *Justice Served* delivers a "crisply written, fast-paced story with twists and turns and keeps us guessing until the final explosive ending."—*Independent Gay Writer*

Lambda Literary Award finalist *Turn Back Time* "is filled with wonderful love scenes, which are both tender and hot." —*MegaScene*

Applause for L.L. Raand's Midnight Hunters Series

The Midnight Hunt
RWA 2012 VCRW Laurel Wreath winner *Blood Hunt*
Night Hunt
The Lone Hunt

"Raand has built a complex world inhabited by werewolves, vampires, and other paranormal beings...Raand has given her readers a complex plot filled with wonderful characters as well as insight into the hierarchy of Sylvan's pack and vampire clans. There are many plot twists and turns, as well as erotic sex scenes in this riveting novel that keep the pages flying until its satisfying conclusion."—*Just About Write*

"Once again, I am amazed at the storytelling ability of L.L. Raand aka Radclyffe. In *Blood Hunt*, she mixes high levels of sheer eroticism that will leave you squirming in your seat with an impeccable multi-character storyline all streaming together to form one great read."—*Queer Magazine Online*

"Are you sick of the same old hetero vampire/werewolf story plastered in every bookstore and at every movie theater? Well, I've got the cure to your werewolf fever. *The Midnight Hunt* is first in, what I hope is, a long-running series of fantasy erotica for L.L. Raand (aka Radclyffe)."—*Queer Magazine Online*

By Radclyffe

Romances

Innocent Hearts
Promising Hearts
Love's Melody Lost
Love's Tender Warriors
Tomorrow's Promise
Love's Masquerade
shadowland
Turn Back Time
When Dreams Tremble
The Lonely Hearts Club
Secrets in the Stone
Desire by Starlight
Homestead
The Color of Love
Secret Hearts
Only This Summer

First Responders Novels

Trauma Alert
Firestorm
Taking Fire
Wild Shores
Heart Stop
Dangerous Waters
Fearless Hearts
Swept Away

Red Sky Ranch Novels (With Julie Cannon)

Fire in the Sky
Wild Fire

Honor Series

Above All, Honor
Honor Bound
Love & Honor
Honor Guards
Honor Reclaimed
Honor Under Siege
Word of Honor
Oath of Honor
(First Responders)
Code of Honor
Price of Honor
Cost of Honor

Justice Series

A Matter of Trust (prequel)
Shield of Justice
In Pursuit of Justice
Justice in the Shadows
Justice Served
Justice for All

PMC Hospitals Romances

Passion's Bright Fury (prequel)
Fated Love
Night Call
Crossroads
Passionate Rivals
Unrivaled
Perfect Rivalry

The Provincetown Tales

Safe Harbor
Beyond the Breakwater
Distant Shores, Silent Thunder
Storms of Change
Winds of Fortune
Returning Tides
Sheltering Dunes
Treacherous Seas

Rivers Community Romances

Against Doctor's Orders
Prescription for Love
Love on Call
Love After Hours
Love to the Rescue
Love on the Night Shift
Pathway to Love
Finders Keepers

Short Fiction

Collected Stories by Radclyffe

Erotic Interludes: *Change Of Pace*

Radical Encounters

Stacia Seaman and Radclyffe, eds.:

Erotic Interludes Vol. 2–5

Romantic Interludes Vol. 1–2

Breathless: *Tales of Celebration*

Women of the Dark Streets

Amor and More: Love Everafter

Myth & Magic: Queer Fairy Tales

Writing As L.L. Raand

Midnight Hunters

The Midnight Hunt
Blood Hunt
Night Hunt
The Lone Hunt
The Magic Hunt
Shadow Hunt
Rogue Hunt
Enchanted Hunt
Primal Hunt

SWEPT AWAY

by

RADCLYfFE

2026

SWEPT AWAY

ISBN 13: 979-8-90035-050-9

This Trade Paperback Original Is Published By
Bold Strokes Books, Inc.
P.O. Box 249
Valley Falls, NY 12185

First Edition: March 2026

Credits
Editor: Stacia Seaman
Production Design: Stacia Seaman
Cover Design by Inkspiral Design

Acknowledgments

In these changing times, I am eternally grateful to the readers who have followed me for the last two decades and supported BSB's authors. I am just as grateful and excited to welcome our new readers and hope you enjoy my books, old and new. Without all of you, authors and publishers will no longer exist, and the power and beauty of our community will be diminished. Thanks also to Stacia Seaman for taking such good care of my words, and Sandy for endless support and encouragement.

Radclyffe

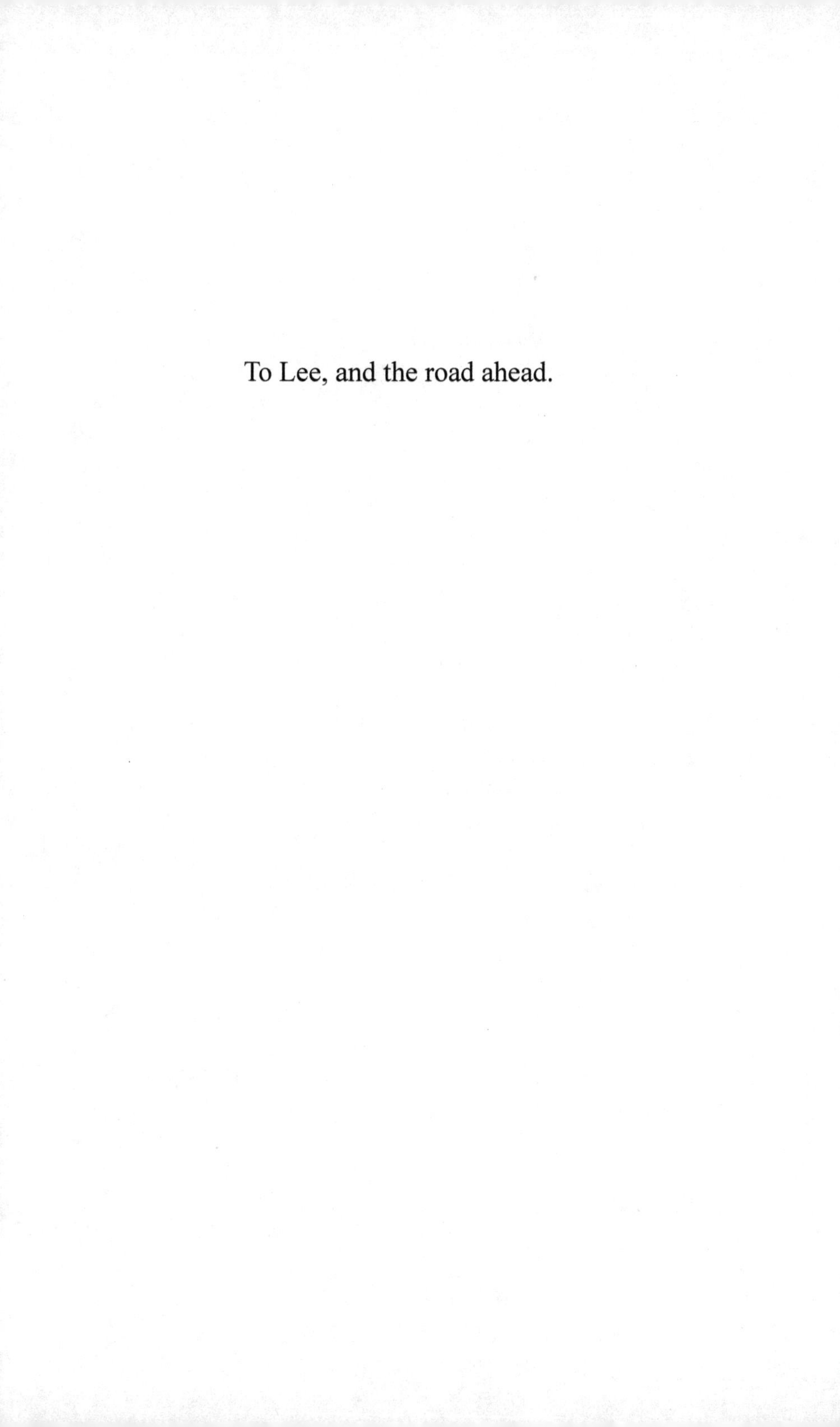

To Lee, and the road ahead.

Chapter One

Boston
April

Sloane Marshall stepped through the automatic doors of Mercy General's emergency department at 6:23 a.m. without breaking stride, steaming coffee mug in one hand, phone buzzing with a page from the ER charge nurse in the other. A gust of April rain and diesel exhaust from an idling ambulance rolled in behind her like a tardy friend.

Three gurneys, all holding patients watched over by EMTs waiting to hand off, lined the hall just inside. The waiting area, TV blaring, babies crying, full as usual. She hit the automatic door panel and entered the combat zone—residents in rumpled scrubs hurried between the central desk and the semicircle of enclosed cubicles, transport pushed patients in wheelchairs to and from the elevators, and everywhere, the noise. Beeping monitors, screaming patients, staff calling for an assist, a suture tray, a second opinion on an X-ray. The big board in the center of it all tallied those being seen, to be seen, and waiting for beds.

"Glad you're here." Keisha handed her a tablet with a patient's chart already open. "Stein needs a little help in cubicle three. We've got a GSW coming in, ETA six minutes."

"Bay two ready for the GSW?" Sloane glanced at the chart, already moving toward Stein's room. *Jose Juarez, soft tissue trauma, left forearm. Age 36, no known medical problems.*

"All neat and shiny. Trauma team's standing by." Keisha's tone held the easy camaraderie of their years working together.

"Thanks. I've got this one, then." Sloane pushed through the curtain where Ari Stein, still fresh-faced and eager ten months into his first year, sat over the arm board staring at the open wound like it might bite him. After pulling on a sterile gown, mask, and gloves, Sloane dragged a stool over with one foot and sat down opposite Ari. "What have we got?"

"Crush injury. No fractures, neuro intact," Ari said, his forehead above his mask beaded with sweat.

Jose Juarez shifted on the stretcher, craning his neck to peer over the sterile green drape covering his arm. "How soon can I get back to work, Doctor?"

"About fifteen minutes sooner if you stop moving around up there," Sloane said lightly. She leaned over to examine the jagged eight-inch wound, and her shoulder brushed Ari's. She eased away from the casual contact. "Okay—keep going."

Ari slowly placed an absorbable suture in the muscle and tied it.

"Cut that with a tail," Sloane murmured.

Ari snipped the suture, his hands trembling slightly.

"Just loosely approximate the rest of the wound." Aware the patient was listening, Sloane kept her tone neutral and businesslike. "It's going to swell. Simple sutures. Don't squeeze the tissue with the forceps."

"I got it," he muttered, hunching over to place the next suture.

Sloane watched another minute to be sure he did. Outside the cubicle, the ER hummed with the usual symphony of beeps, rattling gurneys, and staff calling to one another for equipment or a lab report. Familiar, comfortable, and comforting. The level one trauma center was her happy place, where split-second decisions meant the difference between life and death, her skills mattered in measurable ways, and emotion was a luxury that could cost lives.

Ari started on the skin. Clean edges, good approximation. Mangled tissue salvaged. This man would work again.

"You're good there," she said to Ari. "Send him home on p.o. antibiotics."

She pushed her stool away from the treatment table, stood, and stripped off her paper gown along with mask and gloves. She tossed them into the red contaminated trash receptacle and arched her back to loosen the cramped muscles on her way to the head of the table. Jose Juarez, a thin man in dusty work pants and a faded green cotton shirt, turned questioning eyes toward her.

"How's it look?" he asked.

"Dr. Stein is almost done, Mr. Juarez," she said. "Everything came together nicely. Dr. Stein will put you in a light splint that you'll need to keep on for a week. You'll get follow-up instructions when you leave."

His dark eyes reflected more worry than pain. "What about work?"

"That will depend on the practitioner monitoring the wound healing, but no major structures were damaged. Six to eight weeks is a good estimate. Your workmen's comp insurance should cover the period you're out of work."

He turned his face away, swallowing visibly. "Thank you."

Sloane frowned. "Do you need assistance with paperwork for your employer?"

He shook his head, still not meeting her gaze. Sloane mentally cursed. He either wasn't employed by anyone carrying insurance, or he was undocumented. Possibly both. Either instance meant he might not get the medical follow-up he needed. "Before you leave, we'll give you the number for the surgical clinic. You can see the residents there for follow-up."

"Okay," he said softly.

"Mr. Juarez?" Sloane waited until he looked up at her. "You have to go. The insurance won't be an issue. Are we good?"

"Yes." He took a deep breath. "I will. Thank you."

"No thanks needed," Sloane said gently, embarrassed by gratitude when she was simply doing her job, the one thing she truly loved. Work that mattered, work that filled the spaces in her life with purpose and meaning.

A flurry of voices and rolling carts signaled the trauma resuscitation in two was well underway, so she headed for the intake desk for the chart of the next patient to be seen. As she reached for the tablet, her phone chimed with a call from the chief of the department.

"This is Marshall," she said, pausing in the hallway.

"Sloane," David Jerome said, "sorry for calling during your shift, but the director of Health Resources and Services Administration just called me about a replacement for Kyle Remky."

Sloane frowned. Kyle, a senior attending in the ER, had just had an emergency gallbladder resection and would be out for two months. "I'm not tracking. Replacement for what?"

"Kyle was scheduled to head up a rural outreach mission in North Carolina, but that's obviously not happening. We need to provide a replacement."

Rural outreach. Doctors pulled from trauma centers where

minutes meant the difference between life and death. Sent to—where? A mountain clinic somewhere?

"We'll be pretty thin on staff down here with Kyle out," Sloane said, "but I'm sure we can find someone to fill in."

David didn't answer for a long moment. "It seems that person will be you."

"What?" Sloane's stomach dropped.

"It's only for a few weeks."

Weeks. Her chest tightened. Weeks away from the ER, away from her ordered life, working with strangers in conditions she couldn't control.

"How *many* weeks exactly?"

"Depending on the conditions you find when you get there, four to six. It's a place called Coulter's Gap in northern North Carolina. I gather it's pretty remote. Not a lot of access to medical care."

"I'm not a family medicine specialist. Wouldn't that—"

"There will be team members to assist there, but part of the mission is to train local EMTs or whoever else has any kind of medical training to triage and treat acute injuries and medical emergencies. That's in your job description."

"Come on, David. This would be a great opportunity for a young attending or even one of our senior ER residents to—"

"I suggested that," he said, "but the hospital gets a healthy grant for assisting in these outreach programs, and the director was firm this wasn't a training situation. The administration calls the shots."

"I'm hardly qualified in rural—"

"You've credentialed in field response and treatment. You're it, Sloane. Sorry."

Sloane bit back another argument. The finality in his voice was clear.

"When and where do I go?"

"They want you at the federal building in Asheville for a briefing at eight a.m. the day after tomorrow. They'll email you the flight arrangements."

"I see." Sloane fought the cold anger spreading through her. She'd manage. She'd faced much worse upheavals in her life. "Then I guess I'm going."

"Good luck." He laughed. "Hey, maybe it will be fun."

The line went dead. Sloane stood in the trauma bay corridor, surrounded by the familiar sounds of emergency medicine while the familiar hollow opened in her chest, the one that appeared whenever control slipped from her grasp. She'd built her life on predictability: twelve-hour shifts—often in a row, evidence-based protocols, professional distance. Even her apartment was ruthlessly organized—everything where she could count on finding it. Minimal embellishments. No photographs except the one she kept face-down in a drawer.

She caught her reflection in the trauma bay doors. Outwardly calm and composed. No one would guess she was already calculating ways to maintain distance from whoever these strangers would be. Distance was survival. She'd learned that at twelve, refined it through medical school, perfected it in residency.

Four to six weeks. She could maintain her walls that long.

"Sloane?" Dr. Jennifer Walsh slowed on her path to the conference room for change of shift. "Everything okay?"

Sloane forced a smile. "Well, I'm being sent to rural North Carolina for a month or so."

"Ouch. When?"

"Two days."

"That's brutal timing. But hey, might be good for you—get out of Boston, meet new people, remember there's life outside this hospital."

Meet new people. Jennifer meant it kindly, but the idea upped the uneasiness seeping through her. New people meant unpredictable interactions, emotional complications that could disrupt the careful equilibrium she'd created in her life. Better to work with familiar colleagues whose behavior she could anticipate, where professional relationships stayed within manageable boundaries. Work was safe. Work was controllable. Work didn't require the kind of emotional investment that made people vulnerable to loss they couldn't predict or prevent.

"I should get to this patient," she said, indicating the chart in her hand.

Jennifer smiled, sunny and bright. "Oh, sure. Well, try to enjoy it. Should be a nice break from this place."

A break? Hardly what she wanted.

"See you in a month," Sloane said, turning away. A month wasn't all that long. She could handle a temporary disruption in her life. Medicine was medicine. She'd just focus on that, rather than worry about working with strangers or what they might expect of her. Even if the idea of unpredictable situations in unfamiliar settings made her stomach twist in ways that had nothing to do with medicine and everything to do with the threat to her carefully constructed existence.

❖

Maui

Jax Kincaid stood on the hotel balcony in yesterday's jeans, coffee mug in hand. Early-morning surfers navigated the big Pacific curls with the effortless ease of people who'd found their element. She might have envied them once, when even her stint in the Army hadn't given her that sense of rightness. She'd found that comfort zone now, though, with AERIS and work that saved lives rather than taking them. Even if *belonging* remained an elusive feeling.

Behind her, Claire stirred awake with the soft sounds of someone emerging from sleep induced by excellent wine and even better sex. Jax smiled at the memory of a mutually satisfying and uncomplicated evening. They'd met at the hotel bar—Detective Claire Sasaki vacationing from Honolulu PD, Jax on R&R between deployments. Their chemistry had been immediate and their goals compatible. A little time for conversation, light and not too personal, an impromptu meal, a shared bottle of wine, and a night of casual pleasure.

The perfect arrangement for people whose work required constant movement and left no room for relationships that demanded geographic stability or emotional investment beyond the immediate moment. No expectations, no promises, no complications when duty schedules changed without warning. She'd gotten good at making sure she didn't invite anything more than that after Rodriguez's blood pooled in her bird. She didn't get close. Close meant loss. Close meant someone else's blood on her hands.

Temporary was safe. Temporary couldn't gut you when it ended.

Claire appeared beside her wrapped in the hotel terry cloth robe, sleep-mussed and unhurried. "You're up early."

"Military habit," Jax said, sliding out of the past. "Internal clock doesn't recognize vacation mode."

"Sleep well?"

"Better than I have in months." And she meant it. Physical intimacy without emotional complications, connection that satisfied immediate needs without creating obligations she couldn't fulfill, was all she looked for on the rare breaks between missions.

Claire moved closer, close enough for Jax to catch the scent of expensive shampoo and skin warmed by morning sunlight. “Funny, me too.”

Jax grinned. “We have that in common.”

“We have plenty of that.” Claire, near Jax’s height of five ten, leaned against her shoulder and kissed her. “Plans for today?”

Jax circled her waist lightly. “No plans. I’ve still got three days of R&R.”

“And then where?” Claire took Jax’s coffee cup and sipped with a familiarity that had Jax laughing.

“What?” Claire asked, one brow arched.

“Next thing you know, you’ll be wearing my T-shirt.”

Claire’s eyes sparkled, and she grinned. “You wish.” She sighed. “Something tells me neither of us are made for that kind of thing.”

“Regrets?” Jax asked, unexpectedly curious.

“No. I wouldn’t recognize myself without the badge. You?”

Jax shook her head. “I was born to fly—just didn’t know it right away. AERIS lets me do more than just fly—I like never knowing where I’m going next, what’s waiting down the road.”

“Mmm. Kind of like catching a new case,” Claire said. “AERIS—that’s like FEMA, right? Disaster recovery?”

“Similar,” Jax said. “Airborne Emergency Response & Infrastructure Support is actually part of the Public Health Service. We provide medical services and disaster relief training as well as evacuation and recovery.”

“Big canvas,” Claire said.

“Never gets boring,” Jax replied.

“You know what else never gets boring,” Claire said, threading her arms around Jax’s neck.

Jax kissed her. “I can guess. Want breakfast first?”

“I’d rather work up an appetite.”

Jax took her hand. “That sounds like a plan.”

As Jax slid the balcony doors closed behind them, her phone sounded the particular pattern that meant AERIS dispatch. She wasn’t surprised. AERIS responded anywhere in the continental US, and disasters rarely went on vacation.

“Sorry, gotta take this.” She walked back outside. “Kincaid.”

“Hey, Jax, it’s Bean. Sorry to interrupt paradise, but we’ve got deployment changes.”

“What’s the situation?”

Wes “Bean” Binyama was her team’s crew chief and closest thing to family she had in civilian life. He was also the only person she’d told where she planned to spend her R&R. A getaway she suspected was about to get cut short. She might not get all the rest and recovery she needed, but she wouldn’t get restless either, Claire’s company notwithstanding.

“A rural outreach mission in North Carolina is getting moved up on the calendar. NOAA predicts flood season to start early, and AERIS wants a team in and out before that.”

North Carolina. Terrain she’d flown before, conditions that required navigation skills that came from years of emergency response experience. Not the most challenging assignment she’d handled but work that mattered in ways that made shortened vacations acceptable.

“Duration?” She leaned on the balcony railing, following the progress of the surfers on the big waves.

“Four to six weeks initially, extending as conditions require. Looks like a combo gig—on-the-ground medical care, plus emergency evacuation and disaster preparedness training.”

“Who do we have on the team?” A dual-pronged mission often meant team members with different objectives and disparate skills. Not always a recipe for smooth skies.

“Eli is coordinating. All I got on the medical lead is she’s a first-timer.”

Jax grimaced. An inexperienced team leader on an outreach mission where conditions were never predictable? “Who thought that was a good call?”

Bean snorted. “Way above my pay grade. Can you get to Asheville by 0800 day after tomorrow?”

Jax glanced into the room where Claire, already dressed, gathered her things. She had enough seniority to decline the assignment, especially given she was officially on leave. But if she stayed, no matter how pleasant Claire’s company, she’d be restless in another day, wishing she could be in the air. A duty call made ending her brief interlude with Claire simpler, too. “I’ll get a flight today.”

“You want I should ask the boss to arrange your flights?”

“Nah, I’ll handle it.”

“Outstanding. I’ll let you know what I hear.”

“Roger that.” Jax tucked the phone away and joined Claire inside.

“So, I have a feeling this is goodbye,” Claire said easily, her tone suggesting schedule changes that took priority over personal plans were nothing new.

"What gave it away?"

"Body language. As soon as you took the call, I recognized the alert."

"I'm sorry about the no notice."

Claire shook her head and kissed her, a swift easy kiss. "No worries. It could have just as easily been me."

Jax walked her to the door. "Be careful out there."

"You too."

And then she was gone. No phone numbers exchanged, no *look me up next time you're out this way.* Just unspoken acknowledgment that they'd enjoyed each other's company without expectation of anything else. Exactly the kind of interaction that had defined her personal life since leaving the Army—temporary connections that provided companionship without demanding commitment she'd learned not to offer. Clean breaks, no loose ends, no one waiting around for promises she couldn't keep. Yeah, they understood each other.

Jax called the airport and, while on endless hold, considered the upcoming mission. Basically routine—pre-storm presence and embedded support for the outreach clinic; dynamic rescue, supply drop, and evacuation training; medical assistance as needed. Rural medical support meant flying routine patient transport, providing emergency evacuation for people whose conditions exceeded local capabilities. Not high-stakes disaster response but work that served communities with limited options for emergency medical access. The kind of assignment that reminded her why she'd chosen this line of work after leaving the Army.

Once she had her flight info, she tossed her gear in her duffel and headed to the airport. An hour later, she sat in the Kahului Airport departure lounge, bag secured, boarding pass in hand.

Should make Asheville early tomorrow, she texted Bean.

Her phone buzzed immediately. *Copy that. Lead doc's from Boston Mercy. Rumor says she has the creds.*

Jax sighed. A hospital-based doc in rural conditions. Not ideal. Someone accustomed to unlimited resources and immediate backup? She'd seen the type before—brilliant in controlled environments, less adaptable when conditions got messy. But, not her call.

Either this doctor would adjust to circumstances that challenged standard approaches or she'd spend the deployment wishing she was back in Boston, where medicine meant ordering tests and consulting specialists rather than making decisions with basic equipment and clinical judgment.

Jax typed back. *Should be interesting.*

That's one way to put it.

We've handled worse. Check you when I land.

Bean sent a thumbs-up emoji.

Once boarded, Jax settled back for the overnight to North Carolina with connections. Enough time to transition from vacation mode to operational readiness and prepare for whatever challenges came with supporting medical operations during flood season in a remote mountain community.

Who knew? Working with an emergency medicine specialist in challenging conditions might prove more interesting than usual assignments. Or at least, she hoped so.

Then again, she might spend the deployment counting the days until the doctor could return to the civilized world of high-tech medicine. Either way, it would be work that mattered to people who needed help they couldn't get any other way.

Besides, she'd always liked a challenge.

Chapter Two

Asheville, NC briefing
Cloudy and cool

Two days later, Sloane entered the federal building in Asheville at 7:53 with her essentials in an oversized roller bag and a large cup of decent coffee she'd picked up on the walk from the hotel. If she had no say over an assignment, she could at least preserve some small degree of control over the quality of her caffeine. Inside, the décor embodied government efficiency—beige walls, fluorescent lighting, and the scent of industrial coffee that had been brewing since dawn floating out of half-open doorways.

She followed the signs down one of the many nondescript gray tiled halls to Briefing Room B. A battered credenza on the far wall hosted a big stainless-steel urn of the lethal-smelling coffee. Several people already gathered around the requisite faux mahogany conference table in the center of the room. A stocky but muscular white man of average height in a crisp white shirt and black trousers, looking to be in his mid-forties, raptly examined an array of communication equipment in a foam-lined aluminum case twice the size of a steamer trunk. A Black woman in her twenties wearing a light violet sweater and gray pants sat at the center of the conference table flipping through a file folder. The only other occupant, an older woman with short, gray-streaked brown hair in a blue short-sleeved shirt with chest pockets tucked into tan cargo pants, nodded to Sloane with a friendly smile and sharp-eyed assessment. Her weathered tanned skin said she probably spent more time outdoors than in.

Sloane set her bag against the wall and chose a seat with her back to the row of windows that gave her a view of people entering as well as the screen pulled down on the wall. She opened her tablet and reviewed the mission parameters she'd been emailed, though the details remained frustratingly vague. Rural medical support. Disaster preparedness. Community health assessment. All euphemisms for spending weeks in conditions she couldn't predict with people she didn't know.

"Dr. Marshall?" The young woman closed the folder and scooted down several seats until she was next to Sloane. "I'm Callie Williams, a volunteer RN with the Disaster Corps Program. This is such a great opportunity, and I'm really looking forward to working with you."

"Thank you." Sloane briefly shook the extended hand. Callie's bright enthusiasm echoed that of the young residents who arrived in the ER every July, sure that each day would be filled with excitement and heroics. Like them, Callie might soon find the long days and often simple hard work without much glamour. And out in some backwater area devoid of any medical infrastructure? Everyone would likely be doing double duty and working overtime every day. "First time for this?"

"Yes. I was hoping I'd have a chance to get some flight experience. Do you think—"

"Callie," the older woman interrupted gently, "let's wait until Dr. Marshall gets through the briefing before we start talking about assignments."

Callie blushed. "Oh, right. Of course. Sorry."

"That's fine," Sloane said. "And your request is noted."

With a grateful expression, Callie slid back to her seat.

The other woman held out her hand. "Sarah Hull, field NP and community liaison. I've lived and worked around Coulter's Gap all my life, so I know the people and some of the challenges we'll face."

"What kinds of problems are you managing?" Sloane asked, instantly encouraged. An experienced team member could make her life much easier. Nurses and PAs working in the trenches often made the best allies, with knowledge she hadn't been exposed to in medical school—and sometimes not even in a tertiary care institution with the most up-to-date support in the world. Sarah Hull likely had much more familiarity with the kinds of cases they'd be seeing than she did.

"Mostly chronic medical conditions—hypertension, diabetes, obstructive lung issues." Sarah sighed. "As much prenatal care as I can. Not everyone who needs it wants an outsider involved."

"What kind of social services are available?" Sloane leaned heavily on the hospital social service unit. So many patients who sought care in the ER had no primary care providers or insurance.

"Mmm," Sarah murmured with a head shake. "The farther from a large city, the fewer resources. Of course, sometimes it's just a matter of educating folks as to what's available."

Sloane nodded. That was a very politically astute answer. Translation: Aftercare would be a challenge. "Have you worked with this team before?"

"Some of them. That's Eli Crane." Sarah gestured toward the man with the communication equipment. "He's the guy who manages incoming dispatches, schedules daily missions, and tracks supplies."

Eli sketched a wave in Sloane's direction. Obviously, he'd been listening. "Anything you need, or need to report, come to me."

"So noted," Sloane said. A bureaucrat with actual usefulness in the field. That was encouraging at least.

Now that the professional courtesies were over, some of the tension in Sloane's shoulders relaxed. New people meant unpredictable interactions and personality dynamics that could make for unpleasant surprises. Starting over with strangers felt like being a first-year resident again. Irritation simmered on the verge of annoyance at needing to prove herself.

"Is this everyone?" Sloane asked, mentally assembling a picture of how the team would mesh.

"Not quite," Eli said. "Our flight crew should be here any minute, and we're still expecting a radiology technician. Another last-minute replacement." He grinned wryly. "NOAA threw us a curveball with their latest weather update, so we've had to scramble to get the team together."

"I'm aware," Sloane said.

"I understand you were volunteered," Eli said. "First field experience?"

"Not entirely," Sloane said. "I had a brief field medicine rotation during my fellowship."

"Probably why you got tapped for this," he said. "Our pilot, former Chief Warrant Officer Jax Kincaid, current AERIS emergency response, is a flight paramedic as well, so you'll have plenty of backup."

"Good to know," Sloane said neutrally. Apparently everyone considered her a newbie, or too soft to handle rough country medical care. Well, that was fine. She'd been underestimated before.

Eli glanced over as the door opened and a brunette strode in. "Morning, Chief."

"Eli. Good to see you," she said in a golden alto tone.

Somewhere around forty, taller than average, tanned, and clearly very fit. Her black cargo pants and matching black polo, a flight insignia over her heart, could have been a military uniform, given her bearing. She moved with coiled energy, like a spring under tension. Her short hair looked like she'd finger-combed it, and her surprisingly blue eyes swept the room with laser-sharp focus, as if assessing the threat level.

Chief. She must be the pilot. Jax Kincaid.

"Heard we interrupted your R&R," Eli added.

"Happens." Kincaid's voice carried traces of impatience. She crossed to the coffeepot, poured a cup, and turned back to take in everyone in the room.

"Jax," Sarah continued smoothly, indicating Sloane, "Dr. Sloane Marshall, emergency medicine specialist. Sloane, Jax Kincaid, our wings for the next month."

"Doctor," Jax said, the single word carrying undertones Sloane couldn't identify.

Her gaze swept over Sloane's face, unapologetically direct, as if she was used to measuring a person's capabilities by reading their reactions to being studied. Sloane didn't wither under scrutiny—a lifetime of being judged and catalogued had inured her to the judgment of others. She usually presumed most people looked at her and saw a capable physician. This woman looked at her like she was trying to solve a problem. *That* was different.

Sloane stiffened at the unexpected flutter in her chest—not anxiety exactly, but heightened awareness she wasn't used to, making her momentarily uncomfortable. She dealt with patients she didn't know every day and never found that distracting. Never lost her focus or control. Pushing aside the momentary lapse, she met the woman's gaze directly.

The inspection lasted three heartbeats until Sloane replied, "Sloane is fine, Chief Kincaid."

"Jax will do." Jax Kincaid's smile was indecipherable. Amusement? Challenge? Wondering if Sloane was up to the job?

Jax's directness wasn't the problem—Sloane preferred clear communication, always had. So why was this unsettling? When Jax smiled that sharp, knowing smile, Sloane's pulse stuttered. A tiny, unwelcome crack in the armor she depended on to preserve the calm. In the next breath, she brushed the uneasy reaction aside. Just adrenaline from the unwanted assignment. Nothing more.

"Boston Mercy, right?" Jax continued. "This will be a change."

"Yes," Sloane said evenly. So the pilot had done her homework. Everyone seemed to be one step ahead of her—not the usual situation, and not something she was happy about. "The setting might be different, but the care will be the same."

"Good to plan for that. Not always possible." Jax's tone sharpened, and she nodded so slightly Sloane might have missed it if she hadn't been watching her. "Mountain rescues get complicated. Hope you don't get airsick."

Heat prickled up Sloane's neck. Airsick? *Please.* The comment *could* be taken as just a casual remark, but sparked annoyance. Why should this stranger's opinion matter? Or worse, put her slightly off-balance? Still maintaining her practiced calm, Sloane said, "I've been the flight surgeon on dozens of medical transport runs."

"Hospital transport's different from what we do." Jax sounded slightly amused, like she'd heard similar claims before and considered them naïve. "Uncertain weather conditions, no predetermined landing zones. Limited equipment. Sometimes you make it up as you go."

Make it up as you go. Everything in Sloane's systematic approach to medicine—to life—rebelled against the concept. True, clinical assessment was always situationally dependent—every patient was different, *but*…protocols, evidence-based practice, and knowledge-based decision making led to successful outcomes. Nothing about uncertain weather or lack of equipment would change that. "I'm sure I can adapt to operational requirements."

"I'm sure you can."

Jax's smile was quick and sharp, and Sloane felt heat rise in her cheeks. Irrational and completely inexplicable. Before she could respond to what felt like a professional challenge wrapped in casual conversation, a redhead in a deep green suit and matching heels entered with a tall, thin middle-aged Asian man, his salt-and-pepper hair cut military short, wearing the same civilian uniform as Jax Kincaid.

"Good morning," the redhead said. "I'm Regional Director Holloway. Most of you already know Wes Binyama, your flight crew chief."

"Hey, Bean," Eli said.

"Morning, all," Wes said.

When he looked her way, Sloane said, "Dr. Sloane Marshall."

"Doctor," he said congenially and circled the conference table to stand with Jax. "Most folks call me Bean."

"Thank you all for your deployment flexibility." Holloway stood at the head of the table, her manner suggesting she wasn't the least concerned by their actual feelings about being called up with no warning. She pulled up a weather projection on the screen.

"We're looking at a narrow window here. Current NOAA models show the first major storm system arriving in approximately six weeks, with flood risk escalating dramatically after that. Your mission is to provide medical services and disaster prep training *before* things deteriorate and of course to maintain operations through whatever comes."

"Define 'whatever comes,'" Jax said dryly.

"Historical flooding in this region occurs on a thirty-year cycle. We're at year twenty-nine." Holloway's expression never changed. "Obviously, on-the-ground disaster training is a priority."

A topographical map appeared next, showing mountainous terrain that looked more ominous than Sloane expected. Even without first-hand experience, she could discern the scattered settlements connected by roads that looked like suggestions rather than reliable transportation routes. Geographic features that would affect medical care delivery in ways she'd never had to consider. Mountains, rivers, and isolated communities that might as well have been on another planet compared to Boston's urban infrastructure or even the densely populated communities affected by forest fires in Southern California where she'd done her fellowship.

She studied the map while Jax asked questions about supply routes, weather patterns, and satellite images of potential landing zones—all things Sloane recognized as critical and totally out of her field of expertise. She'd be at a disadvantage in this scenario, dependent on the skill and proficiency of strangers. Something she had avoided all her life. She functioned in a team in the ER, yes, but she depended on her own knowledge, drive, and determination to make the right decisions. To be accountable to no one at the end of the day except herself.

As the briefing progressed, Jax Kincaid emerged as someone used to being in command and experienced with this kind of mission—where Sloane was not—and essential for getting medics to outlying regions for routine care and emergencies. Sloane struggled against her uneasiness over Jax's role. Illogical, and an unwelcome reaction. Jax's main responsibility would be transport logistics, after all. Sloane's focus would be mostly seeing patients in a clinic environment. She'd probably have little reason to interact with the flight crew. So, no reason to give Jax Kincaid any further thought.

"I understand the timeline is four weeks?" Sloane asked.

"*Minimum* four weeks, extending as conditions require." Director Holloway's gaze swept the team with the kind of assessment that suggested she'd managed difficult personalities before. "You'll be largely self-sufficient, Doctor. Communication is limited, helicopter operations will provide primary connection to regional facilities if needed…and navigationally feasible."

Self-sufficient. Navigationally feasible. What Holloway really meant was no backup, no consultations, and limited ability to transfer difficult cases for specialized care. Reality hit harder than it should have, a situation Sloane wouldn't have guessed possible a few days before, surrounded by all the support she could ever need.

"Very well," Sloane said steadily. She'd had years of practice divorcing her personal feelings from her behavior. She wasn't about to let anyone on the team see she had any doubts.

Out of the corner of her eye, she caught Jax nodding with an approving expression, and a frisson of pleasure rippled through her. How strange. She hadn't sought or needed anyone's external validation since she'd learned long ago that none was forthcoming.

"Usual equipment manifest?" Wes Binyama said laconically.

"Transport trucks are on the way. Road access is limited, so semis are out of the question. You'll have whatever we can get there in our off-road RTVs." Holloway slid a binder down the table in his direction. "Field hospital and diagnostic equipment, pharmaceutical supplies, communication systems."

"I'll need a copy of that," Sloane said. Probably basic supplies compared to what she was accustomed to, equipment that required manual operation instead of automated systems, diagnostic tools that would test her clinical skills rather than sophisticated technology. "Is there time to add anything?"

Holloway shook her head. "I'm afraid not."

"Of course," Sloane said mildly and again, across the room, a glimmer of a smile from Jax. How was she to interpret that? Assessment? Agreement? Approval?

As if she needed any of those things from a stranger.

The briefing continued—supply routes, weather patterns. Important details, but Sloane's attention kept sliding to Jax. The way she leaned forward, intent and laser focused. The casual air of command. She caught herself studying Jax's hands as she jotted down a note in a small black notebook about some detail regarding the helicopter that Sloane had missed. Her long, surprisingly slim fingers moved with quick precision, no wedding ring, and carried calluses that suggested someone who worked with equipment rather than just operated it. Details that for some reason remained in Sloane's mind like an afterimage when looking into the sun.

Her heart pounded with the strangeness, and she deliberately angled her chair so Jax was no longer in her field of view. Uncomfortable reactions that made no sense created distractions she couldn't afford during an assignment that would test her professional capabilities under challenging conditions. Better to focus on medical responsibilities rather than whatever inexplicable responses to a woman she'd just met.

Director Holloway distributed final briefing materials—contact information, supply manifests, and emergency protocols that looked woefully inadequate compared to hospital standards. "Departure in one hour," she concluded. "Transport is waiting outside."

The room emptied efficiently, everyone collecting gear and tossing paper cups in the trash. Wes Binyama handed her the equipment and supplies list.

"Here you are, Doctor."

"Thank you, Mr. Binyama."

"Call me Bean, ma'am."

Sloane smiled. "All right, Bean. If you don't call me ma'am."

He laughed. "Understood…Doctor."

Sloane just managed not to flinch when Jax appeared unexpectedly beside her.

"Dr. Marshall?"

"Yes?"

"I'll walk you down. I know you said you've flown before."

"That's right." Sloane grabbed her roller bag and coffee.

"Medevac, right?"

Sloane frowned. "That's correct."

"Mountain flying is quite a bit different. We don't have much time, so I thought we ought to go over a few things."

This close, Sloane caught the scent of leather and soap, or maybe shampoo, that suggested Jax favored practical over fragrant. Somehow that seemed fitting. Aware that Jax was studying her face like she was trying to read something written there, she stepped a pace away as they walked down the hall. Personal space, always important, seemed more so around this woman, like armor against the unsettling effect she seemed to have. "I understand aviation safety basics. And I *don't* get airsick."

Jax's smile flickered again. "Good to know. All the same, mountain flying goes beyond basics. Weather changes rapidly, landing zones can be challenging, operations sometimes require flexibility in patient transport that hospital-based physicians find…" Jax paused, as if searching for diplomatic phrasing, "Difficult."

Hospital-based physicians. The way Jax said it suggested experience with medical personnel who hadn't adapted well to field conditions. Probably doctors who'd expected rural medicine to be like urban practice with different scenery.

Sloane stopped in the middle of the nondescript beige hallway and faced Jax. The rest of the team had already departed on the elevator. "Are you questioning my professional adaptability, Chief Warrant Officer?"

"Just Jax these days. And no, not questioning anything—just noting that rural emergency medical services require different approaches than you might be used to, and when we're in flight, you'll need to adjust as I instruct."

As she instructed? Well, that certainly defined the power structure nicely. Sloane inwardly bristled, but the response was fleeting. Emotions never controlled her reactions. "You are in charge of the aircraft, and I will certainly accept your authority where flight and passenger safety is concerned, but please remember that I am in charge of patient care. On or above the ground."

"I think we understand each other, then." Jax's skeptical smile suggested she'd heard similar assurances before and watched them crumble under pressure. "See you on the aircraft, Dr. Marshall."

Jax pushed open the stairwell door and disappeared. Sloane listened to her receding footsteps before moving off to the elevator. While she waited, she reviewed a morning quite unlike any she'd ever experienced.

The briefing *had* been informative. The team seemed impeccably competent—even the pilot, who reminded her of several trauma surgeons who thought they were the only ones capable of handling a crisis. Competence and arrogance occasionally went hand in hand. Hopefully Jax Kincaid was both.

Nothing she'd heard changed her expectations. Four to six weeks of rural medical practice, and then she would return to Boston to the work, and life, that suited her. She'd handled difficult colleagues before, managed personality conflicts that interfered with patient care, and maintained professional boundaries under stressful conditions.

She could most certainly ignore inexplicable reactions to testy pilots who made simple professional interactions feel more personal, and a great deal more uncomfortable, than they should.

Chapter Three

Flight to Coulter's Gap
Cloudy, rain forecast

Jax circled the Bell 412, checking for leaks, damage, wildlife nests, or anything foreign that might have lodged in the body during transport from the AERIS facility in Virginia. She'd been flying this helicopter or its twin for three years now, and she knew every rivet, panel, and sound the rotors made when something wasn't quite right on both of them. She ran her hand over the fuselage, checking for stress fractures, cracks, or buckled skin. Confirmed the exhaust and intakes were clear.

She cursed under her breath at the squirrel's nest tucked into the angle of the skid support. "How can they manage that in a few hours?"

"Diligence and determination," Bean said, appearing at her elbow with a clipboard.

She shot him a look. "They're *squirrels*."

"Okay—they're sneaky, too." He sent that easy grin that had gotten them both out of trouble more times than she could count. "Maintenance logged everything green before we shipped her down."

"I know. Still checking." Jax completed her circuit and popped the engine cowling. "You read the weather briefing?"

"Twice. Spring storm systems moving through faster than normal, which means we could get caught between fronts if we're not careful." Bean leaned against the aircraft. "You worried about the terrain?"

"Nah. We've flown plenty of mountain ops in-country. It's the mission parameters that have me thinking."

"How so?"

Jax pulled out a flashlight and examined the turbine blades for nicks or foreign object damage. “Four to six weeks embedded with a medical team. That’s not a quick evac or supply drop—that’s living with these people. Eating with them, working with them, depending on them when things get complicated.”

“And that’s a problem because?”

“Because I don’t know them, and none of them are field trained.” Jax straightened and closed the cowling. “We’re not talking about billeting with hotshots or a disaster response team. Hell, the team leader is city-based hospital staff. You know how I am about working with unknowns.”

Bean laughed, leaning down to scan the fuel lines. “You mean how you are about working with people, period?”

“I work fine with people.”

“You work fine with *me*, and people like us who’ve been out beyond the wire. Everyone else has to prove themselves.”

Jax climbed inside to the medical bay and scanned the equipment. Cardiac monitor, defibrillator, IV fluids, intubation kit—everything secured and accessible for in-flight medical procedures. “Nothing wrong with being cautious.”

“True.” Bean filled out the pre-flight checklist as he followed. “So what’s your read on the team?”

“Eli’s solid. Worked with him on that hurricane response in Louisiana two years back. Sarah Hull knows the territory, and she’s got the kind of practical experience that matters when you’re operating outside normal support structures.”

“But you’re worried about the doctor?”

Bean kept his tone casual. Jax paused. Where was he going with this? “What do you mean?”

“You tell me. You were pretty focused on Dr. Marshall during the briefing.”

Jax frowned. “Focused how?”

“Like you were trying to solve a puzzle. That’s a lot more attention than you usually spare for anyone who isn’t a field-trained medic. The rest you always view as passengers who happen to know CPR.”

“Well, she isn’t *just* the medic overseeing a patient on an evac—she’s the team leader.” Jax resumed checking equipment, irritated that Bean had noticed anything. “Besides, she’s different from the usual hospital docs we transport.”

Bean cocked his head. “Huh. How so?”

“Most of them at least *ask* about creature comforts or want to know exactly how primitive conditions will be. She wanted to know about equipment manifests and patient transport protocols."

"Sounds professional."

"It *was* professional. But there was something else." Jax secured the medical bay and moved to the pilot's compartment. "When Holloway told her there wasn't time to add equipment, she just accepted it. No argument, no demands to speak to someone higher up the chain."

"Still sounds professional to me."

"Yeah, but it was the way she said it. Like she'd made a decision to adapt instead of fighting what she couldn't control."

Bean climbed into the copilot's seat and began running through pre-flight checks. "That bothering you?"

"Why would it bother me?"

"Because you like being right about people, and your first impression was that she'd be another soft city doc who'd fold under pressure."

Jax started the auxiliary power unit and waited for systems to come online. "I didn't say she was soft."

"You didn't say she wasn't."

Jax blew out a breath. "Look, she's got the credentials—emergency medicine in a big trauma center, some field experience at least. On paper, she's qualified for this mission."

"But?"

"But credentials don't tell you how someone handles real pressure. How they react when the plan goes sideways and they have to make decisions with incomplete information."

"Like mountain flying in marginal weather?"

"Like mountain flying in marginal weather to reach patients who might die if we don't get there in time."

Bean glanced at her sideways. "You know, I've flown with you through three deployments, and as many years here, and I've never heard you analyze a team member this thoroughly."

"I analyze everyone."

"More like *categorizing* everyone," Bean went on good-naturedly. "Medical personnel, support staff, administrators—you put them in boxes and treat them accordingly. This is different."

Jax focused on her instrument panel, checking fuel levels and hydraulic pressure. "No, it's not. I just want to know who I'm working with before we're in a cluster out in no-man's-land."

"Can't argue with that. Might be good if you stopped watching her like you're trying to figure out if she'll have your back when things get ugly."

Jax stared. She trusted Bean. The guy never missed anything, and if *he* thought that, did Marshall, too? Because that hadn't been what she'd been thinking.

Had it?

"I don't pre-judge people," she muttered.

"Good thing," Bean said, "because here comes our team."

Jax climbed back into the open bay as voices carried across the tarmac. The team approached the helicopter in a loose group, everyone carrying personal gear, Sarah and…Callie?…chatting, Eli dragging his case of electronics, and Sloane Marshall? Walking alone.

"Are we going to fly this bird," Jax said, "or are you going to keep busting my chops a bit longer?"

Bean laughed. "It was fun, but I'm ready for sky."

"Uh-oh," Jax said when Sloane abruptly left her bag on the ground and headed back across the tarmac. "Takeoff delay."

A woman in dark blue scrubs jogged across the tarmac toward Sloane—Black, late thirties, athletic build, carrying a gear bag that suggested she was ready to travel.

"Sloane!" The newcomer hurried toward Sloane.

Jax narrowed her eyes. Who?

Sloane opened her arms. The woman who'd been rigid through the briefing laughed—loud, unguarded. Jax straightened. This was new. Her buttoned-up professional demeanor dissolved into something warmer, more relaxed, as she embraced the other woman. She smiled, the first smile Jax had seen from her.

Jax braced a boot on the skid and waited as the two women crossed the tarmac side by side. Sloane's friend said something Jax couldn't hear, but she caught Sloane's response clearly.

"Mina, what are you doing here?"

"I was on somebody's list to pay my US Health Service dues, and my number got called." Mina tucked her hand around Sloane's arm. "I said yes, because hey—it gets me out of Boston where it's forty-five and raining. But how did *you* end up here?"

Sloane glanced at Jax, her expression closing as if she'd just realized they weren't alone. "Long story. I'll tell you when we have a minute."

"Ooh, that sounds juicy."

Sloane blushed. "It's not."

Watching Sloane with someone who was obviously her friend—or maybe more—Jax's opinion of Sloane shifted. This version of the woman she'd pegged as aloof and wrapped up tight seemed younger, less armored, and more like someone who might be able to go with the flow in a crisis.

"I take it you're Mina Akoa?" Jax said as Sloane and the newcomer paused before the open bay. "Our missing radiology tech?"

"That's me," Mina said, smiling up at Jax. "Sorry I'm late."

"You're not. Yet." Jax held out a hand. "Jax Kincaid. I'll take your bag."

"Thank you." Mina glanced at Sloane, one eyebrow raised for just a second, before handing up her bag. She ducked under the spinning rotors and climbed in with practiced ease.

Jax reached for Sloane's gear bag. "Need a hand, Doctor?"

"I'm fine, thanks." Sloane passed up her bag, stepped onto the skid, and sidled past Jax, their shoulders briefly touching.

"Welcome aboard," Jax murmured, and headed for the cockpit. "Everyone buckle up. Don't forget your headsets, and make sure your bags are secured to the clips."

She settled into the pilot's seat and pulled on her helmet. What had Bean said?

You categorize people. Put them in boxes and treat them accordingly.

Maybe so, but she'd been off the mark with Sloane Marshall. Her transformation at the sight of her friend from cool, distant, and clearly annoyed to warm, open, and happy, for instance. Two different people—or one person with serious walls. What else was Sloane hiding?

Bean slid into the copilot's seat beside her, headset already in place. "You can stop worrying about them now. All the chicks are secured."

Jax didn't look up. "Cross-check for takeoff."

Bean chuckled. "Copy that. Rotors green. Fuel topped. Comms clear."

"All right," she announced to the group over the internal intercom system. "Ninety minutes' flying time. Enjoy the ride."

Jax adjusted her harness and gave the instrument panel one last glance. All green to go across the board, but her mind wasn't. Time to fly. She had a job to do.

Whoever Sloane Marshall was beneath her shields was no concern of hers.

❖

Sloane sank onto the narrow bench, diagonally from Jax in the cockpit. Gear stowed, headset snug around her ears, as instructed. Beside her, Mina, gear bag wedged under her knees, grinned like this was the best adventure she'd ever been on. Mina's surprise appearance still warmed her, their hug on the tarmac something she hadn't realized she missed until Mina's arms encircled her. Their frequent texts and FaceTiming helped, but their schedules made for rare in-person meetings. Having her best friend—okay, *only* real friend—along for this mission made it easier to ignore the faint unease curling in her stomach.

Jax's voice crackled through her headset, unexpectedly intimate in the closed loop of the intercom. "Everybody good back there?"

Apparently the unease had a name. And the source was in the pilot's seat.

Sloane swallowed. "Fine," she said, though it came out clipped.

Mina gave a thumbs-up. "Ready when you are, Captain."

"Not a captain," Jax replied, gaze flicking over Sloane and Mina as if checking cargo, her hands moving over instruments with the same efficient economy with which she seemed to do everything. "Just the one keeping this thing in the air."

All business, something Sloane could appreciate.

So why the same attitude from Jax Kincaid irritated her, she couldn't fathom.

The rotors built to a deep, thrumming growl, vibration running up through the soles of Sloane's boots. Jax lifted them clear of the tarmac, banking smoothly toward the river valley and the mountain range beyond. Out the side window, the runway blurred as the aircraft rose toward open sky. Within minutes, Asheville disappeared into a patchwork quilt of evergreens, rivers, and stony mountain peaks.

Turning from the view, Sloane studied the interior. Inside, the cabin was smaller than she'd imagined from looking at the outside. Not cramped, but deliberate, with every inch claimed by purpose. She'd been inside plenty of hospital-affiliated medevac helicopters, the fuselage usually dominated by a single stretcher bolted to the floor, oxygen tanks strapped down with webbing, and a wall of sterile-packed supplies waiting for the moment a patient's life depended on them. This was different.

Here, multiple stretchers folded up against the bulkhead, freeing the floor. The compact modular medical station held a portable monitor, defibrillator, and suction unit clipped into quick-release brackets. IV kits, airway adjuncts, and trauma packs were sealed in labeled pouches that hung on a rail, ready to be stripped free and carried into the field. Instead of fixed cabinetry, collapsible mesh bins held medications. A compact refrigeration unit hummed faintly beside a rugged case stenciled *Field Surgical Kit.*

This craft wasn't built for stabilizing a patient in flight. This was a mobile ER, built to land on a riverbank or a washed-out logging road and keep someone alive on the ground. If there was any chance of that, Sloane would see that it happened. The idea energized her.

She glanced toward the cockpit, Jax's profile lit by the faint green wash from the instrument panel. She tensed as Jax's gaze met hers. How long had Jax been watching? Shouldn't she be paying attention to where they were going?

As if reading her mind, Jax grinned and toggled a button on her helmet.

"Don't worry, we're more or less on autopilot right now." Jax's voice sounded just a little tinny through Sloane's earphones, but the faintly mocking note was clear enough. "Does it pass inspection?"

More or less on autopilot?

"Is that military humor?" Sloane asked. "Because if you're trying to make me nervous, it's not working."

Jax laughed. "Didn't even consider it. So...do you like the accommodations?"

"Impressive. I'll want a more complete examination when we land."

"Of course you will. I'll give you a tour."

Sloane's pulse jumped. Decidedly unusual. Perhaps the flight *was* making her a little nervous.

"Over there," Jax went on, pointing to a glint of water threading through the trees, "that's the Green Fork. Town's on the other side."

Everyone leaned to catch a glimpse. Jax must be on an open channel to all of them now. Sloane took note not to say anything personal. Not that she would, of course.

The view was breathtaking—ridgelines slashing against the sky, shadows pooling in the hollows, and the mountains an endless palette of green as far as she could see. What she couldn't see were roads.

There must be some, though.

She glanced at Mina and leaned close. "Was that year you spent with public health anything like this?"

"In Honduras," Mina said. "A mudslide cut off a village up in the mountains, and we had to bring the clinic in by mule. This'll be easier. I think."

"I hope," Sloane said, voice dropping though Sloane knew Jax could still hear.

"Most of the access routes around here don't qualify as roads, unless you're in a Humvee," Jax's voice cut in. "You won't see them from the air. That ridge to the north? We'll be running medevacs over it if the roads wash out. Fog sits up there like soup, sometimes for days."

Sloane looked where Jax indicated. The ridge was a sheer wall of green and stone, clouds snagging along its top like pulled wool. She could imagine how quickly weather could close in, sealing them off. As they flew deeper into the mountains, the settlements thinned to nothing. Just folds of forest, occasional glints of tin roofs, winding dirt ribbons that must be roads, all seeming to go nowhere.

"How many people live out here year-round?" Sloane asked.

"A few hundred in the main town. Hard to know about the outer hollers," Jax said. "Some don't come down for months. We're it if something happens."

That reality landed heavier than Sloane expected. Her *normal* meant ER shifts where every tool she might need was a step away. Out here, there would be no reinforcements, no second opinions, no computerized scans. Just their team, whatever equipment they'd brought, and the time Jax could buy her and an injured patient in the air.

A new sensation eclipsed the unease that had plagued her since she'd been assigned this mission: excitement. Nothing much surprised her, but this did. The challenge of the unknown, even working with the sometimes annoying woman flying the helicopter, gripped her in a way that was new—or possibly long forgotten.

She studied Jax again, appreciating the confident way she piloted the craft, one hand light on the stick, the other flicking a switch without even glancing at it. Jax could be infuriating, yes, like the way she'd seemed to size her up in seconds that morning without knowing anything about her, but there was no denying the competence.

"You fly medevac in areas like this often?" Sloane asked before she could stop herself.

Jax chuckled. "Enough to know I don't like bringing patients in unless I have to. Out here, you work on them where they are. Saves lives and rotor time."

A pragmatic answer, suggestive of someone who made decisions fast, who didn't cling to protocol if the situation demanded something else. A good quality in a pilot. Possibly a nightmare in a partner.

She'd find out soon enough. Until then, she could only guess. Worrying about what she couldn't change just wasted energy.

A little over an hour later, Jax dipped the nose and banked toward a break in the trees. "Next stop, Coulter's Gap," she said. "Population… depends on who you ask. We'll come down into the valley over that ridge ahead. It's a bit steep, so hold on."

The descent was smooth but sharp, the angle tighter than Sloane liked. She gripped the straps at her shoulders, trying not to show it, and leaned slightly to look out the window. The deeper they flew, the less approachable the landscape looked. Trees pressed in around narrow switchbacks. Hills folded into each other like secrets. It was beautiful. And entirely removed from the world she knew.

The forest suddenly opened like a cracked bowl—steep walls, a sloping valley, and a scattering of rooftops tucked into the crook of a wide, muddy, churning river—a stark contrast to the beauty of the mountains. A single, narrow main street ran the length of the town, with side roads spilling into the hills. Sloane spotted what could only be the church, given the simple spire that rose above most of the other buildings, and a low rambling structure with a large field behind it—probably the school. The helicopter circled that field, and Jax set them down in the center of it with barely a bump.

"Welcome to the middle of nowhere," Jax said.

Sloane unbuckled, the harness clinking against its mount. The big doors remained closed while Bean and Jax went through the post-flight shutdown of the aircraft. She pulled off the headset, happy to be free of the strange intimacy of Jax's voice appearing in her ear.

"You okay?" Mina asked.

Sloane nodded. "Just adjusting, or trying to."

"To the altitude or the assignment?"

"To all of it." She didn't elaborate. Mina would know better than to press.

She glanced toward the cockpit. Jax's profile was mostly in shadow under her helmet, but the firm line of her jaw was visible, her posture as easy as if she'd been driving a pickup instead of piloting two tons of engineered lift through treacherous mountain ranges. Apparently cool and confident was her baseline state.

Jax's face came to mind as she'd appraised her at their first meeting—unapologetic, entirely unreadable. Jax hadn't even reacted to the greeting she'd shared with Mina, when she hadn't been thinking about being surrounded by colleagues who were still strangers. Not a raised eyebrow, not even a sideways glance. Which shouldn't matter and yet left her wondering what Jax had seen in those unguarded moments.

"We've got a good pilot," Mina said, tracking her gaze.

"Sure of that already?"

"I'm still breathing."

Sloane cracked a smile. "Not a great endorsement."

Mina unbuckled beside her. "You're blushing."

"I am not."

"You're definitely something."

Sloane busied herself with her pack. "I'm just focused."

"Uh-huh." Mina gave her a long look. "You sure this is where you want to be?"

"I wasn't given a choice. You didn't mind the last-minute callout?"

"Not really." Mina grinned. "I've got a thing for remote locations and overworked friends. Plus, I'm due for a detox."

Sloane snorted. "You mean from hospital politics and insurance forms?"

"More like fourteen-year-old twins."

Sloane tensed at the word, a reaction she hadn't had in years. This assignment—or something about it—had definitely thrown her off stride.

"Ah, the daring duo," she said, keeping her tone light. "How are they?"

"Still joined at the hip, which quadruples the trouble factor," Mina said with obvious affection. "Jamal just got back from a dig in North Africa, so he's due for an extended tour of duty with them."

Sloane laughed. "Lucky you."

Mina laughed. "I know it."

Sloane relaxed for the first time since stepping into the aircraft. This wasn't where she was supposed to be. She'd taken this assignment under duress, after all. But now, with her friend at her side and a hum of anticipation in her blood, the tension faded. Her heart beat faster. For the first time since she'd been informed of the assignment, the knot in her chest loosened just enough to let in something else.

Anticipation.

Instead of bracing for the worst, she imagined what else might be waiting to unfold. And what's more, how she was going to work with Jax Kincaid when every one of their interactions left her slightly off-balance.

When the bay doors opened, Sloane hitched her pack higher and stepped out from under the rotor wash. The wind carried the scent of wet earth and woodsmoke, the kind that clung to a place long after the fire had gone cold. Mina fell in beside her, her curls ruffled by the downwash, while the rest of the team emerged dragging their gear.

Sloane exhaled slowly and looked back at the aircraft. Jax remained in the cockpit, head turned toward her, just barely. Watching, maybe. Or maybe not.

CHAPTER FOUR

Coulter's Gap
Misty rain

A group of people waited just beyond the swirling circle of rotor wash. As Sloane and Mina approached, a woman in a weathered khaki slicker and jeans stepped forward with her hand out, smiling like she'd been practicing for this moment.

"You must be Dr. Marshall," she said, grip firm and brisk. "Lynette Ronson, mayor of Coulter's Gap."

"Mayor," Sloane said, nodding.

"Appreciate you bringing your people in." Lynette's smile held, but her eyes flicked to the helicopter and then to the gray ridge behind them, as if she'd rather be measuring the weather than exchanging pleasantries.

"Reggie Inouye," a man who looked built for hauling crates—broad-shouldered, with a shaved head and a faint scar across his jaw—said in a gravelly baritone, giving her a nod instead of a handshake. His navy windbreaker bore the AERIS patch above his name. "Motor transport chief. Good to see you, Doctor. We convoyed in from Asheville with your field hospital modules yesterday. No trouble except the last four miles—some recent rain made for a muddy slog."

Sloane glanced past him to where two heavy-duty flatbeds, painted matte green and kitted out with oversized tires, idled at the far end of the field. Mounds of what she assumed was their equipment sat stacked beneath weatherproofed tarps.

Inouye saw her looking. "That's the last of it. Portable cots, medical supply crates, equipment packs, refrigeration unit, and two portable backup generators. And the fuel to run them."

"And our lodging?" she asked.

Reggie's mouth twitched.

Lynette Ronson cut in. "We've got you set up in what used to be a roadhouse, before the railroad went through down in the flats and the logging business followed it. A lot of jobs around here dried up after that." Her tone, dry and bitter, suggested she didn't see progress as a friend. "Place is just down the road a ways from the school. Shared quarters—bunkhouse style—but you've got a working shower, a kitchen with propane, and we cleaned out the mouse nests. Roof is sound too, for now."

"Luxury," Mina murmured at her shoulder.

Sloane didn't look at her, just kept her expression even. "That'll work."

Lynette started walking, gesturing toward the trucks. "We figured you could set up your clinic space in the school gym. It's the only place big enough and with heat that works most of the time. Got showers in the locker rooms."

"I see." Sloane sighed inwardly. No actual clinic. No exam rooms. Just a gymnasium—echoing, exposed, and almost certainly not designed for privacy or infection control. "Have residents been told we're setting up medical services?"

The mayor hesitated. Just long enough for the silence to be noticeable.

"They know you're coming," Lynette said finally. "And a lot of folks will be glad for it. We haven't had a regular doctor hereabouts for twenty years." She glanced toward the helicopter where the rest of the team milled about getting their gear, her expression softening a moment. "Everyone knows Sarah, though. The rest, well…this is a close-knit place. Outsiders don't usually stay long, and people take care of their own. Some may not see the need for help from away."

Meaning: *Don't expect a line at the door*.

"Understood," Sloane said. "Perhaps once we get the opportunity to let people know what we have to offer, they'll find us useful."

"Could be," Lynette said neutrally.

They reached the first truck, and Reggie swung up into the cab to grab a clipboard. "We'll pull around to the gym to offload the medical supplies first, then deliver the sleeping kits and personal gear at the bunkhouse. Bean'll take one team—he knows the drill."

Bunkhouse. She was actually about to spend a month and a half—please, not any longer—in a *bunkhouse* with people she hardly knew. Jax's face flashed through her mind. She pushed it away. Not a distraction she needed.

"We'll want a triage center and walk-in clinic area outside, with some kind of cover in case it rains," Sloane said to Reggie.

Reggie smirked. "I can guarantee that, Doctor. We'll get a canopy tent and some benches out front."

"Fine. Treatment areas and emergency medical areas inside." She paused, envisioning the flow of patients, how to prevent massive contamination should they be dealing with anything infectious, and the best way to offer some degree of confidentiality. "Do you have curtains—no—tarps or something like that to cordon off treatment zones inside?"

"On the truck. You tell us where you want them."

Jax, who'd apparently arrived to help, said, "Good planning, Doctor. You almost sound like you've done this before."

Sloane vacillated between irritation and pleasure at the vote of confidence. "It's simple mass casualty planning, Chief Warrant Officer. That's ER 101."

Jax grinned. "Just Jax. And all the same, good to know you're not a total rook."

Sloane narrowed her eyes. "Good to know you've flown one of those things before, too."

Bean snorted, and, as Jax walked away, she laughed.

Once Reggie and his crew maneuvered the loaded vehicles closer to the school, Sloane addressed the team. "Let's get everything inventoried as we offload it. Mina, you're with me on the clinical supplies. Eli, you can coordinate with Reggie and Bean for the rest."

The next few hours were a blur of lifting, unstrapping, and checking manifests. The tent frames were heavier than they looked, their aluminum struts slick with condensation. The supply crates rattled faintly with the clink of metal instruments. A faint diesel smell hung in the damp air. Jax passed by twice, hauling a pair of collapsible tables on one trip and a case of IV fluids on the next, her gaze sliding over Sloane without comment.

The gym was exactly what Sloane had pictured—polished hardwood floor scuffed from decades of sneakers, faded basketball lines, and a row of windows below the high ceiling fogged by grit and moisture.

Bean unfolded the first of a stack of free-standing eight-by-ten canvas walls on wheels. "These, along with the dividers Callie scrounged from the storage closet, will let you set up separate treatment areas."

"Just make an aisle down the center with cubicles on either side for now," Sloane said, mentally mapping the space. Triage station under the canopy just outside the big double doors, cots along the far interior wall, treatment cubicles on the other, and the supplies and pharmacy in the rear. Not ideal. Not even close. But workable.

Reggie added, "We set up the generators right outside the west wall in case the power goes. Lynette said it happened three times this month already."

Sloane's jaw tightened. "We can make do without most modern conveniences, but we can't keep people alive without power. What about fuel?"

"We brought our own," Reggie said. "Jax and Bean will make regular runs for medical and personnel supplies, but we can only get you more fuel by truck."

"Understood," Sloane said, crossing that off her mental list. Her job was to manage the medical end of things, not the supply lines. "See that we don't run short."

"Yes, ma'am," Reggie said easily.

As the off-loading neared an end, Mina joined her at center court, hands on her hips as she surveyed the room.

"Well," Mina said, "I've worked in worse."

"Well, *I* haven't." Sloane kept her voice low, for Mina alone. "I was expecting at least a clinic shell. Exam rooms. Doors."

"You can make anything work," Mina said. "That's why you're here."

Sloane let that sit for a moment, watching the team haul in the last of the supply cases. She didn't say what she was thinking—that she was the team leader by default, not experience, and everyone knew it. Jax, in her annoyingly direct fashion, had said what everyone probably thought. *Rookie.*

She ought to be insulted, but she'd survived medical school and residency, where everyone was tested in fire from day one. You either toughened up or you found another career. That experience hadn't shaken her confidence, and neither would this. She'd been battle-tested a long time before adulthood and had survived growing up where no one gave her success or failure a thought.

"You're right. I know ER medicine. This is just a little different window dressing."

Mina laughed. "Wish you'd said that to our pilot."

"I hardly have time to verbally joust with Jax Kincaid," Sloane snapped.

Mina tipped her head, studying her. "Is that what we're calling it now?"

"Calling *what*?" Sloane paused. She sounded snappish. She *was* snappish. And Mina didn't deserve her bad temper. "Sorry. Long day. And I didn't enjoy the mayor's little warning about the community reception. I don't like walking in blind."

Mina shook her head, her expression suggesting Sloane had missed the obvious. "Maybe that's not all that's got your knickers in a twist."

Sloane shot her a look. "Meaning?"

"Meaning," Mina said lightly, "I saw the way you looked at our pilot."

"I *have* to look at her," Sloane said. "We're dependent on her to get us wherever we need to go that isn't right here in this…clinic." Even saying the word made her wince. "That's all you saw."

"It's my eyes," Mina said, unfazed. "And my gut. And, frankly, you're a little less icy than you were this morning."

Sloane exhaled, gazing toward the open gym doors where Jax stood with Bean and Reggie, sleeves pushed up, laughing at something Bean said with the ease of someone who belonged.

Unlike her.

"She's competent," Sloane said finally.

"That's one word for it."

Sloane ignored the insinuation. "And I need to work with her. That's all that matters."

"Sure," Mina said, but her smile said she didn't buy it. "I'm going to go find Callie. She was looking a little lost. See you at the homestead."

"Delightful."

Laughing, Mina clapped her shoulder and headed for the door, leaving Sloane in the middle of the gym, surrounded by the echo of their voices and the low rumble of distant thunder.

She turned back to the stacks of unopened crates.

Work first. Always work first.

But as she bent to pry open the nearest case, the faintest trace of rotor wash still ghosted across her skin, carrying with it the memory of Jax's voice in her headset and the glint of sunlight on the ridge beyond.

And for the second time that day, she caught herself thinking—not just about the obstacles ahead, but about what might unfold if she let herself look past them.

❖

By evening the gym smelled faintly of wet canvas and diesel exhaust, replacing the scent of old varnish and the musty memories of games long past. Sloane arched her back, stretching out some of the kinks from bending over packing crates for a few hours that felt like days. At least the last supply crate had been stacked inside. The team had fallen into a rhythm that boded well for the next month—Reggie worked with Bean on installing the generators and whatever else needed mechanical know-how, Mina and Callie catalogued pharmacy items, and Jax filled in without complaint wherever anything needed doing. Eli had disappeared earlier, saying he needed to set up the comms center in the roadhouse—correction, *bunkhouse*, and Sarah Hull had gone off to meet with the friend she stayed with while on her circuits through the area.

Sloane jotted notes in the margin of her field pad, marking where she'd want the portable lights set up and the crash cart stored. She took one step back and bumped into someone.

"Oh, sorry." She spun around, ending up nearly nose-to-nose with Jax Kincaid. A flutter of surprise—nothing else—brought heat rushing to her cheeks. Jax's amused expression suggested she'd noticed the reaction, which was somehow worse than the proximity itself.

"No damage done. You got a minute?" Jax grinned, her tone not quite casual but not official either. She'd rolled up the arms of her black flight shirt, and sweat gleamed on the tanned skin of her arms and neck.

For some reason, Sloane hadn't expected her to be so tightly muscled. Or to notice that the look was appealing.

"For what?" Sloane snapped.

If her tone offended, Jax didn't show it.

"I promised you a tour of the transport. Figured you might want a closer look before we put it back in the air. Which, considering where we are, could be any time." Jax's gaze flicked briefly toward the crates. "Unless you'd rather keep counting boxes."

"Five minutes." Sloane closed her pad and stowed it in her backpack. "And don't jinx us."

Jax blinked. "Don't tell me you're superstitious."

"Everyone in the ER knows something isn't superstition if it's true. I'm surprised you don't feel the same after being in the military."

"Didn't say *I* didn't believe in jinxing something—I'm just surprised *you* do."

"Why is that?" Really, Jax Kincaid making assumptions about her was getting tiresome.

"You just seem…"

Sloane could almost see Jax trying to think of a way out of answering. The prospect of Jax being uncomfortable was downright enjoyable. She folded her arms. "Yes?"

"Too analytical."

"Analytical." Sloane shouldered her pack. She'd been called worse. "What I *am* is someone who likes to be prepared for an emergency before I'm in the middle of one. You mentioned a tour?"

Jax smiled like she might comment further but just turned and led the way back across the patchy gravel lot behind the school toward the helicopter. The rotors still ticked faintly in the cooling metal, a low, lazy sound. On the ground, the bird looked bigger somehow than it had when she'd been inside—more foreboding.

"She's a Bell 412," Jax said, running her hand over the fuselage with obvious affection.

"Is that like what you flew in the Army?" she asked.

Jax stopped a few feet from the helicopter, her expression unreadable. "No."

"But you flew medevac, right?"

"I flew the missions they ordered me to fly." Jax stepped onto the skid and pulled herself up into the aircraft with the easy fluidity of someone who'd done it a thousand times. "Watch your step."

Sloane got the message loud and clear. Personal questions were off-limits. Not that she minded. She wasn't even sure why she'd asked, not being in the habit of making idle conversation. She climbed in, much more agilely than last time. The interior smelled faintly of machine oil, warmed metal, and something clean and sharp, maybe Jax's soap. Without the team crowding the benches on both sides or the white noise of the comms in her ears, the atmosphere inside felt heavier. Closer.

"Go ahead," Jax said, gesturing to the gear strapped in along the sides. "Start with whatever you like."

Sloane took a minute, visualizing the sequence of loading a patient, stabilizing their vitals, securing them for flight. The layout was as she remembered from the inbound flight—folded stretchers against the bulkhead, modular med station clipped into place, mesh bins labeled in block print. But with the rotors still and the doors open to the damp mountain air, she could take in the details: the scuffed tread plates along the floor; the locking brackets designed for quick release even with gloves on; the way the collapsible med packs were arranged so you could strip an entire set free with one pull.

"How many stretchers can we accommodate?"

Jax's eyebrows rose. Not a question she expected, apparently. "Depends on how many medics we have back here. With the minimum—say two—we can handle six patients on stretchers."

"O2?"

Jax pointed overhead where masks and lines snaked into recesses in the ceiling. "Like in a commercial airliner—each with independent flow regulators."

"Smart," Sloane murmured.

Jax nodded. "Everything in here is set for speed—grab and go. No rooting around for the right tubing or trying to remember which pouch has the epi."

"Can I look inside? I work best with visuals."

"Sure. You can't break anything. Probably."

Sloane shot her a look.

Jax grinned.

For a heartbeat, Sloane almost smiled back. Really, the woman was relentless.

Sloane unlatched one mesh bin. Inside, vacuum-sealed packs of syringes and IV lines nestled in rigid foam so nothing shifted in turbulence. She replaced the latch and methodically checked each bin and cabinet, cataloguing and memorizing the contents.

Jax leaned against the bulkhead, arms folded and booted feet crossed at the ankles, seemingly content to let Sloane take all the time in the world.

"Impressive," Sloane said when she'd finished exploring. "Much more extensively equipped than most medevac setups I've seen. Whoever spec'd it knows how to keep people alive outside a hospital."

"It's basically a Black Hawk in civilian camouflage," Jax said.

"Like you're a soldier in a civilian uniform," Sloane said.

Jax gave her a long look. "You could say that."

"Can I see the cockpit?"

Jax spun on her heel and Sloane stiffened. Had she gone too far?

After all, she knew nothing about this woman. Not enough to make any kind of judgment. "I should apologize."

Jax, already seated in the pilot's seat, turned her head. "Why? I'm not insulted."

"I…" Sloane blew out a breath. Anything she said was likely to be even more embarrassing. "Can I sit up there?"

"As long as you don't want a flying lesson."

"I *was* wondering—"

"No."

Sloane laughed.

Jax swiveled in her seat, meeting her gaze. "Did you just make a joke?"

"Of course not," Sloane said, careful not to smile.

"Riiight." Jax frowned ever so slightly before sliding a switch that lit up the instrument panel. The glow washed her profile in green, turning the angles of her jaw and cheekbone into planes of shadow. "Well, climb in."

Sloane's shoulder brushed Jax's in the close confines as she lowered herself into the copilot's seat. An unexpected jolt shot through her at the brief contact. She touched people every day—dozens of times—but that slight exchange was so unusual she had to resist the urge to brush her arm, as if Jax's touch still lingered.

"You're *not* going to be flying her," Jax said, her hands resting lightly on the stick, "but it doesn't hurt to know what's up here if you ever have to take the second seat."

"Okay—I'm listening."

Jax's voice seemed lower in the cockpit's intimacy, and Sloane focused on the instruments, ignoring the warmth radiating from the pilot's seat beside her.

"Dual hydraulic systems, so I can afford to lose one and still get us down. Glass cockpit with terrain-following radar. Weather scan's solid but not magic—if the mountains want to eat us, they'll eat us." She glanced up to see if Sloane was following. "And these," she tapped a pair of toggles, "let me talk to everyone—inside, outside, or just one person. So if I need to keep something between us, I can."

Sloane arched a brow. "Between us?"

"Operationally speaking," Jax said, but she smirked like she knew how it sounded.

"What's your main concern flying in here?" Sloane asked.

"Wind shear in the gaps. Fog that'll blind you in thirty seconds flat. And nowhere to put down if you miscalculate." Jax's voice had shifted—no tease now, just clean, clipped professionalism. "We'll stage here in town, but if a call comes in from upriver, you and I are wheels up with whoever you need to assist. If it's weathered in, I'll put you on the ground as close as I can get and circle back."

"You trust your team enough to leave them?"

"I have to trust you enough to know your limits. And I trust myself not to strand you if I can help it." She turned again, that hawklike gaze fixed on Sloane's. "If we don't trust each other, this won't work."

Trust a stranger with her life—and more, the lives of her patients and teammates. The enormity of that landed somewhere Sloane didn't have time to examine. She adjusted the harness buckle instead.

"And you can trust I will come back for you," Jax said, "no matter how long it takes."

"Good to know." And for reasons Sloane could not define, she believed her.

The silence surrounded them for a moment, the quiet interrupted only by the soft ping of cooling metal. Jax rested one arm along the back of her own seat, her fingers absently tapping against the fabric.

"You strike me as someone who doesn't like surprises," Jax said finally.

"Not in my line of work."

"Then here's one for free—this place will surprise you. The people. The pace. Maybe even yourself."

Sloane stared through the windshield at the endless green mountain range obscuring the sky. "Is that supposed to be encouraging?"

"Depends on how you feel about surprises."

Sloane finally looked away toward the mist curling over the ridge and over at Jax. "I prefer challenge."

Jax's smile was small, but it reached her eyes this time. "Funny, so do I."

"I should get back," Sloane said, aware of being alone with a woman who at turns annoyed and intrigued her. "We're going to need all day tomorrow setting up in here."

"You're the boss." Jax pointed to the rear. "After you, Doctor."

Sloane climbed out, Jax right behind her. The sounds of the town returned—someone hammering somewhere up the street, a dog barking in short bursts, the low hum of a truck engine.

"See you at the roadhouse," Jax said. "I want to button up the aircraft."

"Of course," Sloane said. "I appreciate the…instructions."

"All in a day's work," Jax said and walked away.

Sloane crossed the field to the gym, where Mina sat on an empty crate outside the now closed doors. "All finished inside?"

"For today at least." Mina stood and stretched. "We'll need to do some reorganizing once we start seeing folks, I'm sure."

"If and when. Ready to go check out our accommodations?" Sloane looked around. She had no idea what the town looked like now that she was on the ground. "Wherever they are."

"I've got directions. Come on." As they started off, Mina said, "Well?"

"Well what?"

"How was the tour? And the tour guide?" Mina's voice was mild, her eyes anything but.

"She's very professional," Sloane said.

"And competent," Mina said dryly, echoing Sloane's earlier assessment. "What else?"

"And I know better what I'm working with."

Mina pursed her lips as if about to comment but just shook her head. "Of course you'd think work first."

Sloane walked on in silence. Of course.

Work first. Always work first.

But under that, the image of the cockpit lingered—Jax's voice low in her ear, and the promise that surprises were coming.

She wasn't sure yet if that was a warning or a reason to look forward to what came next.

❖

Jax ducked her head under the rotor blade, the smell of hot oil and faint ozone from the avionics hanging in the cool mountain air. Bean looked to be halfway through the post-flight checks, moving around the aircraft with the unhurried precision of someone who'd done this a thousand times. He didn't really need her, but she needed the excuse to put a little distance between herself and Sloane Marshall. She couldn't get a handle on her, and that bothered her. At first glance, Sloane looked like the typical civilian doc who'd never seen battle, or a disaster.

Smart—no doubt. Competent—most likely, in the right situation—like the clinic they'd just organized inside the gym. But under fire—because that's what it would be if they had to make a real emergency field run, not a transport but a treat on the ground, save them or lose them emergency—who knew. Before a few minutes ago, her experience told her Sloane would be out of her depth. Most city docs would be, too.

Sloane's questions during the tour had been sharp and specific, her gaze tracking every piece of equipment as if memorizing where it lived. No wasted words, no wasted movements.

So now? She wasn't quite sure how to categorize Sloane.

That wasn't like her.

"I don't like surprises either," she muttered.

"Say what?" Bean asked.

"Nothing."

"Hell of a landing." He checked the tension on the tie-down straps. "That field's softer than it looks."

"Better soft than slick." Jax coiled a headset cord and stowed it in its case. "I've seen worse."

On the far side of the field, the small knot of locals and AERIS personnel clustered near the school's gym. She couldn't see Sloane.

"So," Bean said after a beat, "how'd she like the tour?"

Jax glanced at him over the curve of the rotor hub. "What tour?"

"The one you just gave her. Don't play dumb, Kincaid—I could see you in here." His tone was light, but his eyes were curious, probing.

Jax shrugged, checking the fuel gauge out of habit. "She's the team lead. Needs to know what she's working with."

"Sure," he said slowly, drawing the word out. "That all it was?"

Jax let the question hang in the air, focusing on locking the cowling panel. Whatever he was hunting for, she wasn't giving him any ammunition.

"She strikes me as the type who wants the full picture before she moves a muscle," Jax said finally. "That's not a bad thing."

"Nope," Bean agreed. "Not bad at all. Just wondering if she surprised you."

Jax huffed. "Only in that she didn't flinch. Most docs coming out here for the first time get a little glassy-eyed when they see how far from anywhere we are. She just…absorbed it."

"She's got some fight in her," Bean said.

"Yeah," Jax murmured, more to herself than to him. "She does."

The sound of laughter drifted toward them—Mina's, high and

unrestrained, and Sloane's, lower but warm. It caught Jax off guard, that warmth. She'd only seen flashes of it—on the tarmac when Mina showed up, during the flight when something out the window had genuinely impressed her—but it left her curious.

Bean tightened the last strap on a gear crate and straightened. "So, you planning to bunk in the bird or…?"

Jax shot him a look. "Is that your subtle way of telling me the accommodations are crap?"

He grinned. "I saw the quarters when Reggie and I unloaded over there. Let's just say 'cozy' is the generous term. You might be sharing close air with the doc for the next month."

Jax laughed, shaking her head. "Guess I'll risk it. Not like I haven't bunked with worse."

Still, as she turned back to the cockpit to finish her checks, she pictured sharing that kind of close space with someone as controlled and exacting as Sloane. How would that fly? Exciting, maybe. Worrisome, definitely. Luckily her discipline was solid.

She stowed the thoughts as neatly as she stowed her gear, but the picture lingered all the same.

Chapter Five

Nightfall
Storm brewing

"You're quiet," Mina said.

"Oh." Sloane, startled from her reverie, looked around. They'd already walked half the distance to the roadhouse, if her internal compass was working. "Sorry. Just thinking."

"It's been a heck of a day," Mina said. "Everything okay?"

"I don't have a lot to go by, but I suppose the situation could be worse." Sloane snorted. "At least we're not sleeping in tents."

"We haven't seen the roadhouse yet, so don't get too comfy," Mina said. "But I was thinking more along your impressions of the team."

Sloane hesitated. She hadn't been thinking about the team—at least not all of them. Just Jax. Striding into the briefing and immediately commanding the space even when she wasn't speaking. At the controls of the Bell, cool and controlled. In the cockpit during the tour, so close Sloane could feel the heat radiating from her. Just impressions, really, of Jax—her intensity, her presence like a pressure wave any time she was near, her undercurrent of skepticism about Sloane's ability to handle the mission.

And *her* reactions, swinging wildly from interest to aggravation. Not the kind of response she usually had to anyone. A slight huff from Mina reminded her she was wandering. Again.

"Everyone except Callie seems seasoned and capable. That's a plus," she finally said.

"Mmm. And personally? How do you feel about them?"

Sloane cut a glance her way. "Why does that matter? I don't need to know anything else to work with them."

Mina laughed. "Yes, but now and then, don't you find someone just a little more interesting than most? *Personally*, I mean."

Sloane frowned. "No, not really. I don't seem to have that kind of reaction to people."

"No?"

Sloane sighed at the skepticism and blatant challenge in her tone. "I know you're talking about Maxine. That was ages ago, and *once*. I thought I was curious, but looking back, I think I just *thought* I should be attracted, or whatever. I wasn't."

"That was, what, sophomore year in college?" Mina said. "No one has come along to tweak your antennae since then?"

"My *antennae* are occupied with loftier matters." Sloane slowed as the road, now really more like a wide path, curved along the river and seemed to run right into it. "Are we lost?"

"How could we be? There's only one main street, which is a generous term, and Lynette said the roadhouse is at the far end."

"I hope it's on stilts," Sloane muttered, eyeing the roiling muddy water. "And why are you quizzing me about ancient history now?"

"Because I never get you alone for more than a quick check-in," Mina said. "I know how much time you spend working, and I always assumed you didn't mention seeing anyone because you didn't have time for anything serious."

"You're right. I don't." Sloane picked up her pace. Discussing her lack of interest in a relationship or, knowing Mina, the sex that was supposed to go along with it, really was not what she wanted to dig up. Not even with her best friend. She was quite happy with her current situation—work kept her busy and fulfilled. Why look for problems?

"But—"

"That must be it," Sloane said, sighing internally at the reprieve from a discomforting topic. *She* wasn't bothered by her relationship status, after all. At least, she rarely thought about it, and that was just fine. "Come on, let's see what we've got."

The roadhouse didn't look like much from the street—a long, narrow, two-story structure with plain, weather-worn clapboard siding, a narrow front porch, the blue-gray paint worn pale on the rickety-looking railing where hundreds of hands had probably passed. The front door, a dull brown windowless affair, stood open to either circulate some air or dilute the odors inside.

Sloane hoped for the former. She paused in the doorway to let her eyes adjust before stepping directly into what appeared to be the lobby. The air smelled of woodsmoke threaded through the lingering scent of some long-ago fry oil. Someone had scrubbed the floor hard enough to raise the grain on the pine boards. A long counter ran the length of the wall opposite the door, its old, varnished surface dark as molasses. Square glass cake stands domed on top—empty now—hinted at the pies or donuts they'd probably held when itinerant workers lodged there. The chalkboard menu behind the counter listed burgers, a stew, something called "river fish," and coffee for a dollar if you brought your own mug. The left side of the room was a patchwork of sturdy wood tables, mismatched chairs, a battered piano under a window that framed the last thin wash of evening light. She cataloged exits without thinking: front door, back hall to the kitchen and a rear door she could just make out past a hanging string of metal bottle caps. Windows that stuck half-open on leather straps.

Mina brushed past with a quiet whistle. "Home sweet temporary home."

Temporary. The word settled some of the heaviness in Sloane's chest. Four weeks minimum, six at most. Then Boston again, the ER, the rhythm that never surprised her. She closed the door behind them, and the latch clicked with a sense of finality, as if now there was no turning back.

But then, why would she? She had a job to do.

Work. Always work first.

"Sleeping quarters are upstairs," Eli said as he came down the wooden staircase, a headset draped around his neck. "I'm just getting the comms set up. We can brief just as soon as everyone gets their gear stowed."

"Copy," Jax said, appearing from nowhere, or maybe Sloane had been too busy inventorying the room to register her arrival. She had a duffel over her shoulder, her hair damp at the nape like she'd rinsed off with a sinkful of cold water. Bean followed her in, toting a similar worn green duffel. "Where do you want us, Eli?"

"Follow me," Eli said.

Sloane joined the group trooping up the narrow staircase. The stairs turned once on a tight landing, then opened into a short hall with four doors. Two rooms, one on the left and one on the right, were open: bunk beds with a quilt on each bed, folded in precise rectangles, a single chest of drawers, and a pitcher and basin on a washstand. Like a stage set for an earlier century. The last room on the right was the bathroom. Sloane tried not to think what that might be like, considering the age of the rest of the building.

"I'll set up the comms center in the main room downstairs," Eli said. "It's got the best angle to the satellite. Bean and I will bunk in a room down there, too. That way Bean will know when he needs to get the bird set to go." He pointed to the room on the right. "Mina and Callie there," another gesture to the room opposite, "Jax and Sloane there, since you two are most likely to be called out in the night."

"Right." Jax looked at Sloane and waved a hand toward the first room. "You and me here, then."

Because it made sense, Sloane couldn't argue. Sharing the room meant less time between alert and liftoff, fewer bodies to step over. Efficient. Logical. She nodded once and stepped inside, ignoring the unease coiling in her middle.

The room was larger than she'd first imagined, though the impression might have been due to the window. It ran almost the width of the wall, divided into three panes with old, wavy glass that broke the moonlight—when had night fallen?—into soft shards. A line of hooks she hadn't noticed ran above the narrow dresser. Someone had left a tin of matches and a stub of a candle on the windowsill, the wax smeared on the flaking wood.

"Well, it's clean." Sloane walked to the stacked beds. Someone had already brought her bags up and stowed them by the foot of the bunk bed. The quilts smelled of sunshine. She detected no grit beneath her soles. That was a plus. She preferred clean to comfortable. The awkwardness of sharing an intimate space with a stranger she would endure.

Jax tossed her duffel to the top bunk with a smooth, careless motion and caught the strap with two fingers when it slid. "Top's easier for me. Less traffic."

"I'll take the lower," Sloane said. A concession she didn't need to justify.

Jax's gaze skimmed over her face, not a challenge so much as a read. Sloane kept her expression composed. Jax nodded, the smallest acknowledgment of something decided correctly, and unzipped her bag. Sloane's shoulders inexplicably tightened at the quiet rip of nylon teeth being pulled, as if the act was private and somehow she was an interloper.

Mina's voice carried through the open door. "If anyone's keeping notes, I prefer not to be near a window when strangers can see in."

"I hadn't thought of that," Sloane said. Why hadn't she?

"Curtains look thick enough." Jax slid the plain brown fabric along the brass rod with the same quick, assured movements with which she did everything. She looked over at Sloane and seated the window latch with a metal click. "All secure."

For an instant, Sloane's old habit, to trust herself more than anyone else's assurances, surfaced and then, oddly, the shallow hum of discomfort just below her ribs disappeared. "Thanks."

"Not a problem," Jax said mildly, watching her with that intense expression that always made Sloane's pulse race.

"Comms in five," Eli called from below.

Sloane stripped off her jacket, folded it once, and set it on the bunk. Her bag went under the bed along with the medical bag. That one she placed at the front where she could find it first in the dark.

"You know the bird is fully stocked," Jax said mildly.

"Yes, of course. But I want the essentials with me if I'm going to be working in the field."

"Fair enough." Jax slung her flight jacket on a hook and rolled her shoulders. The motion pulled her T-shirt tight across the long plane of her back. Sloane looked away, not fast enough to convince herself that noticing those little things about Jax was nothing.

"Ready?" Jax asked.

"For comms? Yes." Sloane brushed her hands along her thighs, a habit when she readied for duty. "For everything else? We will be."

"Fair answer." Jax smiled. "Let's go hear how Eli wants us not to die."

Downstairs, Eli had the radio console along with computers and a trio of monitors lit like a small city. The lobby had morphed from lounge to mission control in the short span since they'd gone upstairs. The piano was shrouded with a canvas drop cloth, the chalkboard wiped down except for a slant of block letters: NO PARTYING 2200–0600. The back door stood propped with a wedge of split pine to let in a cool line of night.

"I'm glad I was warned about the partying before I broke the rules," Sloane muttered.

Beside her, Jax laughed. "You *are* hiding a sense of humor."

Sloane tilted her head. "No one has ever accused me of that before."

"Then they weren't paying attention."

Jax's slow smile sent a rush of warmth to Sloane's chest, and she quickly looked away. What was wrong with her? Reading too much into innocent remarks. As if Jax actually gave her any thought beyond wondering if she could cut it when the going got rough.

"Ridge repeaters are cranky," Eli said, tapping a mountain peak on a map projection with a knuckle. "We've got a primary channel for in-town, and a secondary for ridge ops when the weather cooperates. Cell service is an optimism we don't indulge. If I can't raise you and you're due, we assume the worst and start the clock. SAR out of Bonneville, an hour south, will assist. Again, weather and manpower permitting."

"Meaning," Jax said, "we're pretty much on our own."

"Good summary." Eli looked at Sloane. "We'll want to rotate someone in the clinic at night for knocks. Say until eight, then they'll have the radio overnight, and we'll post a call number."

Sloane nodded.

"Sarah's in town, but reachable. You two"—Eli's eyes shifted between Sloane and Jax—"are the fast team. If the call is off-road, I notify Bean, and we spin up the bird if we can't roll the RTV to the location. The mayor's on call, but she'll stay out of our way unless we ask."

"I'll draw up the med call schedule," Sloane said. Eli might be used to coordinating multidisciplinary teams, but assessing who had the medical knowledge to triage was her job.

"Good enough," Eli said. "Questions?"

Jax asked about battery swaps for handhelds, signal shadows on the north ridge, and the schedule for refueling the RTVs. Sloane listened and filed away the answers. So many moving parts, organized so efficiently. Impressive and, for her, comforting. A sense of order settled her anxiety.

"Okay," Eli said finally, flicking off the smaller panel lights until the map stood alone in a ring of hazy light. "We're up at oh-five-hundred once the clinic starts rolling. If something breaks before then, you'll know." He thumbed toward the stairs. "Rest while you can."

Sloane caught up with Mina in the hallway upstairs. "I don't usually go to bed at ten o'clock at night."

Mina laughed. "That's because you're probably working a double most days."

"Why not?" Sloane said. "I really don't need much sleep."

"No?" Mina eyed her pensively as she sat cross-legged on her bunk. "I'd offer you a seat, but…no chair."

Sloane grinned. "I'm not staying. You, as I recall, can sleep anywhere."

"You should try it," Mina said gently. "It sounded like Eli expected us to be busy this month."

"That's fine. At least the time will pass faster." Sloane paused at the door. "In case I didn't mention it, I'm really glad you're here."

"Me too. You going to be okay with the new roommate?"

Sloane stiffened. "Of course. Why wouldn't I be?"

"Oh, I don't know. I got the impression you weren't a fan. Two alphas circling the same territory and all."

Incredulous, Sloane blurted, "What? I'm not…that's ridiculous."

Mina's eyes sparkled. "It's a metaphor."

"Metaphor or not, I am not competing with Jax Kincaid for anything."

"One big happy family, then." Mina pulled a pair of plaid flannel pajama pants from her bag. "Go get some sleep."

"See you in the morning," Sloane muttered and shut the door softly behind her. Whatever was Mina thinking? She and Jax were simply doing their jobs. Nothing more.

Her assigned room was still empty. On impulse, she switched off the harsh overhead bare bulb light and lit the small candle on the windowsill, making sure it was well away from the curtains. In the dim, warm glow, she hurriedly turned down the bedcovers, pulled sweats and a T-shirt from her bag, kicked off her boots and lined them parallel to the bed's edge—toes out for speed—and changed out of her travel clothes. The building, despite the absence of voices, was far from quiet. Pipes ticked, old timbers creaked and settled, and something she refused to think could be anything but a very small mouse scratched in the wall.

She'd just slipped under the soft sheets when Jax ducked back in with a thermos.

Jax glanced over. "Good. You're still awake. I was afraid I'd wake you."

"You don't have to worry about that. Is that coffee?"

"If we need to make a night run, we'll want it."

"Good." Something she hadn't thought of. Then, softer, more for herself, "Good."

Jax's gaze grazed her. Not a smile. Not *not* a smile. "Ready for lights out?"

"Please."

The room went black except for the rectangle of thinned moon through the old glass. The thump of boots and the rustle of fabric. Boards sighed as Jax climbed to the top bunk.

Sloane didn't remember Jax unpacking anything. Was she sleeping in her clothes?

Without clothes?

An image, wholly imagined, flashed through her mind, and she reflexively squeezed her eyes shut. To keep her mind from wandering paths she didn't want to travel, Sloane slowly mapped the bed and willed her body to relax. Hollow in the center, firm on the edge, the strut in the frame near her knee that she would have to remember not to whack in a hurry.

The darkness thickened. Above, Jax shifted once and went still. Sloane counted backward from one hundred, then forward again. She lay there inside herself, senses tingling with the awareness of someone else so close. As she always did when faced with uncertainty, she planned.

This would work. She did not have to like the bed or the rustic accommodations, or the intimacy of another person breathing above her head. She only had to do the next thing right, and then the next.

Chapter Six

Week 1: clinic open
Heavy cloud cover, light rain

Sloane arrived at her usual time in the morning to find a smattering of people waiting on the bench under the canopy outside the clinic. Opinion in town had apparently progressed from curiosity to cautious acceptance. The morning before, she'd seen her first patient—an elderly man complaining of sore joints, likely caused by gout, that had been bothering him for months. Dietary advice and an anti-inflammatory for him. At the end of the day, a young mother had brought in a crying infant who "just wouldn't stop" and now wouldn't eat. Acute otitis would do that to anyone. Sloane had prescribed Tylenol and antibiotics. Simple routine ER cases a med student could handle. Not challenging, yet satisfying. And from the looks of the group watching her approach, successful enough for others to risk coming in.

"Morning," she called as she juggled her travel mug of Eli's excellent coffee and unlocked the double doors, which, thanks to Bean's attention, no longer froze every time she inserted the keys. "We'll be with you in a few minutes."

"That's okay, honey," a matronly woman in a faded cornflower blue housedress and, incongruously, muck boots said with a hint of mountain twang. "We ain't got no bus to catch."

Honey.

Sloane just smiled. Buses were another thing missing in Coulter's Gap, along with reliable cell service, takeout of any kind, and paved sidewalks. She hung her rain slicker on a peg by the door, flipped on the lights, and powered up the computer and portable lab equipment.

She'd worn scrubs, provided by Eli—the man thought of everything—and opened a new box of latex gloves just as Mina came in on a gust of cold, damp air.

"Hoo-ee, I'm sick of rain," Mina said. "And I see we have some brave souls waiting outside."

"Yes," Sloane said. "Good thing Bean and Reggie got the tent up out there."

"Hi everyone," Callie called, hurrying in after Mina with an eagerness Sloane hadn't seen in Boston since the residents arrived the first week of July. "Should I start the triage?"

"Sure," Sloane said. "Let's get started."

As she expected from walk-ins, nothing too startling, but more than the usual proportion of common ailments that had gone unattended because there wasn't anyone to ask. When she stopped to check her watch during a lull, the morning had disappeared.

Mina caught her eye from behind the folding table they used as a desk. "Steady stream."

"Hope you brought sandwiches in that cooler," Sloane said, draping her stethoscope around her neck.

"Help yourself. If I was single, I'd be romancing Eli. The man thinks of everything."

Sloane laughed. "I know."

She ate a roast beef sandwich along with the rest of the coffee and motioned to the next patient, a grizzled mountain of a man in a work shirt patched at both elbows and weeping, psoriatic patches on his hands and neck. Topical corticosteroids from their small pharmacy supply for him.

By late afternoon, the line had trickled to a stop. Callie was restocking gauze and tongue depressors with the focused intensity of someone who thought supplies multiplied when neatly aligned. Mina worked through the stack of supply slips, cataloguing what they'd used.

Reggie walked in the door and called, "We're heading out."

Sloane looked up in time to see the transport crew loading the last of the empty pallets into the big trucks before the door closed. "Hope the roads are drier than the ones around here."

"You and me both." Reggie shook his head. "We'll be back in a month to pack you all out of here."

A month. Sloane's stomach lurched. Why did that sound like forever?

"Try not to get lost out there," Mina said, dry as chalk.

"Not today." He grinned, gave a two-fingered salute, and hurried out.

A moment later the roar of the big engines reverberated through the walls and slowly faded away.

"With them gone," Sloane said quietly, "I feel a little marooned."

Mina tilted her head, studying her. "You're not. We're not lost, and people know where we are."

"Yes," Sloane said. "I'd feel better, I guess, if I could make a phone call. Even send a text."

Mina leaned back in her chair, tapping her pen against the clipboard. "Who would you call? If you needed someone, I mean?"

Sloane stared. Who *would* she call? Not her family. The only friend she had was watching her from a few feet away. The answer crystallized, and she felt herself blush. *Jax.*

Jax, who never seemed rattled, who exuded calm competence and surprising intuitiveness.

Fortunately, Mina seemed not to notice her reaction. "You're not alone here. Everyone on this team knows what they're doing."

"You're right. I think the gray and the wet is getting to me."

Mina huffed. "I hear that. You about ready to wrap it up?"

After five already, and dark beyond the windows. "Yes, let's call it."

Outside, the air had grown heavier, clouds pressing low against the ridge, the taste of rain sharp at the back of her throat. Across the field, the Bell stood in its cleared patch of gravel, blades stilled, cabin door shut. Jax wasn't there, not right now. A refuel and practice run with one of the local EMTs to a nearby town, she'd heard Jax say earlier.

Tracking Jax's comings and goings had become an unintentional habit. She noticed when Jax returned to the bunkhouse at night, sometimes slipping inside for an hour before dawn, sometimes not at all. The night before she'd seen her converse with Eli, then head out into the dark and fog, straight for the Bell like it was home.

Curiosity. That's all it was. That and professional interest. They did have to work closely, after all. But curiosity didn't explain the way her chest tightened when the door stayed shut until morning, or the way her pulse skipped when she caught sight of Jax striding down the path from the landing zone, flight jacket thrown over her shoulder, eyes shadowed but intent.

Mina flicked up her hood. "Big day today."

"Clearly we've passed inspection," Sloane said.

Mina followed her gaze across the lot to the Bell. "She works strange hours."

"Jax?" Sloane concentrated on the muddy path ahead.

"Is there another female pilot I've missed?" Mina asked.

Heat climbed beneath Sloane's collar. She couldn't see Mina's smirk, but she heard it. "Pilots are a breed, at least the ones I've flown with on medevacs. Always restless. Always waiting for the next callout, like that's the only thing they really enjoy."

Mina made a humming noise. "Probably all of them are trouble. Some of them are probably even worth it."

Sloane didn't answer, the unsettled feeling of being thrown into a world unlike any she'd ever known clinging like a half-remembered dream she couldn't shake. And, like the mountain weather, one she couldn't escape, only endure.

❖

Jax debated returning to the roadhouse after midnight, but she'd had a feeling. Just one of those itches between the shoulder blades that something was coming. She'd learned pretty quick on her first tour that ignoring those feelings could get you dead. If trouble was coming, she wanted to be close to the team. To Sloane. She was Sloane's partner, after all.

She eased into the room, climbed to the top bunk. Sloane wasn't asleep yet—she could tell by the measured cadence of her breathing. Sloane was trying, though. Jax recognized the technique. That had worked for her. Before.

"You should get some sleep," Jax said quietly in the stillness when Sloane shifted in the bunk. This sleeping arrangement might turn out to be too close. Not physically. She'd slept in tighter quarters. But Sloane wasn't another soldier. She occupied the space differently. Filled it in a way that made the distance between them shrink.

"I'm sorry. I thought I was being quiet." Sloane turned over again, making the bunk bed shake a bit.

"You were. I could hear you thinking."

"Could you read my mind?" Sloane sounded half-teasing and half-worried.

"Something along the lines of you wondering how you ended up here."

"Actually, that was last night." Sloane shifted again. "This is strange."

Jax imagined her sitting up. "Sleeping in bunks?"

"Sleeping with…*near* someone."

"Yeah, I get that." Jax's chest tightened. Only strange when you cared.

"Did you bring enough coffee for two?" Sloane asked.

"Yes." Jax laughed. "It will still be there in the morning. Get some z's."

"Fine," Sloane muttered.

Jax folded her arms behind her head and smiled in the dark. Prickly. Out of her natural element. But word had it the clinic was humming and folks were showing up. Sloane might be overqualified for walk-in clinic cases, but she was meeting the need. Good for her. Jax closed her eyes on that thought, still smiling.

Somewhere in the middle of the night, she awakened to the soft, staccato crackle of Eli's radio downstairs. Eli's deep baritone and another voice, rapid and adrenaline-pressured, triggered her awareness as similar calls had done for a decade.

From below, a whisper of fabric as Sloane rolled over. "I'm awake."

"I know."

She'd never been asleep. A question for another time.

The hall door opened with a soft snick, and Eli's square silhouette filled the opening. Jax vaulted off the end of the bed and grabbed her pants. A second later, she dug in her duffel and tossed a flight suit to Sloane. "You'll want this."

"Thanks." Sloane rose, pulled on the suit, and stepped into her boots.

Eli said flatly, "Ranger crew clearing a line on Walton's Spur reported a male down, leg pinned under a felled trunk, conscious but shocky. No road access."

"Landing site?" Jax asked, tugging on her flight suit.

"We can get you within a quarter of a mile—dry creek bed. They'll meet you. Bean has the coordinates."

"Copy." Jax headed for the stairs. This was the kind of call she lived for—urgent, clear, no space for anything but movement. Sloane was already beside her, medical bag in one hand, the thermos in the other. No wasted words from her. No scramble—just ready.

"Any details on the injury?" she asked Eli, who led the way down the stairs, her voice even.

"Crush from a roll," Eli replied. "They've stabilized the tree but can't lift it. Crew says distal color's bad."

Sloane said, "He'll need fluids before that log comes off, then." Her jaw tightened almost imperceptibly, the kind of reaction Jax only noticed because she was watching for it.

"Reperfusion syndrome—yeah," Jax said, already mentally mapping the gear they'd need to move the log and make sure the guy didn't crash when they did. "We'll take the FP kit and fluids with us from the Bell."

Behind them, hurried footsteps, and Callie blurted, "I'm awake. Can I—should I—could I come?"

Sloane looked over her shoulder, gave Callie a single measuring look. Jax had seen it countless times on drill sergeants. Sloane nodded once, tight, no time wasted deciding. "Stay on my shoulder and do exactly what I tell you."

Callie's face lit up like she'd been invited to fly the aircraft herself. "Yes, ma'am—uh, yes, Doctor."

"Sloane," Sloane replied without breaking stride. "Remember, act first, question later."

"I understand," Callie said.

Jax really hoped she did.

Jax sprinted out the back door and across the short gravel run to the RTV, Sloane keeping pace at her side. Eil hopped behind the wheel, and less than two minutes after he'd come upstairs, they were en route to the airfield. They made it in under three. The Bell's rotor thumped—Bean readying for flight. The night air had an edge sharp enough to bite, bringing with it the scent of sap, river water, and the faint tang of oil that clung to the helicopter no matter how well it was cleaned. The sight, the sounds, charged her with energy that verged on joy.

Bean had the side doors open, the panel lights pooling across the cockpit.

Jax glanced at Callie and Sloane. "Buckle up. Wheels up as soon as I hit the seat."

Sloane jumped onto the skid and into the bay as if she'd done it a thousand times. Callie followed almost as quickly.

Impressed, Jax vaulted into her seat in the cockpit. "Flight check?"

"Battery hot, rotors clear," Bean reported and tipped his chin toward Sloane and Callie. "Surge kit and traction splint are loaded.

Weather's holding, but fog's forming on the north ridge. We've got a window—small one."

"Good enough." Jax brought the panel from dark to alive, the green glow reflecting off her gloves as she ran her pre-flight. Fuel where she wanted it, hydraulics steady, rotor RPM in the sweet spot. She toggled the intercom. "Seat belts, headsets. Secure all gear."

"Secure," Sloane's voice answered in her ear, small in volume but close, as if she'd leaned in to speak directly to her. Callie's quick "ready" followed, breathless but pitched low.

"Launch in three-two—" Jax said. "Eli, we're airborne. ETA to LZ sixteen minutes."

Beyond the windshield, the obsidian sky, stars obscured by clouds and rising fog, was layered in shadow and shifting air she read with her body as much as her instruments. Bean fed her terrain notes in short, precise bursts.

The ranger crew, a half dozen headlamps bobbing in the gloom, lit the LZ—a narrow ribbon of rocky creek bed between towering evergreens. Jax eased the 412 in, nose to the thin breath of wind, keeping her descent slow. Young pines on the far edge of the scant clearing trembled in the rotor wash. The skids touched soft mud, and she let the power drop to idle.

"We're down," she said. Bean waited for the wash to settle and dropped the doors. "Go."

Sloane jumped out first, steady and balanced, and reached up for Callie to pass her the med packs. Callie exited with a smaller pack, swaying slightly as she fought for balance on the uneven ground. Men and women in hard hats and headlamps converged on the helicopter, grabbing equipment as Jax passed fluids, splint, monitor, and the basket stretcher from the medical bay.

"Where's your vehicle?" Jax called.

"This way." The man leading the ranger crew, eyes wide and urgent but voice steady, brought them down a rough slope to where two off-road vehicles idled. Everyone piled in with the gear, and minutes later, Jax caught sight of a swath of cleared forest where felled trunks crisscrossed like giant pick-up sticks. A man lay on his back, one leg trapped beneath a trunk thick as a barrel. The crew had cribbed smaller logs to keep it from shifting, but the thing was wedged against rock. He was pale under the stubble, chest rising too fast.

Jax carried resuscitation equipment, motioning Callie and Bean to follow with the stretcher, as Sloane hurried toward the injured man.

"Hey," Sloane knelt, headlamp angled to spare his eyes, "I'm Dr. Marshall. We're going to get you out."

"Can't feel my foot," he rasped.

"I hear you," she said, voice low and steady. "What's your name?"

"Rafferty. Butch Rafferty."

"Okay, Butch. I'm going to touch your leg—tell me what you feel."

Jax wrapped a BP cuff around Butch's arm and checked the reading. Eighty systolic. Sloane quickly but thoroughly examined Butch's lower leg, subtle tension escalating in her jaw as she checked for a distal pulse. Sloane looked her way, shook her head subtly.

"Pressure's eighty," Jax said. "Not much getting down there. Callie, got the IV in?"

"Yes," Callie said, just a bit breathlessly. "Roger?"

Jax smiled fleetingly. Good for her. She'd already passed the first test. She'd set to work without a single question.

"Callie," Sloane directed, "run the saline wide open. Hang the second bag as soon as that one is in." Then, to Butch's crew, "Do not move that trunk until I say." No raised voice, no barked orders, just the kind of authority that made others listen.

Callie crouched beside Jax, hands shaking only slightly as she prepared another bag. A moment later, her voice stronger, she announced, "Second bag running."

Sloane leaned closer to Butch. "We're giving you something for the pain. You'll feel a little floaty but you'll stay awake."

Butch's breath hitched. "Want to stay awake."

"You will." She glanced at Jax and murmured, "Ketamine."

"Right here." Jax pulled the prefilled syringe from the med kit. Working this close to Sloane in the flickering light, she couldn't help notice the determined set of Sloane's jaw, how she never flinched despite the groaning logs, the way her hands stayed rock steady even as Butch's color went gray. When their knees touched as they shifted positions, neither pulled away. The contact shouldn't have registered through all the chaos, but it did.

Jax shook her head. *Focus.* "Start with half a dose?"

"Yes," Sloane said.

Jax inserted the needle in the IV port. "Copy. Going in."

A moment later, Butch, voice slurred, muttered, "Think I can walk now."

"Not just yet." Sloane, one hand on Butch's arm, looked to Jax. "We need traction before we roll that trunk and a tourniquet placed high on the leg. Don't tighten it unless I say."

Jax looped the strap of the CAT tourniquet over her wrist, ready to pass it around the leg and secure it above the wound. "Bean, bring the traction splint in close."

"Set," Bean said, kneeling opposite her.

Sloane motioned to the ranger crew chief. "Get ready to lift it."

"Yes, ma'am."

Moving quickly but methodically, four of the crew reinforced the cribbing, then positioned pinch bars.

When Sloane met her gaze, Jax nodded. "Ready."

Sloane called the count. "One…two…lift."

The trunk shifted just enough to free the leg. Jax rapidly placed the strap and windlass around the thigh but left it slack. "Bean, get that splint on. Callie, watch his pressure."

Bean drew the splint into place and Sloane guided the stirrup under the heel. As the loggers eased the trunk back onto the cribbing, Sloane checked the ankle pulse again.

"There it is," she said quietly, satisfaction evident. "Faint, but there."

Kneeling in mud, a streak of something—maybe blood—on her cheek, Sloane looked and sounded like the tricky maneuver was just an everyday thing. She grinned at Jax.

Jax grinned back. "Outstanding."

"Indeed." Sloane held Jax's gaze a moment longer than necessary, an expression in her eyes that Jax couldn't read. Pride? Surprise? Something else? Then she looked away, back to Butch, but not before Jax caught the slight flush on her cheeks despite the cold.

Jax pushed the observation aside. They had work to finish. "Well done, Doctor."

"Excellent work yourself," Sloane said, busy checking Butch's vitals. "Couldn't have asked for a better assist."

Jax's shoulders tensed, the unexpected praise lodging beneath her ribs like shrapnel as she and Bean secured the straps on the litter. She didn't want thanks, had stopped deserving it when she'd zipped Rodriguez's body into the bag.

"We're set, Doctor," Jax said, carefully avoiding Sloane's gaze. Duty done, time to keep her distance.

"Let's move him," Sloane said.

With the splint secured and Butch bundled in blankets, they got him on the RTV and back to the Bell. Jax's territory now.

"Load him onto the forward bench for in-flight monitoring," she advised and climbed back into the pilot's seat to radio Eli. "We're ready to deliver for ground transport."

Eli gave her the all clear to lift.

"Forty minutes to transfer," she called over the intercom as she set the course. She glanced back for a visual check. First-timers, after all.

Callie, seated aft of Sloane, smiled for a second when their eyes met before quickly looking away, as if she'd been caught doing something she shouldn't. Jax toggled the intercom to Sloane's setting.

"We're set for liftoff, Doctor. How's our guy?"

Sloane came back, her voice warmer than usual, "Vitals are holding. Fast as you can, Chief."

Chief. Not anymore, but no point hammering on it.

"Roger that." Jax adjusted their altitude to skim the valley, rotors steady against the rising fog on the ridge. "Hold on."

"Avoid the bumps if you can."

Jax grinned. "Always do."

Sloane laughed, and Jax switched off the intercom. The patient was stable. The job wasn't done, but that had been good teamwork. Sloane had worked under pressure without wasting a second or a word. Competent. Unflappable. And damn it, she'd even looked like she might be having fun.

The tension in the cabin dissipated as the miles ticked away. Jax watched Sloane in the medical bay through the mirror—her gentle touch on Butch's shoulder, the way she tucked a strand of hair behind her ear with the back of her wrist to keep her gloves clean. Utterly focused, but tender all the same. When Sloane looked up and caught her watching, Jax didn't look away. Couldn't, for a heartbeat that stretched too long. Maybe, just maybe, she'd been wrong about a few things where Sloane was concerned.

Chapter Seven

Week 1
Steady rain, the river rises

Sloane awakened before dawn, the three hours' sleep she'd managed after Eli had picked her and Callie up on the airfield more than she'd expected. And enough. Jax had never returned. Had she and Bean gone out on a supply run? Found a late-night bar in town—if the town even had one? Slept in the helicopter? Jax couldn't know anyone in town well enough to spend the night with, could she?

And what did it matter where Jax had gone last night?

She crept downstairs, hoping not to wake anyone.

Eli lounged in one of the threadbare floral armchairs in the big lobby, a steaming mug in hand. "Coffee's hot back there in the kitchen. Couldn't sleep?"

"Early riser," Sloane said. "You too?"

"Lousy sleeper," Eli said, apparently less concerned about appearances than her.

"You sure it's okay if I steal a cup?"

"We're all in this together. If you empty the pot, just put on another."

"You should make a sign," she said, heading for the kitchen.

Behind her, Eli laughed.

Strange, waking up in a place where she'd never choose to sleep in this lifetime and conversing with a man she didn't even know, and somehow it all feeling right. She found a clean-looking cup with a bluebird on the side in a battered cabinet, decided that was hers, and filled it with excellent-smelling coffee. There was even milk in the ancient refrigerator.

"Need a ride?" Eli asked when she walked back into the lobby.

"No, I'm going to walk." She sipped the coffee. As good as it smelled.

Outside the front window, morning arrived as thin sunlight slipped over the far ridge in long, pale ribbons. When was the last time she'd actually seen dawn break? And when had she suddenly gotten whimsical?

"I'm headed to the clinic to get organized. Should I…I don't know…sign out or anything?"

Eli chuckled. "I won't keep tabs on you, but I *will* need to reach you twenty-four seven. There's a radio over there on the counter with your name on it. Don't lose it. We don't have spares."

"I never lose anything," Sloane said. Not anymore.

"Today should just be another getting acquainted day for the townfolks. Walk-in clinic, essentially. Some may come by just to take a look and see what we're about. Shouldn't be too busy."

"That's fine." She clipped the radio to the waistband of her jeans and pulled on the light denim jacket she'd packed. She'd only brought jeans, plain shirts, and boots. Eli, she assumed, had left a neat pile of scrubs on her bunk. Fashion was not an issue out here.

"Community potluck dinner Saturday at seven at the church," Eli called as she headed for the door. "Our official welcoming party."

Frowning, she turned. "Mandatory?"

He grinned. "'Fraid so, Doctor."

She sighed. "Wonderful."

"By the way," Eli said casually, "heard the run last night went smooth as silk. Nice work."

"Really." Had Jax reported on her performance? A prickle of annoyance warred with pleasure. They *had* done good work. "The patient was stable when we transferred him. I think he'll keep his leg."

"Yep, nice work."

"Just doing my job," she said softly, and stepped out into the day.

Fifteen minutes' brisk walk later, she fit the old brass key into the lock on the gymnasium door and let herself in. She set her bag on the table—correction, intake desk—and stood still, taking in the repurposed gym that didn't look like much of a clinic. She'd never cared about the bright and shiny. There'd been nothing bright and shiny about the night before.

She'd knelt in the mud on a slope slick with needles and worked with the bare essentials by the light of a half dozen flickering headlamps while the cribbing groaned and Butch's breath grew fainter with each passing moment. No X-rays, no anesthetist to manage pain and fluid resuscitation, no blood transfusions if he'd crashed when they'd moved that damn log. But she'd had what she'd needed all the same—two experienced field medics, no matter what other titles they went by, a cadre of determined wilderness firefighters, and a shared mission to save Butch Rafferty *and* his leg. Jax had worked beside her as if they'd done it a hundred times before, anticipating her steps without jostling for control. Surprising, now that she thought about it. Not the competence—anyone with Jax's training and experience would be steel in a crisis—but the ease with which Jax had matched her rhythm, an easy fit where she'd been braced for friction.

Even Callie had been steady under pressure, and Jax had helped there, too, overseeing Callie's actions without being asked.

The thrill of success came back to her in a rush, and her heart raced. Taking in the curtained cubicles on either side of the center aisle and the treatment table, monitors, portable ventilator, and crash cart in the emergency bay, she nodded with satisfaction.

Not bright and shiny, but efficient, organized, and ready for whatever came.

Anticipation buzzed through her, quite unlike anything she'd experienced before. So far this mission had been filled with surprises. And surprising people—none as much as Jax Kincaid. Jax was different from the pilots she'd flown medevac missions with before. Jax didn't just transport her from place to place—she was a skilled member of the trauma team on the ground. Plenty of ego, but not that got in the way of her fitting in where needed. Maybe that *was* due to her confidence—she knew when to lead and when to take the second seat.

The door opened, letting in the smell of rain, and Mina barreled in, her curly hair damp and wild. She dumped a cooler on the counter and pinned Sloane with a questioning look.

"So," Mina said, dragging out the word. "You snuck out awfully early today. Avoiding anyone in particular?"

"I did *not* sneak," Sloane said evenly. "Ask Eli. We had a lovely conversation."

Mina laughed. "I can imagine." She hiked a hip on the edge of the table. "How did it go last night?"

Sloane pulled a towel off a metal rack against the wall and tossed it to Mina. "You're dripping. Did you get the details?"

Mina dried her hair and tossed the towel into a nearby canvas laundry hamper. "Just that you all had a trauma callout in the boonies somewhere."

"That describes it pretty well." The starless sky and endless black of the impenetrable mountains flashed in her memory as she recounted the events for Mina. "I was waiting until after shift change to call the receiving hospital for an update."

"Sounds like a save," Mina said. "So how was it, working with the hot chopper pilot?"

"Forgive me," Sloane said, sidestepping the remark, "but I've known you for twenty years, and you're just now telling me you're bi?"

"Not bi," Mina said, grinning, "but hardly blind. What was she like, then? Besides the fact that the entire ranger crew is probably ready to put her face on a church candle for even trying to fly in there."

Sloane stacked charts in the intake area to buy a few seconds. "Exactly what you'd expect—focused, totally prepared, exceptionally solid in the field."

Mina's smile sharpened. "That's a summary you'd put on a quarterly review." She angled her head. "You liked working with her."

Sloane resisted the urge to smooth the edges of the chart stack again. *Liked* had nothing to do with it. The work had clicked. The save had been flawless. All as it should be, as she'd done hundreds of times before. And yet—Jax's solid presence beside her in the flickering lamplight, the way she'd anticipated her every move, as if reading her mind, the way she'd anchored the ranger crew with calm directions, and the way she'd murmured *Good work, Doctor* in the Bell had settled under her ribs like a warm embrace and refused to move.

That was inexplicable. And unsettling.

"She gave Callie room to learn without control of the situation," Sloane said at last. "Didn't crowd me. Didn't need the last word."

"Wow," Mina said, expression brightening. "Now we're using adjectives. Next thing you know, you'll say she's nice."

Sloane pursed her lips. "Let's not go crazy."

Mina snorted, then sobered. "Word is the river's already high out by the approach road. Eli's fussing about fuel and batteries. We're in for more of this." She flicked a glance toward the windows, where rain played off the glass in soft, relentless ticks. "You sure you slept?"

"Enough." Sloane opened Eli's preliminary schedule for the coming week—more like wish list if any emergencies arose, but that was the name of the game. Today was supposed to be walk-ins and vaccinations, pretty unthreatening for a population uncertain of their presence. "We'll handle what comes."

Mina shrugged. "Including reluctant locals and pilots with eyes like trouble."

Sloane didn't rise to Mina's poking, and fortunately, the door creaked open and their first walk-ins arrived. A grandfather who'd run out of insulin and his grandson for a tetanus shot after stepping on a nail. Callie arrived soon after, and in minutes, the clinic found its rhythm. Call a name, coax a laugh, stitch or swab or reassure, keep the line moving. Mina's humor loosened clenched shoulders. Callie, cheerful and willing to undertake anything asked, prepped syringes with a carefulness that made Sloane's chest ease a notch, and assured anxious parents and children alike that it *wouldn't hurt a bit.*

As morning passed noon and turned to after, the rain thickened, a steady undertow behind the voices and the low hum of the refrigerator. Somewhere after two, Jax rolled in on a wave of cold air, flight jacket unzipped, hair damp at the ends, carrying a second cooler she handed off to Callie. Scanning the room with a narrowed gaze, as if searching for hazards, her focus landed on Sloane and held, brief as a metronome tick—but something in it hummed.

"Fuel's topped for the generator," Jax told Mina, tone clipped-soft, the way people talked when they didn't want to rattle the quiet. She pointed to the cooler. "Made a run this morning to pick up extra doses of DPT. The mayor called Eli and said the schoolteachers contacted parents and said the kids needed the shots, so he ordered up extra."

"Good call," Mina said. "We're going to need the rest of our backups for the outreach in the mountains next week."

Listening to the exchange, wondering when and where Jax had made the flight, Sloane studied the consent form for the next child. When she looked up again, Callie had gravitated to Jax with tie-down straps in her hands and appeared to ask a question. After a moment, Jax answered and then half turned away. Callie hesitated for a second, disappointment crossing her face, before heading back to her station. Jax shot Sloane a quicksilver glance over Callie's shoulder, so brief it was almost nothing, a thin thread pulled taut across the room. Sloane felt it anyway.

"She has a crush," Mina murmured beside her.

"Who does?" Sloane reached for a clean pair of gloves.

Mina shot her a look. "Callie. On our pilot."

"That's…not my concern."

"Hmm." Mina sounded skeptical. "Jax doesn't seem to notice. She keeps looking over here."

Sloane carefully did not look in Jax's direction. No matter what Mina thought, Jax's interests, in Callie or anyone else, were *not* her business.

The next lull lasted four seconds. A woman shouldered in with a girl limp in her arms, breath hitching in quick, shallow pulls. Everything in Sloane snapped to.

"Back here," she said, already pulling on the fresh gloves. "Set her down on the table."

The child's cheeks were scrubbed raw with fever, lashes clumped with tears. Each exhale whistled through tight airways.

"Kaylee," the mother got out, voice ragged. "She—she couldn't lie down. I couldn't—"

"It's okay." Sloane found the girl's hand, held it, and put her stethoscope to the narrow chest with the other hand. Wheezes, high and musical through both lungs. No crackles. Not drowning yet. "Mina, pulse ox. Albuterol neb. Warm the mask." She pitched her voice for Kaylee and made it gentler. "You're going to be fine. You hear your breath? Like a tiny flute. We're going to help it play easier."

"I'll draw up the meds," Mina said. "Callie, can you get the mask?"

"I've got it," Jax said, sliding up to the other side of the table without Sloane's having to ask. Leaning down to eye level with the little girl, she held up the nebulizer mask.

"I wear a mask just like this when I fly the helicopter," she said, voice low enough to smooth panic. "Want to see something cool?" She lifted the mask so Kaylee could watch the mist gather. "It's medicine turned into air. Fighter-pilot stuff. You can hold it yourself if you want."

Kaylee's eyes flicked from Jax to Sloane and back. She reached for the mask, her fingers trembling. They steadied when Jax curved her palm around the girl's hand and helped her place the mask on her face.

"Yep, just like that. Good job, Kaylee," Jax murmured.

The first soft hiss of aerosol met the next hitching breath. Sloane listened again. Wheezes still there, but the exhale turned less ragged. Her shoulder muscles eased by a hair.

"PO2 ninety-one," Mina said, watching the tiny monitor climb. "Ninety-two. Ninety-three."

"Good," Sloane murmured. "Let's ride this round, then prime another."

Callie hovered at the end of the table, anxious to help and probably afraid to guess what came next.

"Set up a second neb, Callie, and epinephrine as a backstop—but leave it capped."

Callie's chin jolted once. "Yes, Doctor." Her hands were steadier than her voice.

Sloane angled toward the mother. "Does she have a history of anything like this?"

"We…" The woman's eyes filled. "I work mornings. We haven't had…" She shook her head. "She wheezes sometimes. It passes."

"You were right to bring her in," Sloane said. "We'll get you a plan." She didn't add *We'll find the funds*. She'd talk to Sarah about contacting the county about programs to fill the gaps the system had cut in people's lives.

Kaylee's color improved with the second treatment, the shaky blue rim at her mouth warming toward pink. Jax kept her palm where it was, helping Kaylee hold the mask, unshowy, steady as ballast. Sloane tried not to watch that hand and failed. She tried not to notice the way Jax's attention stayed wholly on the child and yet somehow seemed aware of everything else in the vicinity.

"PO2 ninety-six," Mina said. "Heart rate down to ninety."

Sloane exhaled and the knot under her sternum unwound. The room expanded enough to admit ordinary sound again: rain beating at the windows, the murmur of patients waiting to be seen, the reassuring hum of the fridge.

"Kaylee," she said softly, "you'll be able to go home soon."

Kaylee blinked solemnly and, with grave ceremony, handed the mask back to Jax. "You can be a fighter pilot, too."

Jax smiled, guiding it back to her face. "Maybe, but I'm not as tough as you."

Kaylee closed her eyes, a faint smile on her pale pink lips. Sloane watched her a moment longer, then wrote instructions which she knew without asking Kaylee's mother would follow. Inhaler schedule. Fever care. When to come back. She folded the paper and met the mother's eyes. "We'll give you meds for two days. Then come back and Callie will check her. If anything feels wrong before that, just come back. There's a number here you can call at night, or if that doesn't work, contact the mayor."

"I surely will. Thank you." Her voice broke and she looked away. "Thank you all."

With one arm around Kaylee, the instructions and med package gripped in her other hand like a lifeline, she led Kaylee out.

Silence hung for an instant until Callie released a small, surprised breath, as if she'd been holding it without realizing it. "That was—" She stopped and gazed at Jax, cheeks flushing for no reason Sloane could see but one. "You were *awesome* with her."

Jax gave Callie a small nod. "Just lending a hand. Mina, you want me out of the way now, or should I get in the way somewhere useful?"

"Useful is fetching and carrying," Mina said cheerfully, already moving. "You can start with that cooler you abandoned."

Jax's gaze slid to Sloane and held. "Hope I didn't get in your road—you had it covered."

Sloane hated how easily heat rose under her skin. "You calmed her down. That sped up the treatment."

"Team effort." Jax shrugged, smiled so briefly Sloane might have missed it if she hadn't been looking. But she was. "Anytime. You call; I'll come."

It wasn't a promise, but it sat inside her, refusing to budge, warm and sure in a way Sloane didn't care to examine. She turned to the sink to wash her hands and caught her own reflection in the small, wavy mirror. Softer, as if looking at a stranger. She told herself it was just the release of tension after a good save. She told herself many things. The rain ticked on as if it knew better.

Mina bumped her shoulder as she passed. "Potluck Saturday night. Eli wants a show of faces."

"I know," Sloane said. "I'm going."

Mina's grin was all nurse and a bit of friend. "Wear something that says *I am a friendly* and not *I am a porcupine*."

Sloane reached for the next chart. "I don't do porcupine."

"Everyone does porcupine," Mina said. "Some of us just hide it better."

"I'll be sure to hide mine, then."

Sloane didn't look toward the door but she knew Jax had left. The air inside cooled just a bit, as if the sun had slipped behind a cloud.

Chapter Eight

Week 1
Deluge, the banks hold

Jax walked into the church basement aka community center a little after seven and stood for a second at the threshold, reading the room the way she read the sky—who congregated in clusters, where the currents gathered and flowed. Not looking for anyone in particular.

She didn't see Sloane.

From behind her, Eli said, "Got another weather update."

"Yeah? Let me guess—more rain."

Eli huffed. "And then some. Unseasonably early and unseasonably heavy."

Jax raised a brow. "We staying?"

"Sure. But we might want to bump up the schedule on the supply runs."

"Say the word," Jax muttered, moving aside as a stream of people hurried in, shaking rain from hats and slickers. Across the long hall, a cluster of teenagers pretended not to be seen—or interested in anything—though most of them eyed the locals setting out cornbread, beans, salads, and a mountain of bread and pies. The tables pushed into long, irregular rows practically groaned with the weight.

"Here comes the boss," Eli muttered.

"Thought that was *you*," Jax said and nodded at Lynette Ronson. "Mayor."

Eli covered a laugh with a cough. "Evening, Mayor."

"Lynette is fine." She surveyed the room. "Looks like the whole town has come out to get a gander at you all."

"Better now than later," Eli said.

Lynette hummed in agreement. "Best to jump right in, I always say."

Jax didn't comment. She was used to being categorized and judged—the new kid in school, the green recruit, the field-promoted officer. Like most small, tight, self-sufficient groups, Coulter's Gap radiated wariness toward those who hadn't earned the right to belong yet. Outsiders sorted into *Maybe* and *We'll See* boxes. She didn't mind. She preferred clear lines.

She eased away toward the refreshment area, grabbed a mason jar of what she hoped was cider, and leaned against the wall in an out-of-the-way corner. The milling crowd drifted by, conversation floating over her in snatches. An octogenarian vet who wanted to talk about his war experience cornered her, and she obliged him by listening. A half hour tops, and she'd have done her duty and could slip away.

And then she saw Sloane.

Jeans, soft-looking scoop-necked top in a lighter blue, and honey-blond hair, damp with rainwater, caught back in a clip that had given up and let a strand escape to curl along her temple. The change from clinic to off-duty wasn't dramatic, but the first glimpse was enough to spark a small catch in the chest. Like a breath stopped halfway. Not a familiar sensation.

Neither was her questioning her first impressions the way she'd been doing most of the day. She relied on swift assessments and sound judgment to keep herself and others alive. Where had she gone wrong with Sloane Marshall? True, Sloane in professional mode was exacting and precise. No wasted words, no room for second thoughts. But rigid and brittle? Not this Sloane. This woman, with her softer edges and easy smile, appeared to have shed armor Jax hadn't appreciated at first glance. She didn't want to notice that now. She noticed anyway.

"Sweet or unsweet?" Callie appeared at her elbow with two mason jars, the question more an offering than a choice.

"Got one for now." Jax lifted the cider. Callie's eyes lingered a beat longer before she set one jar aside. Jax recognized the look from the clinic earlier. A little bit of interest that would burn out fast enough unless someone tossed kindling on it.

She didn't plan to.

"Food's over that way," Callie said, pointing. "Do you want a plate? I'm going for one."

"Thanks, but I can get it." Jax waited a beat, then added, "Come on, let's get in line."

She kept a careful, friendly distance between them, as Callie chatted about the amazing day at the clinic. Jax didn't need to add much, so she tended to her potato salad and roast ham slices while watching Sloane move through the crowd. Brief stops for brief hellos, her smile genuine but reserved. She'd probably worked rooms like this a hundred times in some big city fundraiser or other.

When Mina appeared and dragged Callie off to talk with Sarah, Jax got in the dessert line. When she reached for the last slice of blueberry pie, a hand going for the same plate grazed hers.

"Sorry," Jax said, pulling back.

Sloane laughed, close enough for Jax to catch the faint scent she'd noticed earlier—vanilla or bergamot, delicate but not cloying. "Don't apologize. You flew a bleeding man off a mountain. You can have the last slice."

"I didn't do it for pie. Besides, you did the heavy lifting." Jax heard the ease in her own voice and wondered where it came from. "But I'm not stupid."

Sloane smiled when Jax took the pie and popped two brownies onto a paper plate.

Mina walked up and grabbed a piece of apple cobbler. "Got a couple of free seats at our table."

Jax glanced at Sloane. Maybe she preferred other company. Or none.

Sloane met her gaze. "Sure. I've done my share of socializing."

"I probably haven't, but I did talk to the mayor," Jax said.

"Counts double," Sloane said.

Grinning, Jax followed and sat beside her at a round table with the rest of the team. Bean was halfway through a story she'd heard before about a trout the size of a pickup that got away. Sloane laughed like she enjoyed the telling. She didn't laugh much, but when she did, her eyes lit up and her face glowed. Jax caught Mina watching her from across the table and eased back in her chair. Staring. She'd been staring at Sloane.

"Heard you two worked well together," Mina said at last, the nudge in her tone not subtle.

Jax lifted a shoulder. "We got the job done."

Sloane added, "Bean and Callie were there, too. Teamwork."

"Oh, no doubt. Still, your first big trauma in the field," Mina said. "Some people just…sync."

"Sometimes," Jax said, "you get lucky."

Sloane's fork stalled halfway to her mouth. She didn't look at Jax. "Sometimes."

Sloane could have meant anything—and probably meant nothing special. But the way she said it—as if turning the thought over in her mind and deciding it could stay—gave Jax a jolt all the same. Surprise followed by pleasure. That kept happening around Sloane.

Conversation around the table picked up, casual and easy. Jax listened. Sloane's thigh brushed hers in the close quarters. She could have moved away. She didn't.

Before long parents began corralling kids, and people straggled out in clumps. Mist swirled in every time the door opened. The actual rain had stopped for a while at least.

Eli rose and picked up his paper plate and mason jar. "I'm headed back. Anyone for a ride?"

"I'll take it," Mina said. "My feet are reminding me I've been standing on them all day."

"No, thanks, I'm close by," Sarah said.

Bean cleared his throat. "Think my legs need a stretch."

Sarah said easily, "Come on, I'll give you a tour of the town—ought to take a minute or two."

Laughing, Bean followed her out.

"Callie," Eli said, "there's room in the RTV."

Callie hesitated, casting a questioning look at Jax.

Jax indicated her half-full mason jar of cider. "Gonna be a bit yet."

"Oh, okay then," Callie finally said to Eli.

Sloane said, "I want to say good night to a few people."

As the others left, Jax said, "You really going to socialize more?"

"Actually, no. What I really want is a little quiet. I'm going to walk home."

Jax stood. "I'll give you some space, then."

"I haven't noticed you're a big talker."

"Not usually." Jax hesitated. "It's more than a mile in the dark."

"I doubt I'll need protection, but I don't mind company."

Jax blew out a breath. That hadn't come out right. "I didn't mean you needed a bodyguard."

"I know." Sloane rose, that rare smile blooming. "Let's try this. I'm walking home. Want to walk back with me?"

Unearned familiarity usually made her itch, but this didn't feel like some kind of trespass. More like the way a cockpit goes quiet when two people know what they're about and trust each other to do it.

"Yes," Jax said, "I would."

She meant it and didn't question why.

❖

Outside the church hall, the only light in the gravel lot came from the few brave stars peeking through the storm clouds. None of the bright halogen lights Sloane was used to when leaving the hospital in Boston. No security guards watching her walk away either. The faint sound of voices carried each time the church door opened and closed. A few trucks angled toward the road, dark mounds reminiscent of boulders viewed from the air. Off to the right, the river rushed, an impatient sound as if it had somewhere important to go. The night air carried traces of woodsmoke with undertones of evergreen, a scent she was starting to recognize as the mountain's. Sloane angled toward the narrow path that ribboned along the water, and Jax fell wordlessly in beside her.

She'd said she wanted quiet, and Jax didn't try to fill it, just matched her pace, hands tucked into her jacket pockets, her stride loose and easy. For a while, their footsteps scuffing in the gravel path, the wind clattering the pine boughs, and the rumble of rushing water was conversation enough. Sooner than she expected, the tightness in her shoulders and the turmoil of the potluck—rapid-fire introductions, halting questions, and well-meaning scrutiny—evaporated into the mist.

"What did you think of it?" she asked finally. "The potluck."

"The usual kind of first look from people who aren't sure what you're about. Mostly friendly curiosity, some folks questioning without committing to anything." Jax shrugged. "Not all that different from arriving in a village in Afghanistan."

Sloane slowed. "*That* is a scary analogy."

"Didn't mean it to be," Jax said quietly.

"So tell me what it was like," Sloane said, walking on.

"When we rolled into town with our transports and our command centers, people greeted us with a mixture of hope and suspicion. Always took a little time for them to trust us. Feels a little bit like that here."

"That tracks." Sloane angled around a root and, when her foot slipped, grabbed a branch, slick with rainwater, and teetered unsteadily.

"Whoa," Jax exclaimed, a hand on Sloane's back. "Okay?"

"Yes, fine." Sloane edged away from the side of the muddy trail.

She *so* did not need to fall into the river. Jax's hand remained where it was a second longer, solid and oddly reassuring. Even when she moved it, the phantom heat lingered like a brand. "I've never had that kind of experience. I'm used to patients mostly trusting me, especially in the ER when it's clear, I hope, that I'm there to help them."

"I've watched you with your patients," Jax said, flicking wet hair off her forehead with a careless gesture that said she was so used to physical annoyances she didn't even notice. "You have a way of focusing on them that makes them feel safe."

"I…" Sloane's breath caught and heat bloomed in her chest. The sound of the roaring river vanished, drowned beneath the static in her ears. Jax had been watching her work? "I hope you're right. I fielded quite a few questions tonight that didn't sound all that trusting."

"They'll come around." Jax laughed. "Sounds like I had it easier than you tonight. Most of them wanted to talk about the helicopter."

"Makes sense," Sloane said, on stable ground now that the conversation wasn't about her. "It's got flash. Why ask about hypertension when you can ask about top speed and lift and…whatever."

"Seven separate versions of that, actually. Also one request to hover low enough to knock walnuts off a tree."

Sloane laughed, the brightness of it strange to her own ears. "Please tell me you declined."

"I referred the gentleman to the general store for a ladder." Jax glanced sideways. "How about you? Tight circle of people gathered around every time I saw you."

Every time? How many times had Jax noticed her? Sloane's mind caught up with the questions, and she said, "It was a lot more polite hellos and questioning eyes than I'm used to. But the food was good. Whoever made the cornbread should be in charge of morale."

"Lynette's mother," Jax said. "She also asked me if we could airlift her pie to her sister two valleys over since the road's out."

"And did you say yes?"

"Absolutely not." A beat. "I said we *might* be able to refuel there the next time we made a supply run and *might* be able to drop off a pie. If there was one for the airfield crew."

"Pragmatic."

"That's me." Jax walked a few steps, hands tucked in her pockets. "You laughed."

"I reserve it for special occasions."

"I'm honored, then," Jax said teasingly.

Such a strange conversation, so easy and yet so…personal. Quite unlike any she could recall. Damp wind lifted the hair along Sloane's temple, and she pushed it back, brushing fine grit from her skin. The rain had picked up, and she raised her collar.

"Cold?" Jax asked.

Did she notice everything? Sloane shook her head. "Just a little damp. I'm glad you're here, though. It's damn dark out here. I don't think I've ever been anywhere there's no artificial light."

"Never been deep in the mountains before?"

"Ski trip, once."

Once, *before*.

"So did you always know medicine was it for you?" Jax asked, tone casual, non-threatening.

Maybe that was why she answered. The memories snapped into focus—of sitting alone in her bedroom with the single bed, the solitary desk, the aching void stretching as far as she could see. Weeks that became months, when no one noticed, even after she eventually emerged. "I happened to see an episode of *ER*—by accident really. And something clicked. Some people probably saw excitement or drama or heroism when they watched that show. I saw order and logic and problem solving. I saw myself doing what I could be good at while keeping people alive at the same time."

Order out of chaos.

"That's definitely what emergency medicine is all about," Jax said mildly. "Restoring order, in just about every way."

Sloane flushed. Had she actually said all that out loud? She pulled herself back to the moment. Needing to escape the past, she asked, "How long were you in the Army?"

When Jax didn't answer, she added, "You don't have to talk about it, if it's too personal."

"Not that much to tell," Jax finally said. "Just over a dozen years."

"Flight medic?"

"Warrant Officer. Rotary wing. I joined at eighteen."

The path widened and the river swung away from them, leaving a narrow shelf of saplings leaning precariously out over the water. In the distance, lights flickered through the trees. The roadhouse.

"What made you join?"

Jax's breath paused; her stride didn't. "My grandmother died."

Sloane waited. She understood some memories were too fresh, some wounds too unhealed, to uncover.

Jax's voice, softer than Sloane had ever heard, whispered on the wind. "She raised me. With her gone, I had no reason to stay. A recruiter looked at my scores and asked me if I'd ever thought about flying. I said *I have now*."

"What did she do—your grandmother?"

"Work. All kinds." A small laugh that wasn't really one. "Drove a school bus. Cleaned the post office. Collected me from places I probably shouldn't have been and made me a sandwich like that solved it." The quiet again. "She had a small house with a tin roof. When it rained like this, the sound drowned out everything else. Felt like safety." Jax's gaze flicked toward the river. "I haven't heard that in a long time."

"You should be glad the roadhouse roof isn't tin. The roof is about two inches over your bunk." Sloane paused. "I guess it doesn't feel much like safety, either."

"I'm not a kid anymore," Jax said easily. "How about you? Family. Siblings?"

"No." The denial came so quickly, the pain took a moment to surface. With it, the shame. "That's not true."

"What isn't?" Jax's voice gentled. Calm and patient.

An image rose, buried but never forgotten—matching clothes in a closet, separated only by color—hers more subdued; sneakers with colored-coded shoelaces, hers white, of course, Sybil's always bright and sparkly; school photos indistinguishable except for the smile. Sybil's, not hers.

Don't speak of it. Ever.

Her mother's voice. Cold, distant.

Sloane forgot to watch the path, stumbled on a rock. Jax caught her sleeve above the wrist and held. Steadied her.

Sloane didn't pull away.

She took a long breath. "A twin. I…I don't…my family isn't close."

Jax's hand didn't move, the pressure light, enough for Sloane to know it was there and enough to tell her she could end the contact. She didn't. The river continued its soliloquy, a warning to stay away. Somewhere in the dark, a night bird made a single sound and stopped.

"Everyone always wants to know about family." Sloane swallowed the bitterness. "Sorry, I don't usually say that out loud."

"Say whatever you need to," Jax said, her voice low and vibrating with certainty, "or nothing at all. I'm here."

This was where she closed the door, locked away the past, and retreated to the order and logic of her world. Jax's hand on her sleeve changed the moment just enough to keep the door from swinging shut.

"Our house…our life…was ordered and predictable, with rules to keep it that way. We learned young about expectations, and what was acceptable behavior and what wasn't. I followed the rules. The rules were all I could count on. Order out of chaos." She huffed. "Not altogether logical, I suppose. But then what about life ever is? It's not important now."

Jax's thumb shifted the smallest degree, tracing the curve of her wrist.

"Nothing illogical about finding a way to cope. That's sane. And damn strong."

Sloane released a breath that had lodged in her throat. "Yes, well, whatever doesn't kill you makes you strong. Isn't that how the saying goes?" She walked a little faster toward the beckoning light of the roadhouse. Out of the past.

Jax dropped her hand, striding silently beside her, as if waiting for her to decide their direction. The absence of her touch left a void Sloane wasn't quite ready to embrace. "Was there only your grandmother, then?"

"When I was young my mother dropped in every few months—we never knew when she might appear," Jax said, voice flat. "Whenever she showed up, it was like Christmas. Presents and laughter and hugs. Then one morning she'd just be gone again—no number to reach her, no address. No warning at all."

Sloane ached at the image—a child, abandoned, over and over. "Just the two of you, then, you and your grandmother?"

"Yep, just us. My father is a name on a form somewhere."

"It sounds like she was enough."

Jax laughed faintly. "She was pretty much everything—provider, caretaker, warden, and most of all, my advocate. She always told me I could do anything, be anything, I set my mind to."

"She sounds wonderful."

"I hadn't figured out what I wanted," Jax said, "and then she was gone. The Army did the shaping after that. I wanted to fly. The Army, and now AERIS, gave me that."

A downed trunk bridged a shallow run where the bank had washed out, and Sloane set her foot on the wet bark, hesitated. Jax offered her hand without speaking. Sloane grasped it, not surprised to find it warm and steady. She got her balance, and they were across in two strides. She dropped Jax's hand when they reached the opposite side.

"You do a lot more than fly," Sloane said, "even if you want people to think you're just a helicopter jock. You save lives. You train others to do the same."

Jax turned, the light from the roadhouse stronger now, illuminating the blaze in her eyes. "Helicopter jock, huh?"

"That and more." Sloane waited for the denial or the affront.

Jax laughed. "Kinda like the image."

Sloane rolled her eyes, certain Jax couldn't see her. "Of course you do, ergo—"

"Oh, now you're just looking for a fight." In the hazy light, Jax's smile, so easy and free, made her look even more handsome.

Sloane retreated from the image. "Entirely untrue. Only a sound conclusion, given the facts."

"You're a surprise, Dr. Marshall."

"I don't see how that is likely. Ask anyone…I'm organized, rational, and logical. Personally and professionally."

"Well, then, they don't see what I see." Jax's tone left no room for debate.

Sloane didn't ask what she saw. She might not be comfortable with the answer. Their conversation had already veered into territory she didn't broach with anyone, not even Mina. Thankfully, the roadhouse came into view, and the reality of why they were there drenched her more than the rain. Work. Work always came first.

She stopped at the edge of the clearing where the bunkhouse light flared a bright circle in the black night.

"Thanks for walking back with me," Sloane said.

Jax turned to her. "Sorry, it wasn't all that quiet."

"Oh, it was quiet in a different way. A few minutes' respite from a very long to-do list, starting with home calls in town tomorrow." Sloane stepped up onto the porch and turned when Jax didn't follow. "You coming in?"

"A bit later. I want to load some gear in the RTV. I've got evac training with the local volunteer firefighters, all three of them, and the two-man police force bright and early tomorrow."

Jax looked like she might take her hands out of her pockets. She didn't. For a second, Sloane wanted her to. Wanted that earlier touch again without the excuse of a slick log. A foreign desire, impossible to categorize. Without a logical explanation, she only had questions.

Jax scanned the sky where the ridge disappeared into a bank of dark clouds. "Weather's gonna sit on us for a while. Cold and wet."

"Lovely," Sloane muttered. "We'll have a fresh round of coughs, sore joints, and people slipping and falling in the mud."

"Small-town medicine, Doc." Jax's grin lifted Sloane's spirits despite the worsening forecast. No one had ever presumed to call her that before.

Strangely, she didn't mind.

"You should try to get some sleep," she said before she thought better of it.

Jax studied her, curiosity and a nearly brooding shadow in her eyes. "I don't want to wake you, coming in late."

"I'm a light sleeper," Sloane said, "so at least if you're there, I won't lie awake wondering where you are."

"Ah, okay." Jax sounded unsure.

That was new.

"I'll see you later, then," Sloane said.

Jax dipped her head once and nudged a small stone out of the path with the edge of her boot. Her hands stayed in her pockets, which made Sloane very aware of them all over again.

"Good night, Sloane," Jax said at last.

"Good night." Sloane stepped through the bunkhouse door and turned back once. Jax had already pivoted toward the river again, shoulders set against the rain.

Sloane clicked the door shut, surprised to see the lobby dark and quiet. In one week that felt like a month, she'd gotten used to seeing Eli ensconced at the comms station or relaxing in the big ugly chair he'd claimed with a coffee in hand or, on some evenings, what she suspected was a finger's worth of golden liquid. Scotch, perhaps. Upstairs, muted voices drifted from behind Mina's closed door. What sounded like a child's laughter followed her into her own room—one of Mina's children. Of course Mina would keep in touch with her family while away.

Sloane set her radio on the floor by her bunk and sat on the edge to unlace her muddy boots. She had no one to call to say good night. No one who would wonder how she was doing in this foreign land. Instead, she'd opened up without the slightest hesitation to a near stranger about ancient wounds she did her best never to revisit. How had Jax Kincaid, a woman vastly different from her in temperament and experience, slipped so easily through the armor she'd erected and seduced her into nearly talking about Sybil?

Without an answer, she sat a moment longer, letting the rhythm of the rain soothe the turmoil in her heart. Jax should come with a caution sign, one she would do well to heed.

Chapter Nine

Week 2
Weather warnings, forecast: rain

"So," Mina said, not looking up as Sloane picked up the next patient's chart, "how does it feel—getting through the first week?"

The rain had settled into a steady hiss on the clinic roof, a constant backdrop that edged from soothing into distracting as the morning wore on, making the hours feel longer than they were.

"*Through*," Sloane said, tossing her used gloves into the red trash bag. "Not sure *through* is the word."

"What word, then?"

Sloane exhaled slowly. Nothing in Coulter's Gap had turned out the way she'd expected. Not the town, with its yin-yang of equal parts warmth and suspicion. Not the makeshift clinic that had settled into its own rhythm within days and somehow seemed more familiar than the ER in Boston. Not the weather that pressed low and never quite cleared. And not Jax Kincaid, who moved through all of it, flying in and out with supplies or simulating rescues with volunteer firefighters, with a grin and attitude as if the air itself took instructions from her.

The first few times Jax had popped into the clinic unannounced, Sloane had barely registered her presence. She was working, after all. But then a day passed where Jax hadn't appeared, and by evening, Sloane worried something was wrong. The unfamiliar anxiety hadn't waned until Jax and Bean barreled into the roadhouse, rainwater dripping from their slickers, with a box of homemade cookies they'd "scored" from one of the trainees.

This...habit...was becoming a problem. She listened for Jax's return at night, relaxing only when she heard boots on the stairs. During clinic hours, she tracked Jax's schedule without meaning to—supply run at dawn, EMT training at ten, weather check at three. She was a doctor. She had work to do. Important work. She didn't have time for… whatever this was. This distraction that made her pulse skip when Jax smiled that particular way, the one that started slow and bloomed into something deeper.

Really, all she had to do was focus. Focus. She could control this. She controlled everything else in her life, didn't she? Except she couldn't control the way her breath caught when Jax appeared unannounced.

"Confusing," Sloane finally answered.

Mina looked up, eyes narrowing. "Want to elaborate?"

Sloane shook her head. "I'd say I feel like a fish out of water, but considering the weather, that's not accurate."

"Oh my God, that is *so* bad." Mina lifted a shoulder. "But I get the drift. This place isn't exactly Mercy."

"No," Sloane said softly, "it—"

The front door banged open and a mountain-sized man, rainwater cascading from him in sheets, rushed in with a blanket-shrouded figure in his arms.

"My wife," he rasped. "Something's bad wrong."

Sloane dropped the tablet on the desk and pointed toward the treatment area. "Over here. Tell me what's going on."

"It's the baby," he panted. Despite his obvious alarm, he placed the young woman in a plain white cotton nightgown stretched tight over a swollen abdomen down with extreme gentleness. "She says it's too soon."

The woman—more a girl really—appeared at first glance to be in her final trimester. She also seemed barely conscious.

"Mina, ultrasound," Sloane said, wrapping a BP cuff around the woman's forearm. "Callie! We need an IV here."

"Getting it," Callie called back.

Mina was at her side in a second. "How far along?"

"Thirty-two weeks," the woman whispered, eyes squeezed shut.

Her husband blurted, "Started with the cramping last night. She can't keep nothin' down. Feet all swole up, and then her hands, too.

The BP cuff inflated with a hiss. A moment later the readout appeared. 182/114. Sloane glanced at Mina. Severe hypertension. Vomiting. Disorientation. "Edema?"

"Plus four," Mina said, her fingers on the woman's swollen ankle.

"Is this her first pregnancy?" Sloane asked the man. "What's her name?"

"Yes, ma'am. Ruby." His voice broke. "Like the jewel, her ma says."

"Has she had problems before this? Did the doctor tell you her—"

"Ain't had one." The man's face twisted. "She been fine and the women—my ma and hers—said she was coming along like expected."

"I see," Sloane said evenly. "Ruby? Do you have a headache? Visual…uh, trouble seeing?"

"Bad," Ruby answered, her eyes still squeezed shut. "Head hurts. Lights all blurry."

Mina leaned close. "The fetus is small for dates if they're counting right."

"IV's in," Callie said.

Sloane straightened. "Callie, radio Eli. Tell him we need to get this woman to a hospital. Preeclampsia with severe hypertension."

Mina said, "Magnesium?"

"Yes, a loading dose first, then hydralazine."

Sloane turned to Ruby's husband. "What's your name?"

"Hap. Hap Brown."

"Hap, Ruby needs to go to a hospital where she and the baby can be monitored. Her blood pressure is too high, and that's bad for both of them."

"Can't she take medicine or tea or something at home?" He swayed slightly, his face pale.

"I'm sorry, no."

"We ain't got a hospital closer than a day's ride, and the roads are all washing out…we couldn't hardly get down the mountain in the wagon."

Wagon.

Sloane took a slow breath. "I understand. You did an amazing job getting her here. We're going to fly her in that helicopter out there."

"I…" He looked from Sloane to his wife. "Can I come?"

"I'm sorry, no, but I'll call you—"

"No phone," he whispered.

"Then I will find you," Sloane said firmly. "I promise you."

He met her eyes. "Yes, ma'am. If you say she needs a hospital."

"I do."

Eli's voice, steady as always, crackled over the radio. "Bell's spooled and waiting. Jax says the ceiling is dropping. If you're going, go now."

"Ruby," she said, not sure Ruby could hear her. "We're going to move you soon. We're going to give you medicine to keep you from seizing and help protect your baby. You might feel warm and a little nauseated."

Mina injected the meds. "Good to go."

The door opened again, and Bean rushed in with a stretcher aided by a man Sloane didn't recognize. Thick blond hair, White, about thirty, wearing a blue ball cap, brown canvas pants, heavy work boots, and the usual regalia common to all EMTs hanging off his belt.

Sloane motioned to Ruby. "We're ready here."

The EMT with Bean glanced at Hap Brown. "You're from up the valley a ways, aren't you? One of the Browns? I'm Jeb Whitcomb from down in the Gap."

"Mighty glad to see you." Hap looked and sounded relieved. "That there's my wife."

"We'll take care of her," Jeb said as he and Bean gently transferred Ruby to the stretcher.

"Mina, you and Callie have the clinic. I'm going with Ruby." Sloane grabbed her med bag and hustled for the door, the stretcher wheels catching in the threshold before popping free.

Mina's brows rose. "Got you covered here."

Rain blew sideways under the eave. The path to the landing zone had turned slick. Sloane tugged her hood up against the rain and concentrated on keeping her footing as gravel shifted under her boots. Across the field, the Bell crouched like something alive, blades ticking slowly as the wind teased them. Jax stood at the skids, headset already on, flight jacket half-zipped. Her lips pressed into a straight line, her gaze calculating.

"Status?" Jax shouted over the rising wash. She grabbed one end of the stretcher and Bean slipped past her toward the cockpit.

"Thirty-two weeks," Sloane called while Jax helped Jeb lift Ruby inside. "Severe preeclampsia. If we can't get to Asheville, we need the nearest OB-capable facility on the radio." She didn't look away from Jax's face when she added, "Time is short here."

"Asheville's ninety miles in this soup. Johnson City's closer and they've got OB on standby." Jax reached for her hand. "I'll give you as smooth a ride as the sky allows."

"Fast as you can, Jax." Sloane took her hand, even though she could jump the skid as well as anyone now. No time to question why the move seemed so natural, or why Jax's wide, warm palm grounded her in a way she hadn't known she needed. She turned and looked back out the open bay. "Jeb, you're with me."

His face lit up as he jumped in. "Yes, ma'am. But I never made a flight run before."

"First time for everything," Sloane said. She pulled on her headset.

For her, too, it seemed.

Jax's voice in her ear. "Buckle up. Secure your lines."

Sloane took the aft bench, knees bracketing the stretcher, left hand on the IV line, right hand on Ruby's shoulder. Jeb, across from her, attached the monitors, confirmed the pulse ox was secure, and checked the IV insertion site.

The Bell lifted and Sloane's inner ear popped. "Jeb? BP?"

"One-eighty over…one-ten."

Sloane clenched her jaw. Better, but not good enough. "Draw up the hydralazine…there in the med box behind you."

Jeb braced himself against the sidewall as the Bell lurched, tugged the orange med box from its bracket, and snapped it open. He rifled through, hands not as steady as she'd have liked, until he came up with an ampule and held it out for her to see that he had the right drug. His grin was boyish, relieved. "Got it."

"Good. Draw up five cc's and push it slowly."

"Talk to me," Jax said in her headset.

"BP's still too high. We're pushing a second round of hydralazine." Sloane watched the numbers tick, keeping one eye on Ruby and the other on Jeb, steadying the line while he inserted the syringe. "We're already running a magnesium drip." She gently palpated Ruby's abdomen, and Ruby moaned, barely aware. "How's our time?"

"Ceiling's down to eight hundred. Rain band ahead is heavier than it looked leaving the pad," Jax said. "Right now, we're at fifty-two."

"Fifty-two isn't good enough," Sloane said. "Her pressure's still climbing, and she's got upper abdominal tenderness. If she seizes up here, I can manage it, but I'd rather hand her to an OB team before that happens."

Jax didn't answer immediately. When she did, her voice went flatter, the way it had that night they'd treated the ranger trapped under the downed tree. When her face had looked carved from granite and her hands as steady as a compass needle pointing true north. "I can try

Caldwell Gap and cut five to seven minutes if the wind doesn't shear us off the ridge. It'll be rough."

"Take the rough," Sloane said. "I'll keep her on the stretcher."

The radio spat static. Then Eli: "River's up two feet in the last hour—low fields flooding on Mill Road. If Caldwell is ugly, don't be a hero."

"Copy," Jax said.

The Bell tilted and the world tilted with it. Rain slammed the windows like a handful of thrown nails.

Ruby's eyes fluttered open. Her face was pale and sweaty, her voice a whisper. "Is he…okay?"

"We're getting you to the hospital." Sloane didn't lie. She didn't promise. She brushed Ruby's cheek with the back of her hand. "People are waiting there to help you both."

The cuff cycled. 168/104.

"Better," Sloane told Jax. "Borderline, at least."

"Copy," Jax said. "Terrain ahead gets ugly in three. Hang on."

The Bell jolted down and right. Sloane's shoulder dug harder into the wall. The IV pole rattled. She caught it with a quick flick of her wrist and reset the clamp. Ruby made a choking sound.

"Breathe," Sloane said, holding the O2 mask to her face, preparing to pull it off if Ruby vomited. "We're almost through this."

She hoped.

Ruby's eyes rolled for a second, and Sloane turned up the drip. "She's on the edge back here."

"Copy." Jax said.

For some reason that single word steadied her racing heart. She watched the BP readouts, her pulse slowing as the numbers edged down.

"She's quieting."

"And the baby? You monitoring?" Jax. Steady. Involved. Not challenging.

Sloane shook her head. "Too much vibration for monitoring in flight. Our best chance is keeping the mother alive."

"ETA forty-three," Jax said. "If Caldwell gives me a clean line off the shoulder, I can make thirty-eight."

"Make thirty-eight." Sloane said.

The cuff cycled. 172 over 100.

Rain hammered the fuselage. Ahead nothing but gray and darker shadows. That had to be the ridgeline. Sloane stuffed a folded blanket under the right side of Ruby's back to relieve some of the internal pressure, checked the IV flow rate, checked the O2, checked the clamps. Calm lived in the checklist. Calm lived in the next action. So did survival.

Success meant tending to the small details in the midst of chaos.

The radio crackled again. A different voice—county dispatch: "Any aircraft in the sector, reports of trees down along Route 19. Avoid the valley floor."

"Already avoiding," Jax answered. "We're high."

"Jax, time?" Sloane asked.

"Ten to the ridge."

The Bell rocked again, then steadied as the nose dipped.

Jax muttered something Sloane thought was a colorful curse. "What?"

"Caldwell's dirty but doable," Jax said.

"Define dirty," Sloane said, not taking her eyes off Ruby's face.

"Winds shifting from two directions at once where the hollers meet. Like paddling across a confluence. I've got it," Jax said, and the way she said it made Sloane believe her.

Thirty seconds stretched and snapped. The Bell skated through the turbulent seam and found smooth air on the far side, as if someone had ironed the sky.

"ETA thirty-seven," Jax said.

"Thank you," Sloane said, and meant it more ways than one.

"Hospital's online," Jax said. "OB team wants your report. Hold on." A click, then Jax, "Go ahead."

Sloane held the mouthpiece as the helicopter rocked. "This is Dr. Sloane Marshall with AERIS medevac. We have a thirty-two-week gravid patient with severe preeclampsia…initial BP 182 over 114 and systemic symptoms. Diastolic now fluctuating in the 110 range post hydralazine and magnesium drip. Ongoing infusion at two grams per hour. No seizure activity. Fetus growth-restricted by fundal height."

"This is Johnson City ED," a woman said, her voice crisp and welcome. "L&D is ready. We'll meet you on the pad."

Sloane signed off and took Ruby's hand. "You hear that? The OB staff are waiting for you. They'll take good care of you."

"On final," Jax said. "Bit bumpy for a minute. Crosswinds trying to nudge us off-line."

Sloane resisted the urge to relax, even as relief slowly sapped the adrenaline. Not until she'd seen Ruby into capable hands. Four people in blue cover gowns converged on the Bell the minute the skids set down with a surprisingly gentle thump.

Sloane rattled off the essentials again as they transferred—last BP, meds, estimated fetal age—then gripped Ruby's shoulder. "They'll take care of you here. We'll tell your husband you were a star."

Then Ruby and her rescuers were swallowed by the automatic doors. The rain kept at its mission to drown them all.

Sloane stood in the lee of the Bell a moment longer than she had to, rain running down her hairline, headset crooked around her neck. Her pulse steadied. *Her* mission, at least, was done.

When she turned back to the Bell, Jax stood in the open bay. Waiting.

Sloane held her gaze as she ducked under the rotors, "Nice flying, Chief."

Jax grinned wryly. "Precious cargo. Ready to go home?"

Home.

It wasn't that. It was the valley and the gym and the bunkhouse that smelled like woodsmoke and disinfectant. It was Jax's moonlit shadow in the roadhouse bedroom at odd hours. It was the mountain and the relentless rain and a week that had challenged what she thought she knew about herself.

But maybe, soon enough, it might be something close.

"Yes," Sloane said with a nod. "I am."

❖

By the time Jax settled the Bell on the gravel pad and tied down the blades, evening had thinned the town to a handful of lights and a single truck using its wipers more than its brakes. She ran her pre-shutdown sequence by touch, and when she stepped down, Sloane was already waiting outside the wash, jacket zipped, face in that calm, neutral set Jax was coming to recognize now. The one that hid any number of feelings—irritation at being sent somewhere she didn't want to go, determination not to let a trapped man die, sadness when she spoke of family, and maybe, just maybe, the beginnings of trust.

Now, though? Exhaustion, adrenaline letdown. And intensity in the way Sloane's gaze tracked her as she approached that was new. An appraisal that had heat flooding her weary muscles. Without looking away from Sloane, she called, "Bean, you done in there?"

"Just tidying up," Bean called back. "Me and Jeb here are gonna go tap our thirst at Barny's after Jeb gets word to Hap Brown about his wife."

"How?" Sloane yelled.

"Phone tree!"

"Of course," Sloane muttered, pushing damp strands of wet hair back with both hands. Why hadn't she thought of that.

"You need to eat," Jax said. She wasn't asking.

Sloane studied her for a heartbeat longer, as if deciding whether to argue. Then she nodded. "There's not a lot of options, I'm afraid. I guess it's Eli's stew." She sighed. "Again."

"How does a foot-long hoagie sound?"

Sloane's eyes narrowed. "Surely you jest."

"Follow me."

To Jax's surprise, Sloane fell in beside her without question or comment. The main street—mostly a wide gravel track with patches of what had once been the tarmac surface—was three blocks long. One block past Barny's bar, the cleverly named General Store cast a rectangle of yellow across the road. Inside, a glass-fronted cooler hummed. Inside—various meats and cheeses, and miraculously, lettuce and sliced tomatoes.

"How is that even possible," Sloane murmured, as if witnessing a miracle. "There's no market here, and it certainly isn't harvest time."

Jax grinned. Sometimes Sloane reminded her of a much younger woman, one whose sense of wonder and adventure still breathed. Before something, or a long chain of somethings, had trampled the joy from her spirit. Whatever the cause, finding the small things that stirred these moments gave her pleasure.

"Whenever we can, we take a list from the businesses in town and try to fill them on our runs."

Sloane studied her for a moment, as if she'd just been introduced.

"What?" Jax asked after a moment.

"You hide it very well."

Jax frowned. "Hide what?"

"Your soft side."

A flush crept up her neck, and Jax looked away. "Don't be fooled, Doc."

"Oh," Sloane murmured. "I never am."

"Get you two anything?" The clerk, a man with shoulder-length jet black hair, chiseled cheekbones, and deep brown eyes, regarded them impassively.

"Turkey hoagie, extra turkey, extra mayo, Steve." Jax turned. "Sloane?"

"If that roast beef is rare, I'll have that with just lettuce and light mayo."

"Help yourself to drinks from the cooler," Steve said, pulling out sandwich fixings. "On the house."

"Coke? Water?" Jax asked.

"I'm feeling adventurous," Sloane said dryly. "That root beer I see toward the back."

Jax pulled out the cans, dug bills from her pocket, and grabbed the two hoagies Steve slid across the counter. "Looked dry out on the porch. Outside okay with you?"

"Perfect," Sloane said.

The bell over the door clanked as they went back out. They sat on a long bench, its faded green the color of the mountains at twilight, with sandwiches on their laps. Sloane slid closer, out of the dripline, her shoulder pressing into Jax's. The casual contact, surely unintentional, shouldn't even have registered. But it did.

Jax cleared her throat. "Okay?"

A surprisingly rotund ginger cat materialized from somewhere and threaded itself under the bench, then decided they were not interesting and vanished again.

Sloane took a bite, chewed, swallowed, and tipped her head as if cataloging the experience. "Couldn't be better."

Jax's relief left her feeling just a bit stupid, but then a lot of things about Sloane Marshall left her wondering what was wrong with her.

They ate in the quiet as twilight gave way to night. Rain stitched the tin roof. The air had that metallic smell it got when the river had been working on outstripping its banks.

"Eli's last report is that the low ground's going under. We're going to need to move the mountain outreach run up from next week if this gets worse. We can't wait for a dry day that isn't coming."

"How long can we wait?" Sloane asked.

"Another day—not much longer. You should stay here—keep the clinic going now that people are coming."

Sloane shook her head. "You don't know how much time you'll have up there, or how many families need to be seen. All boots on the ground—isn't that it?"

Jax smiled. "Close enough. It's going to be ugly weather and uglier on the ground."

"I'm going."

"You'd have made a good combat medic," Jax said finally.

Sloane smiled. "Why?"

Jax laughed. Sloane's answer to praise was to dissect it. All right. She could give her that. She kept her gaze on the flickering streetlight—the only one at that end of town. "You didn't rattle. Even when the sky tried to shake us loose. I've had civilians totally lose their shi—composure—on rough rides like that."

"I don't lose my shit," Sloane said quietly.

Jax studied her. Sloane never said anything offhand. Everything with Sloane, she was coming to appreciate—was intentional. "Why is that?"

"It's called survival." Sloane dusted off her hands and rolled up the paper sandwich wrapper. "Don't you think?"

Jax didn't answer right away. She wiped a thumb along the edge of the sandwich paper. "Yeah, I do." Almost to herself, she added, "Maybe we're more alike than I thought."

Sloane chuckled. "Oh no, Chief Warrant Officer. *You* live to fly into danger. I live to prevent it at all costs." She stood suddenly. "Ready to head back?"

"Sure." Jax stood and stepped out into the rain.

Annoyance nicked at her ribs, hard enough to bruise. Not anger. Curiosity sharpened into want that was going to go unanswered. She was used to silence. She wasn't used to wanting the silence filled. Tonight she'd wanted to ask for more. Wanted to know why. More questions about Sloane every day. But Sloane had already shut the door on her secrets.

At least for now.

Chapter Ten

Two nights later, end of Week 2
Waters rising

Just past midnight, Jax left Bean to finish securing the Bell as the wind cut in from the southwest, pushing rain across the field in blinding swaths. Hunching her shoulders, she jogged down the path to the roadhouse, mentally rerunning the checklist: fuel topped, survival kit repacked, fresh med box strapped, course charted to the ridgelines they'd run at first light. The lobby ceiling light, a big domed affair that played host to what looked like a hundred dead flies, flickered the way old fixtures did when they were about to give up for good. Still, as she pushed inside, trying to keep the rain out, the dim illumination provided a welcome beacon. In all the years since Gramma Gladys had passed, she hadn't found a place on land that felt as much like home as the sky. Until now.

If she asked herself why, she'd have to say the people and not the place. She didn't put a name to the one who mattered most.

She paused inside the door, scanning for Eli. He'd rarely left the comms station the last few days as more and more reports came in of increasingly weather-related washouts, rising river levels, and vague remarks about integrity issues with the Goldman Dam upriver at Colson Gap. Movement in the shadows caught her up short.

Sloane, merely a shadow slumped in a twin to Eli's overstuffed chair, saluted her with a raised coffee mug.

"Couldn't sleep?" Jax asked.

Sloane traced a finger around the cup's rim as if searching for answers inside. "Tried. The rain's loud."

"It's the quiet that keeps most people up." Jax kept moving—

habit—checked the weather printout on Eli's corkboard even though she already knew what it said. "We're out at first light."

Sloane did that almost-smile that made Jax feel like she'd misread something. "So Bean said."

"Sarah's already packed," Jax said, proceeding cautiously. Sloane wasn't acting like herself. Few words, true. But she was always direct—no games, no verbal traps. This Sloane wasn't just quiet—she projected an aura of finely controlled tension, a whole lot of force held back by a hair-trigger thread. A dam ready to release a torrent. Jax shrugged out of her flight jacket and draped it over a straight-back chair to drip on the floor. Couldn't hurt those boards any more than they already had been. "If the ceiling holds, we hop the spine and make it to the cabins before the next storm front moves in."

"A new one?"

Jax blew out a breath. "More like the next in line. This weather pattern is moving faster and getting heavier than expected."

"But you still think it's safe to fly?"

"If I didn't, we wouldn't be going up." The question was a fair one—Sloane didn't know her, after all.

Sloane stood, the chair feet scuffing linoleum. The lobby smelled like wet wool and old floor wax. They were still the only two in it. "I heard you talking to Eli earlier."

Jax winced. So that was it. "You mean when I told him I thought he should order you to stay behind?"

"That would be the time, yes." Sloane crossed the space between them. Still composed, still radiating seething energy. "Did you really think that would work?"

"You're pissed about that, right?" They'd gotten far enough into this dance to let the coals catch fire.

Sloane laughed. "Actually, I thought it was kind of cute."

Jax frowned. "Cute?"

"That you thought Eli could actually tell me how to do my job, and I'd listen."

"Oh for…" Jax pushed a hand through her hair. "I *thought* if an experienced field agent suggested that you're safer and more valuable here on the ground, you'd *logically* agree."

"Why don't you want me to go?"

Jax stared. Where did that come from? That wasn't the point. Was it? "I…"

"You're taking Bean and Sarah."

"Bean is my copilot. Of course he's going."

"And Sarah?"

"She knows these people. They trust her."

"The weather is a problem, isn't it?"

"Damn right it is."

"So speed is important. You want to get in and out ASAP?"

"Yes, I do." Jax's jaw started to ache, and she unclenched it. "I know you have a point."

"I reviewed Eli's census. There are fifteen families up there, spread out over several miles. You need a bigger *medical* team than the three of you."

"Jeb—"

"Jeb is a newly hatched EMT. Why him but not me?"

"Because I can't..." Jax snapped her jaws shut to hold the words in.

"Can't what?"

Her control wavered. Her throat ached. No. Saying it could make it true. *Because I can't lose someone else.*

"Can't what, Jax?" Sloane stepped closer.

"Because I can't guarantee your safety." Jax jolted, a shock wave rippling down her spine. Where the hell had that come from? This wasn't about Sloane—this was about her. She didn't want the distraction. She didn't want to worry about her. She didn't want her hurt. *Fuck.* What was that all about?

"I understand that." Sloane gently circled her wrist, her fingers like simmering embers. "But you're taking the others. Why am I different?"

"Because you're—" Jax turned away. Forced the words back down. "You're the only doctor we have. We can't afford to lose you."

I can't lose you.

If Sloane heard the lie, she didn't show it.

"I see." Sloane's expression never changed, as if Jax hadn't just opened a door to somewhere neither of them wanted to go. "Well, you'll need me on this run—along with glucose, fluids, antibiotics. If these families haven't had any access to regular medical care, been snowed off from clinics, they're probably out of any meds they'd been convinced to take. Plus insulin, test kits, basic vaccines."

"Sarah's put in a supply list." The pressure in Jax's chest eased. Sloane had just let the door shut. "Did you wait up to tell me what else I might have forgotten?"

Sloane didn't blink. "I've covered everything I needed to say except this. I've never been in battle, but I fight a war every single day. My enemy is death. Don't underestimate me."

Jax's chest did that faint, annoying clench again. She covered it with a shrug. "Then be on the pad at oh-five-hundred." Silence stretched. She filled it. "You should sleep. You look—"

"Don't say tired." Now Sloane smiled for real, just a bright flash and gone. "I don't lose my composure, remember?"

"I remember." Jax felt the wobble of a laugh and let it out as air instead. She picked up her pack. "Don't be late."

"Jax?"

"Yeah," Jax asked warily. *Fuck.* She had really blown this.

"Thank you."

Jax's head spun. "For what?"

"For caring." Sloane still held her wrist. Her thumb brushed a soft circle over the top of Jax's hand. "Night, Jax."

Sloane released her and walked away.

"Night." Jax didn't watch her go. She didn't need to. The quiet left behind wasn't simply silence, it was emptiness.

❖

Morning rolled in on a pale gray tide of heavier rain beating against the windows. Sloane judged the time to be a little after four. Plenty of time to grab her pack, already stocked with med essentials, her duffel and, most importantly, coffee and a shower. She eased to the side of the bunk and slipped into her boots.

"Did you sleep?" Jax asked from the shadows above.

"Surprisingly well." Sloane carefully didn't look up, aware per routine that Jax had hung her flight suit on a hook opposite the bunk. Leaving her to sleep in what, Sloane wasn't sure. As if to answer the question she had pretended not to obsess over, Jax vaulted off the bed in one graceful pivot, landing just a few feet away.

Jax slept in a tank top and briefs.

Sloane had only imagined her body beneath her flight suit and jacket before, but she hadn't been wrong that Jax would be muscled and sleek. Used to taking in a situation in one quick glance, she didn't need any longer than that to know the image was now indelibly stamped on her brain. She still didn't look away.

"I can't believe you came in after I went to sleep and didn't wake me up."

Jax pulled on her flight suit. “I employed stealth maneuvers.”

Sloane laughed. “Really.”

“No. Actually you were snoring, so I wasn’t even quiet.”

Sloane flushed. “I do not snore.”

“Says who?”

“Says—” Sloane swallowed a retort. What could she say? No one slept with her, not even in the same room. Until Jax. “No one needs to tell me. I’m a doctor. I know these things.”

Jax paused in the half-open door, the hall light revealing her grin. “Not to worry. I thought it was cute.”

Before Sloane could fire back, Jax turned and walked away, whistling faintly.

Cute?

Sloane snorted. *That* remark was a little payback for last night. She probably *had* ambushed Jax about the conversation she’d overheard, but she hadn’t intentionally eavesdropped. If Jax wanted a private conversation, she shouldn’t do it in the kitchen. And since *she* had been the subject, she didn’t feel an ounce of remorse.

In the shower, blissfully hot and surprisingly strong, Sloane returned to Jax’s words of the night before.

I can’t guarantee your safety.

Not Bean. Not Sarah.

The implication had been clear: Jax was worried about her, in particular. And when pushed, she wouldn’t say why. She could have said she didn’t trust Sloane’s lack of experience in the field, but one thing was certain—Jax did not lie. And Jax trusted her ability. Sloane knew it. Had known it since that first night they’d freed the trapped ranger. This wasn’t professional concern. It was something else.

Something she didn’t understand. Something she wasn’t sure she wanted to know.

She toweled off quickly and set the ruminations aside. Unproductive, and ultimately, what did it matter? Soon enough she’d be back in Boston, and this whole experience, including the unsettling effect of Jax Kincaid, would be forgotten.

Downstairs, Eli sat at the comms station as a terse voice said from the radio, “River’s up another foot in the last twelve hours. If the present rate continues, the dam may breach.”

“Has the governor ordered evacs?” Eli asked.

“Low-lying counties are on alert.”

Eli grimaced. Jax swore softly.

Sloane turned to Jax. "What?"

"Typical bureaucratic inertia. Evacs are costly. Disrupts supply chains, impacts businesses, upsets voters."

"That seems…understandable."

Jax nodded. "It is, but delaying until it's too late comes with a higher price tag. People die."

Sloane's throat tightened. "We're not calling off the mission, are we?"

"Not yet," Eli said from beside her. "Our being here is more important than ever."

"Good," Sloane said briskly. "Let's go, then."

Jax held the door, her duffel over her shoulder. "Could be bumpy up there."

"Isn't it always?"

Jax laughed. "Pretty much. Two weeks in, and you're sounding like a vet."

"You get us there. I'll handle the medical end. That's how it works, right?"

Jax paused, her gaze moving slowly over Sloane's face. "That's how it works, Dr. Marshall. Ready to ride?"

"Yes, Chief, I am."

Not just ready. Excited. Adrenaline buzzed through her system as she piled into the RTV with Jax and Sarah.

"You'll want this," she said, turning to the rear to pass Sarah a notebook. "Glucose logs. They'll swear they remember. They won't."

"Copy that," Sarah said, grinning. "Doctor coming along. We're fancy now."

Beside her, Jax whistled softly. Sloane smiled.

Inside the bay, Sloane settled onto the bench and grabbed her headset, strapped in, and quickly checked that all the equipment was secured. Automatic and natural now. On Jax's way to the front, she reached down to lock Sloane's harness and tug the strap once, checking tension. A small, practiced move that shouldn't have made Sloane's breath catch or her pulse jump.

But it did.

At liftoff, the Bell's blades blurred the rain into a gray disc. Mist lifted out of the valley like breath on a winter morning. Sloane's headset pinched at the crown of her head in the way it always did for the first ten minutes. After that she forgot it was there. As the land peeled away below them, she mentally organized what she knew of the people she would be seeing. Sarah's list had been sparse. In her words, people moved away, died, were born, and always developed new ailments. Any medical census was inaccurate a day after she drew it up. But at least it was a start.

Jax rode the ridgeline until a scatter of rooftops appeared—tin gray, tar black, the same color as the sky. Jax set the Bell down on a bald patch above a thin trail.

"We'll have to walk the rest of the way," she said. "Not enough clearing down there for us."

The path down was slick with moss-covered stones. Sarah, born to it, moved with light, sure steps. Jax covered the ground in long, steady strides. Sloane gritted her teeth to keep her footing and tightened the strap on the med bag slung across her back. At one drop-off, Jax offered a hand. Sloane hesitated, took it, and smiled when Jax murmured, "Looking good, Doc."

The cabin, a dark, ramshackle single-story box with walls built from a hodgepodge of plywood and unpainted lumber, sat amongst a graveyard of rusting machinery.

Sarah knocked on the windowless front door. "Hello! Mrs. Merckle? It's Sarah Hull from the county med service."

A moment passed.

When the cabin door opened, a blond boy of about seven in a faded T-shirt and jeans a size too big stared before vanishing like he'd been pulled backward by a string. The woman who replaced him was young, blond, and might have been his sister.

"Hi, Frannie," Sarah said. "How's your mother doing?"

"She's worse today," Frannie said without preamble. "Ma's hardly peed. Can't keep tea down. The sugar stick says 'HI' but won't give no number."

Sloane filled in the blanks. Hyperglycemia, dehydration, probable acidosis. "I'm Dr. Marshall. We'll fix this. Can you take us to your mother?"

Frannie hesitated, glanced at Sarah, then nodded. "Here."

Frannie's mother, who Frannie said was just called Meemaw, lay under a quilt in a room at the rear of the cabin with a window but no working light. Sloane knelt and pressed her fingers to the artery in her wrist as she introduced herself. Respirations and pulse elevated. Fingers cool.

"When did you last take insulin?" Sloane asked.

"Ran out," Meemaw whispered. "I…stretched it. Then…none."

Sloane nodded once. "We'll fix that."

She snapped open the glucometer Sarah handed her and pricked a finger. 498 flashed. The monitor beeped like it had been insulted.

Jax moved through the room quietly, clearing space, setting the med kit where Sloane's right hand would fall without looking, nudging a chair closer so Sloane didn't have to kneel.

"We're going to start an IV," Sloane said. "Give you some insulin to get your sugar down."

They worked as the storm pressed harder. Sarah found a vein and grinned at her clean stick. Jax sifted through the med kit and passed the insulin and a syringe to Sloane before she asked.

"Is she gonna be okay?" Frannie asked, the boy a shadow behind her.

"She's sick," Sloane said, because the truth was the only answer. "But we came with what she needs."

Sloane gave her a bolus of insulin, hung a drip, and waited.

Wind hit the cabin in bursts. Jax drifted between door and hearth as if she could keep the weather back with her shoulders. Her radio emitted a garbled string of words and died in static.

"Say again?" Jax stepped closer to the door. Nothing. She looked at Sloane.

Sloane held up a finger. One more minute.

"Glucose 412," Sarah said on the next check. "Coming down."

"Another dose—half of the initial," Sloane said. "Sip water. Not too much." She shifted on the stiff, narrow chair to ease the knot in her hip, sensed Jax at her shoulder.

"What?" Sloane asked, softer than she intended.

Jax shook her head once. "Just watching you make it look easy. And everyone else feel safe."

Sloane didn't know what to do with that. She filed it under *later* and turned back to the patient.

"You're getting better," she told Meemaw, and behind her Frannie let out a sound like a sob.

By afternoon, dispatch came back as a smear of words. "…rivers…downed trees…don't try the valley floor…stay high ground…" before it died to static.

Jax stepped into the bedroom doorway. "We should pull out before dark." Her eyes flicked to Sloane, not the sky. Asking, not ordering. "We might make the next stop before dark. After that I'll never find an LZ."

"Not yet." Sloane kept her voice even. "I need another hour."

"That could buy us a night on the ground," Jax said mildly. Still giving Sloane the lead.

"Then it buys us a night," Sloane said.

By late afternoon, Meemaw's breathing slowed, and her glucose came down notch by notch. Frannie squeezed Sloane's hand.

"We didn't think you all would come in the storm."

Sloane glanced at Jax. "Of course we came. That's what we do."

While Sloane went over instructions with Frannie, Jax made a circuit outside. When she came in, her jacket was wet through, hair plastered to her temples. She shook her head. "No safe way out tonight. Heavy clouds along the ridge. We're down for the night."

Sloane exhaled. "Where?"

"The Bell," Jax said. "She's weatherproofed better than we are."

Sarah exchanged a look with Bean, who'd come in with Jax.

"Not to worry, Doc," he said with a twinkle in his eyes. "She's plenty comfortable."

Sarah put in, "Neighbor up the ridge sent word she has a sick boy. I've got enough light left to get up there to check him."

Instantly, Bean said, "I'll go with her."

That left Sloane and Jax walking back up the trail in steady rain, packs heavy with quilts the family had pressed on them. The Bell crouched in the shadows. Sloane had never been as happy to see it.

Inside, Jax pulled blankets out of the cargo pouch, laid them over the deck, and put the quilts on top. "She'll keep us dry."

Sloane stripped off her wet boots and set them by the door, just as she did every night. She glanced at Jax, at the narrow space the body of the Bell allowed. "So it's you and me tonight."

Jax shrugged out of her jacket. "Looks that way."

The storm pounded outside, steady, insistent. Inside, silence crowded closer than the walls. The Bell was only big enough for two people lying shoulder to shoulder. Jax knew it.

Sloane knew it, too.

CHAPTER ELEVEN

Night in the mountains

Sloane settled with her back against the Bell's inner wall and pulled the quilt Frannie had pressed into her hands with another fervent thank you up to her chest. The metal at her back pushed the outside cold straight through to her spine. Damp crept in through her pant cuffs, the bottom of her sleeves, and the gap around her collar. Her boots steamed where she'd set them by the hatch, and the thought of pushing her feet into them again made her wince. Beside her, Jax mirrored her position, but despite her soaked hair and the insidious wetness, looked infinitely more comfortable—arms behind her head, legs stretched out across the width of the floor, rangy body relaxed. As if a vibrating metal shell in a storm was no more precarious than a bunkhouse cot.

Of course, Jax had probably had a lot of practice resting in places no one should ever have to. Sloane caught her breath when the whole frame shuddered. Jax didn't flinch. Or if she did, she hid it well.

Rain hammered the fuselage in endless sheets, as if the night itself wanted inside, the endless beats drumming out any sense of time. Even Jax's radio was silent. Closed inside, they could have been anywhere. Or nowhere at all.

"Tired?" Jax asked, her voice crystal despite the savage roar of thunder and pounding water.

Bean had shut everything down earlier, and the small flashlight Jax stood upright by the door threw a brave circle of light over the deck and the edge of the quilts. Beyond it, details melted into suggestions. Except for Jax's face. The flickering beam caught the length of her throat and edge of her cheekbone—an elegant arch in the slanting glow. Her eyes, the deepest blue in sunlight, gray now, gleamed as she watched Sloane, alert and focused. Her profile, softened by shadow, no less strong.

"Not really," Sloane said. "Too revved still."

"Worried about the patient?"

"No, actually—I'm confident she'll be improved by morning." Sloane sighed. "Of course, nothing is going to change unless she gets regular medical care—and out here? Not likely."

"At least she'll be on Sarah's radar," Jax said.

"Yes." Sloane reached for a towel Jax had magicked out of a bin somewhere and dried her hair. As if that might warm her up. She *wasn't* tired. Just the opposite—wired and wakeful and too aware of the two of them in the small space. "It's the circumstances."

"Me?" Jax asked. "I could climb up into the cockpit."

"No." Sloane quickly grasped her wrist. Warm. How could Jax be warm when she was definitely on her way to icing over? "You're fine. Just the strangeness of it all—the storm, so close I feel like it wants something from us. The helicopter—somehow I feel like it's protecting us." She shook her head. "That's weird, and I am *not* a whimsical person."

Jax chuckled. "I think given that this is all new, you're allowed to feel a little weirded out."

"Huh. I don't get—all right, maybe I am, a little." She tossed the towel aside. "Do you often sleep in here?"

Jax didn't answer at once, then exhaled as if she'd been holding her breath. Or holding something else in. "More times than I can count."

"How often is that?" Sloane asked lightly, giving Jax space to brush it off. She hoped she didn't. The sound of Jax's voice dissolved the strangeness pressing in, but more than that, she wanted to know. What had it taken to create such calm in the literal belly of the storm?

"Enough that I could probably diagram the location of every rivet in my sleep." Jax's fleeting smile didn't reach her eyes.

When Sloane said nothing, after a moment, she went on.

"In Afghanistan, we'd set down on a forward operating base, or a field somewhere somebody *decided* was a landing zone, or whatever dirt strip the brass called a landing zone. Didn't matter if the roof over our heads was canvas or tin. When the calls came, we had minutes. Sometimes less. Better to sleep in the machine, strapped in, fuel topped. Then we could lift the moment airspace cleared."

Sloane pictured the Bell under a different sky—the air blowing hot instead of cold, sand finding the seams the way water did here, people shouting in a language she didn't speak. And Jax, exactly as she was now, outwardly relaxed but poised for action in the space between heartbeats. Efficient, sharp. Dangerous.

"And did you *sleep*," Sloane said, "or did you just practice not sleeping until you were good at it?"

"Are there points for either?" Jax asked.

"You keep track of points?"

"Depends. I keep track of the fuel," Jax said. "I keep track of the weather. I keep the course."

"Do you keep track of people?" Sloane stilled, unsure why she'd asked. Or what she wanted to hear.

"Sometimes," Jax said after a long stretch. "If they want to be kept."

"And if they don't?"

"I keep my distance," Jax said. "That's the other thing I'm good at."

And which am I? But Sloane kept her silence. She'd already asked too much, intruded too far into realms that were foreign. She didn't explore other people's private lives. Didn't share hers. Exposure only led to pain.

Lightning sketched a white line across the sky beyond the window. Thunder rolled over the ridge and echoed from the valley below. The Bell creaked, protesting.

Sloane flinched.

Jax's hand shifted to her thigh, grounding her as if by reflex. Only an instant, and then gone. But just like that, Sloane understood something she hadn't before. Jax didn't only sleep in the aircraft because it was expedient. She slept with it because it let *other* people sleep. She was offering the same to Sloane without asking to be thanked, or even to be recognized for it.

"Distance comes in all shapes," Sloane said. "Do you miss it? That may be a naïve question, but it wasn't just war, was it—you were saving people every day."

Risky to ask. Curiosity was its own kind of storm.

Jax stayed quiet long enough that Sloane considered apologizing for treading on sacred ground.

"When we came home," Jax said finally, "everything felt too loud and too slow at the same time. Supermarket aisles. Traffic lights. The sound the refrigerator makes at three a.m. The whine and thump of rockets incoming still buzzed in my brain. At first I couldn't sleep in the bed—afraid I wouldn't wake up fast enough if I needed to *move*. And then I'd lie awake…just waiting." She exhaled, a small not-quite laugh. "That's not the story I'm supposed to tell."

"Who says?" Sloane asked.

"People who like the made-for-TV version."

"I don't." Sloane curled her fingers in the quilt. The icy stiffness lingered. "I like the one where people say what is true and then keep breathing."

"Copy that," Jax murmured, the phrase somehow right, there in the shadows inside the Bell.

"The waiting is the worst, isn't it," Sloane murmured. "You know it's coming, you just don't know when."

"Yeah." Jax shrugged. "The quiet? Not the time to sleep." She tipped her head against the sidewall. "Quiet meant the questions would start."

"What were you questioning?"

"How far, how many, how bad." Jax's hand fisted on her thigh. "What we didn't ask? How many *wouldn't* make it. That answer was always the same—nobody, not on our watch."

Sloane nodded. Not so different from her world. "That's the non-negotiable, isn't it."

"Too right." Jax said, her tone darker than the night pressing in. "You must feel that way, in the ER."

"No one is trying to kill me while I do my job," Sloane said, "but I understand the urgency. And the battle—against time, against the fragility of the human body, against the fear of failure."

Jax snorted. "Move fast. Then there's no time for doubt."

"Mmm, doing is always better than waiting," Sloane said. In another place, another time, she might have stopped there, but Jax's openness made it easier, somehow, to talk. And Jax had been brave enough to revisit some part of a nightmare. She could be, too. "My first mass casualty was a ferry accident. A barge collided with it. Dozens of injured, a lot of them in the water. We got the alert and every available person in the hospital showed up. We pulled sterile instrument packs from the OR. Readied every trauma bay for surgeries. Stacked wheelchairs and gurneys outside to meet the ambulances, lined stretchers down the hall."

The blare of the overhead intercoms calling the alerts, the rush of adrenaline, the acrid scent of sweat and fear. Still fresh after all this time. "And then we waited."

"The fucking quiet," Jax murmured.

"Yes." Of course Jax understood.

"I remember standing there," Sloane went on. "The corridors empty, everything ready. And nothing yet. Just…waiting. I imagined them pulling people from the water. I could practically feel the cold creeping in. Immobilizing."

She shivered. "I knew that cold. Knew that paralyzing darkness everywhere."

Jax stirred, her thigh brushing Sloane's as she turned toward her. "What do you mean?"

She hadn't meant to go there, but the memories crept in with the storm, and now the pressure in her throat wouldn't let her retreat. She stared at the faint circle of light on the floor. Like a beacon from a search ship. If only she could have reached it. "We were on vacation, out on our Jet Ski. A boat…coming so fast…we couldn't swerve. Then we were flying…the sun swirling like a pinwheel before…just blackness."

Jax didn't speak, but her shoulder edged a little closer, as if she too was waiting.

"We both went under. The water was so cold. The waves—they kept pushing me back down every time I surfaced. I heard her call my name. Water closing over my head. So, so cold."

Jax pressed a hand to her thigh, outside the quilt, but warm. The only warm spot anywhere. The only thing keeping her from floating away into the cold darkness of memory. She caught Jax's fingers and held on like she should have held Sybil's.

Softly, Jax said, "What happened?"

"I grabbed for her hand. Her fingers kept slipping through mine. I think…I keep trying to remember." Sloane's breath caught. She forced it out anyway. "Had to find air. I think I let go." She squeezed her eyes closed. "A patrol boat came…pulled me out. Not Sybil. Sybil drowned."

"I'm so sorry."

Jax shifted before Sloane was aware of the movement, sliding her arm around Sloane's shoulders. Easing her closer—not a tug, more a question.

Is this okay?

Sloane wanted to say no. Didn't want to need anything. But she did. Jax's shoulder beneath her cheek was warm despite the damp, Jax's palm where it cupped her shoulder steady and warmer still. She didn't want to remember, but the warmth, so fleeting but so pure, carried her through the rest.

"My parents…my parents were devastated it was me they saved. Not Sybil. I was, too. I wished it had been me. I still do." The sounds of the storm retreated, or maybe that was just the blood roaring in her ears. She trembled and couldn't seem to stop. "God, it's so cold."

Jax drew her closer against her side, voice low in her ear. "Hey. Hey, you're right here. You're safe."

The words, simple and steady, cracked something inside. Sloane pressed her forehead against Jax's shoulder, quilt slipping. "I'm so cold."

"I know, baby, I know," Jax murmured, the word too soft, too instinctive to be anything but truth. She sounded like she didn't expect it to be remembered.

But Sloane would remember.

"I'm sorry," she said after a moment and let go of Jax's hand.

"For what?"

"I don't talk about them," Sloane said, her voice sounding like sandpaper on stone. "I don't talk about Syb."

"You don't have to talk about anything—or anyone—you don't want to," Jax said.

Sloane huffed. "I've made a mission out of that, believe me."

Jax's cheek brushed the top of her head. "You okay?"

"No," Sloane said. "Yes. Both. I'm…" She couldn't find a word that made sense. "Here."

"Good enough," Jax said, her tone lighter, giving Sloane permission to retreat from the dark. "You should now make a mission out of getting some sleep. We've got another shift out there tomorrow if the Bell will fly."

"I'll try." Sloane shifted, not away, just settling. She'd inventory the night in the morning, the way she inventoried a shift when it ended—what worked, what broke, what she would do again. Right now, she reeled from what she hadn't expected—the warmth without asking, the word *baby* coming from someone who didn't use words like that, and being watched over—cared for—with boundaries set every bit as strong as her own.

She closed her eyes, let herself rest in the circle of Jax's arm, because she could without fear. She assessed her body. The wired edge had dulled a fraction with the telling. The cold had retreated to something else—fatigue with a pulse.

"Head here," Jax said, and nudged her shoulder—a small invitation into a better angle.

Sloane adjusted. Not enough to call it curling, enough to accept a corner of Jax's body as a rest stop. The quilt slipped. Jax pulled it back over Sloane's hip with one hand without making a production out of it.

Sloane let her mind do the thing it did when she was twelve and trying to learn not to panic. She counted breath in and the breath out. Jax's heart beat under her ear, steady as a metronome, slower than she'd expected.

"You won't remember," Sloane said, half-asleep already.

"What," Jax said, low.

"Calling me baby," Sloane murmured, eyes closed now, the words coming from some unsupervised corridor of her brain.

There was a pause she felt more than heard.

"Probably not," Jax said, the humor a shade softer than usual.

Sloane smiled into the jacket. "I will."

"Okay," Jax said, and Sloane heard the permission to keep a thing without having to apologize.

The storm pounded, the Bell rocked, but Sloane focused on Jax's heartbeat beneath her cheek. Steady, relentless, impossibly grounding. Like Jax.

Touching her in a place she hadn't thought could be touched, that hollow that lived inside her since Sybil had gone.

Jax eased back against the Bell, working her shoulders to ease the stiffness. The storm kept up its chorus of thunderous percussions joined by the furious tympani of rain pinging off the skin of the Bell and the wailing notes of the wind. Sloane slept in fits—if her barely beneath the surface of wakefulness could be called sleep. She'd go slack against Jax's side, breath steadying, then in the next minute jerk when the rhythm of the barrage shifted—or more likely, some remnant of memory pierced the thin veil of exhaustion.

Bean's flashlight had died to a weak cone of pale yellow on the deck. Not that she needed it. Sloane's restless murmurs told her everything she needed to know. She'd lain awake enough nights in the top bunk to recognize Sloane's usual sleeping pattern. Sloane would lie quietly until a few hours before dawn, and then a restless sleep held in rigid check. The pattern resumed inside an hour, and when Sloane's breathing hitched, Jax tightened her hold just a bit until Sloane shifted and settled again. She probably shouldn't be holding her, even so carefully, but the same instinct that had her grabbing for Rodriguez, trying to stop the pumping artery while she bled out, had her sliding her arm around Sloane.

She'd failed then. The people who mattered to her died. Her mother, leaving over and over until she didn't come back. Her grandmother, quietly in her sleep. Rodriguez, gasping her name. She shouldn't comfort Sloane. Shouldn't create this connection. But some reflexes went deeper than fear, and she didn't let go.

Tonight was nothing like that last flight with Rodriguez, but then, nothing about tonight was typical either. The last thing she expected was to spend the night in the bird—which she did on the regular—with Sloane Marshall. Or to end up sharing war stories with her. And Sloane's revelations sure as hell qualified. She lost her twin in a horrible accident, and her parents were pissed she didn't die instead? At least *her* mother pretended to care about her on her infrequent visits.

Anger rode in with the fury of the wind. Not at Sloane, for curling up into a protective shell, deciding no one was worth the risk. That's what Sloane had done, even if she didn't see it herself. No, anger for her. She knew what loss did to people—she'd seen it firsthand, felt it like a punch to the heart. Some grew cold, hardened even to the living. Others broke under the guilt. Twelve years old, and Sloane did neither. She kept her humanity alive. She fucking saved people at no small cost to herself. Always a cost—in blood, in sweat, in tears. Because no one could save them all.

She didn't have a fix. She didn't have any words. What words could ever touch that pain? She could do one thing, though.

She stayed.

Baby.

Well. That cat was out.

No idea what Sloane would make of that, if she even remembered. Hell, *she* had no idea what to make of it. Reflex, maybe. Some way to purge her own pain. To beat back the ache of imagining Sloane's.

Sloane shifted again, a small restless drag of cheek against her shoulder. Jax smiled, a short thing, gone quickly. She could at least keep her warm. And when the time came, fed.

Jax slid her hand out to reach the side bin, finding the latch without looking. MREs. She cracked one quietly, ran the heater with a splash from a bottle cap, tucked the steaming pouch into the crook of her knee to muffle the hiss. Chili mac. The gods had a sense of humor. She tore open a second pouch for the hot drink, shook the powder down into the sleeve.

Sloane stirred at the sound and straightened fast, pulling away like she needed to do something critical and didn't know what.

"Easy," Jax said. "You're in the Bell. Everything is fine."

She offered the hot drink first, because heat mattered more than calories just then. "Here. It's not coffee. It's not even honest cocoa. But it's hot."

Sloane took it, no questions asked. The small bit of trust hit Jax like a gut punch. Sloane always assessed, calculated, judged risks. Not this time.

Sloane's hands weren't shaking now. Good. Jax kept that to herself. Sloane would not appreciate having been observed, especially while asleep.

The first sip was a bit tentative, but not the second. Sloane looked at Jax over the rim, her expression clear even in the dying light. Hesitant—judging what Jax had seen, what she'd revealed. A private person, used to protecting her secrets, wondering if she'd been exposed.

"I—" she began.

"No." Jax gently touched a finger to Sloane's lips, as if to say *I heard the apology forming and I'm not interested in it.* "I'm honored you told me. And so damn proud of you."

Sloane blinked. "Why?"

Her confusion reminded Jax that Sloane really didn't know how damn special she was. Her chest ached, to soothe her, to shake her. To say *you deserved to be held, loved, protected.* To say more than she should.

"For who you are." Jax didn't do speeches. She didn't need one. "That you didn't let the cold take you back then, or after. That you never let up, even when waiting's the job. You're a damn warrior, Sloane." A beat. "I'm not wrong much. I was wrong about you, back in Asheville."

"Maybe we were both wrong, back then."

She should let it go. They'd both probably regret the night in the morning. But she couldn't. "What do you mean?"

"You said you couldn't guarantee my safety out here, but that's exactly what you've been doing all night." Sloane's voice was soft, pensive. "Your mission is to save lives. Still."

"I managed to keep you a little dry. And handed you an MRE." Jax snorted. "Not exactly lifesaving. And I don't always succeed."

"But what I needed tonight." Sloane tilted her head. "Does the one who haunts you have a name?"

Jax sucked in a breath. Time to end this conversation. The silence stretched. "Rodriguez. Magdalina. Mags."

"A friend?"

"Yeah. And my copilot." More than a friend, but that didn't matter now. "We got caught in a flurry of RPGs. Our bird was hit. I tried to stop the bleeding while fighting to keep us airborne." She swallowed the familiar acid taste of self-loathing. "I made it back. She didn't. The last thing she said to me was 'I'm so cold, Jax. So cold.'"

"Oh God. I'm sorry."

"Me too," Jax said softly.

"It's hard, isn't it, when you can never find a way to make it right."

Jax closed her eyes. Just for a second. Sloane knew, of course she did. Jax pulled her closer, knowing this was dangerous, knowing this was something that would hurt to lose. "Yeah."

Sloane studied her a long moment, like she was assessing a trauma patient, searching for the hidden truths. Whatever she saw eased the strain in her shoulders. She leaned, not much, just enough to rest her head on the edge of Jax's shoulder again.

"Do you mind? You're an excellent pillow."

Jax snorted softly. "Happy to be of service." She slid her arm around Sloane's shoulders again, fitted her in. Didn't worry about it this time. "Go back to sleep."

Sloane settled, faster than before. Her breath stuttered once, then smoothed, regular and deep. The MRE steamed against Jax's knee, and she tucked it aside for later. She'd feed her in the morning, pretend she was only thinking about Sloane needing to be sharp for the grandmother up the hill, the boy across the ridge with the bloody cough.

She kept watch the way she'd always done—eyes on nothing, ears on everything, mind on what was needed to keep everyone safe. The pouches cooled. The storm changed keys. The Bell rocked to a new beat.

"I've got her," Jax whispered when the wind paused.

She did not sleep.

Chapter Twelve

Week 3, first morning
Flood plains under water

Sloane drifted, rose from the depths of sleep, drifted again. Once, thunder rolled hard and close and she jerked nearly awake, but the arm around her tightened, and she went under again. She didn't fight the pull. At some point in the long middle—an hour that could have been three—Sloane came up enough to feel that the rain had worked its way through some seam and Jax had set a cloth of some kind under the drip. Jax had apparently managed that without moving the arm she had wrapped around her. Sloane made a small approving sound and accepted the comfort.

If she dreamed, she couldn't find the edges of it when she roused. Only the sense of being held in a way that didn't set off alarms, of the Bell surrounding them—securing them inside a metal cocoon—and Jax's steady breathing and untroubled drum of her heart. In the brief time between almost-waking and sleep, the river rushed in the distance, rolling over its banks with the sounds of a new language—dangerous and unsympathetic to any in its path. Knowing what raged outside should have unnerved her. It didn't. She knew why, but making sense of the reasons would have to wait until morning.

When gray finally arrived, it came from nowhere and everywhere at once, a softening of the dark that made the failing flashlight beam unnecessary. The Bell's interior shifted from black to the color of nickels. Sloane opened her eyes, dawn being the only alarm clock she'd ever needed. Heat came first, the quiet kind that sinks into muscle and bone. Her forearm lay across Jax's waist, her hand somehow having found its way inside Jax's unzipped jacket. Her palm cupped the hard line of an oblique through flight shirt and fleece. Beneath her hand, Jax's chest rose, strong and steady.

Jax's arm still curled around her shoulders as if it belonged there. Warm, gentle, carrying no threat. Sloane lay still, tempted to pretend not to be awake yet, just to linger a few more minutes in the strange otherness of the night. She didn't. She'd promised herself years ago not to lie in small ways when she could help it.

She did not reach for her mental checklist. For once, order could wait its turn. Curiosity slipped in instead, not about a lab or a scan, but about things she'd been avoiding for days. She traced the line of Jax's flank unconsciously, and movement gave her away.

Jax's arm loosened but didn't leave. Her breathing changed. Deeper, preparing for the day.

Sloane lifted her head a fraction, and every muscle along the length of her spine complained. Their faces had somehow come closer during the night. Jax's hair had dried and gone a little wild. Sloane stifled the impulse to smooth it.

"You okay?" Jax asked, her voice a little hoarse. Her hand slid from Sloane's shoulder into her hair, fingers combing once, twice, the touch light, the unthinking gesture of someone who forgets to guard against softness when she is still half-asleep.

The sensation struck like lightning. Bright and burning.

"Yes. Thanks for letting me sleep." She could have said *thanks for taking such good care of me*, but maybe that wasn't how Jax thought of it. Better not to assume and embarrass them both.

"What happened to the people on the ferry?" Jax asked a minute later, as if their conversation had never ended.

"We saved a bunch," Sloane said. "We didn't save all. That's always the math."

"Still count them?" Jax said.

"Not anymore. The numbers still favor the win."

"That helps." Jax's hand moved—just a thumb stroke at Sloane's collarbone, careless as a breeze.

"Do you ever regret anything?" Sloane asked, then winced. Not because it was a stupid question. Because it was unfair. People who flew into places like the places Jax had flown didn't have the luxury of pretty answers. "Wait, you don't have to—"

"All the time," Jax said in her flat, matter-of-fact command tone. "Differently than people think. Not the calls I made on the fly. Not those. The calls I sat with too long. Waiting for an all clear when I should have rolled the dice and lifted."

"That sounds like survivor's guilt," Sloane said.

"That sounds like the job," Jax said. "But yes."

"You could be gentler to you," Sloane said, thinking *she* sounded like Mina. Or a lifetime ago, Sybil.

"You first," Jax said.

Such an irritatingly right answer, Sloane laughed into the jacket beneath her cheek. "That's the hard one, isn't it."

"The hardest." Jax's thumb still traced soft, slow circles, as if echoing her musings. "I'm sorry about your sister."

"Me too." Sloane stared at the edge of the light and the dust motes that flickered in and out of it like a constellation that couldn't decide whether to stay or go. "For a long time, I didn't know who I was without her." The admission surprised her—how it sat more comfortably than she'd expected in the air between them. "Not sure I do yet."

"Maybe you don't have to know all the way," Jax said. "Maybe knowing enough to get through every day is enough."

"You say that like you've practiced it." Sloane raised her head to search Jax's face. Looking for the recognition she heard in Jax's voice, as if Jax saw her without her needing to explain.

"I have," Jax said. "I practice a lot."

Jax was close. Closer than Sloane had ever been to anyone who mattered. She took a deep breath. Jax met her gaze in the cotton-soft morning light. Sloane had catalogued Jax for days without realizing it. Her purposeful gait, her easy air of command, her refusal to fill a silence with useless words. She had not catalogued this. Jax unguarded. Jax without her cocky smile. Jax looking at her with singular attention. Not casual, but only her.

The intensity in her eyes hit Sloane deep inside. Her body, a traitorous stranger, quickened in a way she'd never experienced. This was dangerous territory. She knew it. Could feel it in the way her skin seemed too tight, in the way every nerve ending had become hyperaware of exactly where their bodies touched. She should pull back. Create distance. Return to safety. Instead, she leaned closer.

As if in a dream, Sloane slipped her hand from inside Jax's jacket and rested her fingers on the column of Jax's throat. The bounding pulse was a match striking tinder in her blood—heat flared and rose through her with a mind-blinding roar. A soft sound, almost a moan, escaped her.

Jax went very still under her touch, her gaze never wavering from Sloane's. Jax's fingers curled around the base of her neck. Firm, grounding. Sloane's lips parted, but no words came.

"Sloane."

Just her name, rough and barely controlled, sent arousal spiraling through her. The way Jax said her name, like a prayer and a warning all at once, answered every question she'd never asked. Why me? Why her, and no one else?

The space between them thinned until it hardly existed. Sloane shifted, angling into Jax's side, and cupped Jax's throat. A pulse beat wildly against her palm.

Jax moved first. Not a flinch. Not a retreat. A hand to Sloane's wrist, careful but deliberate, easing Sloane's palm a millimeter from her throat. Not so much a rejection as a gentle nudge off a ledge onto solid ground.

"Last night," Jax said softly, "in here, we weren't strangers. So no regrets. No apologies. Just truth."

"I know," Sloane whispered, grateful and resistant all at once. Of course Jax was right—the night had been a catalyst for something she'd never known. A connection so effortless she'd forgotten to be cautious. Forgotten to protect herself. Had trusted Jax, without completely knowing why. She'd let her emotions lead, not her head. "I wasn't entirely myself."

"Here's another truth." Jax cupped her hand and drew it away now, still gentle. "I'm no hero. And I'm not strong enough to say no right now, when a big part of me doesn't want to."

"I could pretend I don't know what you're talking about," Sloane said. "But you deserve more. Part of me wants to argue, and that's not like me. I'm not a reckless person."

Sloane drew her hand away and pressed it to her thigh. Safe there. "But it's not for you to say if you're a hero. That's for those whose lives you've changed."

Jax closed her eyes. "You make me think of things I don't want to think about."

"I'm sorry."

Jax met her gaze. "I'm not."

Sloane eased away until her back was to the Bell's outer shell once again, careful not to jostle the MRE wrappers and the folded foil blanket Jax had tucked along the deck. She drew up her knees, wrapped both arms around them. Sense crept back in, and with it, her control.

The night had rules—or maybe none at all. Dawn, though, had different ones. Ones she guided her life by.

Outside, the wind lifted and fell, an invisible hand pressing against the airframe. The storm had stepped back in the night, but it was out there waiting. She cleared her throat.

"Thank you for last night." The words were not enough, but they were true.

Jax shifted onto an elbow, the movement quiet. "We were both there."

"You carried the heavy weight."

"All right," Jax said. "You're welcome."

Jax's radio hissed, saving Sloane from struggling to resume their working relationship at some safe distance. Jax rolled onto her back and reached for the radio, the motion fluid, taking her outside their makeshift quilt shelter. Alone, awake, aware of her duty, Sloane snapped back into her professional mindset with relief. She didn't need irrational emotions complicating her judgment when lives were at stake. She had more to thank Jax for than just a warm, dry place to sleep, a shoulder to lean on, and a sympathetic ear. Jax had saved her from forgetting why she was there. The afterimage of the near kiss, if that's where they'd truly been headed, faded, replaced by the familiar quickening she recognized.

Duty called.

"Bell One, this is Coulter's Gap Ops," Eli's staticky voice announced. "Gauge at Green Fork up twenty-two inches since zero-six-hundred. Road to Black Run compromised at mile four. Lynette reports community shelter filling."

Jax glanced at Sloane, tipped the radio toward her.

"Eli, this is Sloane." She sounded steady. She was. "Do you have a shelter head count? We'll need an ancillary shelter if we're nearing capacity. Have Mina send you a pharmacy inventory. We'll need med supplies replaced. Ditto on portable O2."

"Copy, Sloane. Shelter head count sixty-three at last check. Two reported missing out past Miller's Bridge. Lynette says town power is flickering again."

Jax said, "Abort the outreach mission? We can lift in ten and make a run for Miller's Bridge."

"Affirmative, Bell One. Advise search and extricate if possible."

"Copy, Coulter Ops," Jax said, already moving, already in that rhythm that made other people keep up or get out of the way. "We'll spool up—get the rotors turning—and take a look at the bridge first. Bell One out."

Jax rose and offered a hand without thinking about it. Sloane took it, heat rising through her palm. The contact lasted half a second longer than necessary. Jax let go first.

"You should eat more than three bites so you don't get cranky." Jax nudged a second MRE pouch toward Sloane on her way to the cockpit. "Bean will have heard—he and Sarah should be on the move."

"I don't get cranky." Sloane heard the cranky coming through and smiled. "Not clinically."

Sloane ate four more bites because Jax was right and because her body seemed to be making a lot of decisions for her lately.

Jax's radio pinged again.

Bean. "ETA five, Chief."

"Copy," Jax said, working through the pre-flight without looking like she was working. "We eyeball Miller's Bridge. If it's passable, we'll call for transport. If it's not, we set down upriver, find the subjects, and haul them out."

"They'll be hypothermic," Sloane said. "Callie can stage for rewarming at the clinic if we can't transport."

"Copy." Jax clicked off the radio, turned to look back at Sloane. "You good to go, Doctor?"

Sloane took in the set of her jaw and the steadiness in her shoulders, and a memory stirred of a hand easing her away from a move she would have made without regret and regretted later. She ought to be thinking about blood gases and hypothermia protocols, and she was, but awareness of the woman at the controls rode beneath it all. She drew a deep breath, her mind clear and calm. "Yes, Chief. I'm good."

The words slid into the place where a kiss would have gone. For now.

Jax grinned. "Then let's go keep people breathing."

❖

Jax cracked the door and the cold came in, sharp as a blade. Behind her, Sloane readied the med kit and checked the straps on the litters. "You checked all that yesterday."

"That was yesterday," Sloane murmured without turning.

"Knew you'd say that."

"Then why ask?" Sloane sounded amused.

"Because sometimes people surprise me."

Sloane finally looked over. "Do I?"

"Pretty much every day." Jax touched her radio. "Bean? Perimeter check?"

Bean's silhouette moved past the window, a thumbs-up in the gray. Jax gripped the tiller. The last thing she'd held had been Sloane's hand. Her pulse skipped for a second and she pushed the thought aside. Last night was last night. Today was a new day.

Bean and Sarah climbed in, and Bean dropped into the seat beside her. "Some fun, huh, Chief?"

"Running hot, Bean," Jax said as every system checked green. "Bell One to Ops command. Lifting for Miller's Bridge recon."

"Copy lift," Eli replied, radio now crisp and clear. "Heads-up. Sheriff Langley just reported water over the road by the old feed store. If it keeps rising, Main Street will flood."

"Understood."

Sloane came on over the intercom. "Eli, have Mina move the oxygen-dependents closer to the generator side of the gym now. If we lose power, I want them on concentrators within a minute."

"On it."

Below them, the river was a slate ribbon that twisted through brown fields and black stumps. The uprooted trees rode the current like dead soldiers. The road connecting Coulter's Gap to the far side of the river had disappeared, buried beneath rock and mud.

"Bridge," Jax said.

Miller's Bridge made a valiant stand. Water licked the lower struts and coursed over the span on the near side. Debris wedged sideways against the support pillars. The road on the far side ran with brown soup past the first bend. On the near bank, a pickup sat with its hood angled into the river, driver's door open, no one inside.

"If anyone tried to cross, they're either somewhere on the far bank or they're in the water," Bean said.

Jax clicked on the floods, raked the muddy ground below. "Far end of the bridge. Two people."

"See 'em," Bean said. "Can't hoist over the bridge."

"I'll set us down on the near side gravel bar, but we'll have rotor wash in the water. Your call."

"No choice," Bean answered in her ear. "I'll rig a line."

Jax hovered over the narrow strip of almost solid ground. "Sloane? You carry the kit. I carry you if the bank goes."

"You won't need to," Sloane said, her voice perfectly cool. "But I won't argue if you try."

Jax spared enough breath to chuckle and set the bird down. That bit of unexpected humor—dry and edgy—nearly distracted her from the floodwaters trying to tear the last sliver of solid ground out from under them. The Bell shuddered, then settled. Wind flung spray off the river in their faces as the bay door slid open.

Bean made the lines ready, his arm a bracket across the opening, his grin tight. "Just a little morning exercise."

Jax clipped in. The cold slapped at her, sharpening every sense. She and Sloane dropped to the muddy gravel, in sync. Jax gripped the back of Sloane's harness, not protective really, more a guide and an anchor. If it eased her worry at the same time, that was fair. The slight hitch in Sloane's shoulders said she noticed. "I have you. Ready?"

"Yes. Go."

"Two," Sloane called after a minute.

On the far bank, a figure waved, small and urgent, another shape half-hidden behind a guardrail.

"I see them," Jax shouted. "We'll go as far as we can, then we talk them across to us."

"What if they can't walk?"

"Then I carry."

Even in the rain and wind, Sloane's head shake was clear. "You'll get swept away."

"You just hold the line." Jax met her gaze. "Copy?"

Sloane looked at her. She didn't blink. "Yes. I copy."

The exchange took half a second, but it was all Jax needed. She stepped off into what had been a shallow river turned raging floodwater. Testing the sweep of water and stone before each step, she worked her way across. She rigged a second safety line as she approached the two people who edged toward the river on the far bank. The current threw a branch at the guardrail. It spun and raced on.

Jax, the water to mid-thigh, shouted instructions. The world had narrowed to current and rope and breath and pale faces watching. She leaned into the swirling murk and did not look down. She looked at Sloane—hair plastered to her cheeks, chin up, fearless eyes steely with resolve. Determination carved in alabaster.

All she needed to carry her the rest of the way across. And back again.

CHAPTER THIRTEEN

Week 4
Disaster stirring

Jax nosed the Bell down through the last veil of cloud, the bird shuddering in crosswinds as Coulter's Gap rose out of the mist like a half-remembered dream. The ridgelines in the high country had slumped and cracked under the weeks of punishing rain. Fresh scars ran red with earthy debris where whole swaths of trees had uprooted, clinging to the sides of newly carved rivulets like desperate fingers grasping a crumbling ledge. The river below the Gap was a wide brown gash now, bleeding muddy water that overflowed its banks, drowning fields gone to soup, lapping at barns listing in floodwater to their eaves.

Jeb said over the intercom, "Can't even recognize anything down there. That's the McBride place, but I don't see the house."

"Make sure to let Eli know," Jax replied, checking on him with a quick glance back. "He'll need to scan the rolls to see if the family has sheltered somewhere."

"Copy, Chief." Jeb sat on the rear bench, one gloved hand braced against the litter where the old man lay strapped in place, a traction splint on his right leg. Fractured femur, high risk for shock, but he'd stayed lucid through the load and lift, had even made a crack about finally getting that ride into town he'd been putting off for forty years.

"Tell Ezra we'll have him warm and cozy in ten." The guy was tough, despite his obvious pain, but she wanted to get him to Sloane. She banked hard enough around a washed-out gully to make her own ribs ache. Every minute mattered now—for him and whoever would need them next.

"Bell One to Ops," she said now into the mic, circling the town. "Inbound with male, late seventies, isolated closed femur fracture, splinted, vitals stable. Be advised, the ridge track to Martin Hollow is gone. Entire west shoulder's in the ravine. No ground access until it's rebuilt."

Eli's voice cracked back, so sharp she could almost taste his urgency. "Copy. Advising medics. You see anything on the flats to the east?"

Jax let the Bell drift lower, tilting so she could sweep the valley. "River's over its banks as far as I can see. Feeder roads from the south all underwater. I count three houses submerged to the second floor and a propane tank loose in the current. North access still holding, but the road's breaking up by the culvert. Anything heavier than a pickup's going to chew through it."

Beyond the flooded flats, the distant shadow of the dam crouched against the gorge. They all pretended it would hold. No one really believed it.

"Copy all," Eli said, voice tight. "Will advise Reggie to hold the transports in Asheville."

"How's our shelter census?"

"We're at eighty-nine," Eli said. "We'll need a food run."

"Air drops?" Jax pulled the collective gently, dropping them toward the field behind the clinic. Below, the town hunched small and stubborn against the dark sweep of mountains, the sandbag barriers on Main Street meandering like a lost army on the march, the clinic lights bleeding thinly through the plastic sheeting tacked over the windows. Even from the air, the overflow from the community center shelter was clear—lines of bright tarps blooming like mushrooms in the parking lot and abandoned vehicles left helter-skelter in side streets swollen with runoff that climbed above the wheel wells.

The Bell's rotors clawed at the mist. Jax's shoulders locked into that familiar tension between relief and refusal—relief they were home, refusal to unclench until she was sure they'd make it home again the next time.

His laugh over the radio sounded like a whip cracking. "We're down the list. Assume we're on our own."

"Copy," Jax said, more to herself than to him. She always assumed she was on her own—her and her team. Five days now since the river tried to take the couple stranded on the riverbank. Nearly a week since the storm stopped pretending it would break. In that span, the ground had come apart piece by piece—first the feeder roads sloughing off into ditches, then the backcountry bridges snapping at their joints, then whole access tracks vanishing overnight. Families from the lowlands had trickled into town with laundry sacks and pets in crates, soaking wet and white-faced, leaving dark lines on the shelter floor where they tracked in the muddy red clay. Supply trucks couldn't get within ten miles now. The whole town hummed like a hive of riled hornets, in full survival mode, with daily town meetings to decide on everything from school closures to food lines. Eli's hourly updates relayed to Lynette, her response grimmer by the minute as the rain gauges ticked up and stayed there. Nature ran its own course, heedless of pleas or prayers. The dam twenty miles upriver wanted to fail.

Everything the town counted on to survive, it had because the Bell could still fly.

And because she kept flying it.

She didn't mind the nearly twenty-four seven duty. She needed to keep moving. When she was *doing*, she wasn't *thinking*. When she wasn't flying a sortie, she doubled her equipment checks, ran sling-load drills—practice flights carrying cargo slung beneath the Bell—because they sure as hell were going to need to up the supply deliveries soon. When Bean rolled his eyes and told her she was wearing a groove into the gravel, she just shook her head and scheduled another test run.

She avoided the roadhouse at the times she knew Sloane would be there, because being near her and pretending she didn't want to be closer was getting harder. Not the work—the work was fine. It was the other stuff. Noticing things that didn't matter. How Sloane took her coffee. How she bent over patient files, that little furrow between her brows, tucking her hair behind her ear in that way that shouldn't matter. The way she hummed when she thought no one could hear. Rodriguez used to say Jax collected exit strategies like lucky charms. She could hear her saying, *You know what your problem is, Kincaid? You think caring about someone is the first step to losing them.*

Mags had tagged her right back then. Was probably laughing her ass off now, wherever she was, watching her catalog Sloane Marshall's habits like intel she needed to survive. And running the other way.

No, the problem wasn't that she kept thinking about Sloane up on the mountain caring for Meemaw—patient, gentle, and steely with determination. Or the night in the Bell—gentle, tender, and heartbreakingly vulnerable. Or even the terrifying few seconds in the middle of the wild river during the rescue, when she feared she could lose her and the fear nearly paralyzed her. The problem was how her body reacted whenever she thought of her—like a hand clenched deep inside her. Or that involuntary way her breath caught whenever Sloane appeared. Or the way she lay motionless in the dark, *feeling* Sloane awake beneath her, her own heartbeat so loud she thought Sloane might hear it. When she'd realized she was timing her returns to the roadhouse to coincide with when Sloane would be awake, she'd started sleeping in the Bell. When she slept at all.

Fine—Rodriguez would've called her on it the first time she saw her stand a half second too long in a doorway. *You're gone for her, Kincaid. Just admit it.*

But she couldn't. Admission had a cost. She had learned that in blood.

"Doc's on her way," Eli reported as Jax set the Bell down, yanking her awareness back to the present.

Sloane. Of course Sloane was on her way to meet them. The only reason she hadn't insisted on making the run up the mountain to retrieve Ezra was an outbreak of measles among the refugees at the shelter that needed urgent attention.

The skids kissed gravel uphill from the clinic, and Jax powered down fast, rotors still ticking as she swung into the Bell's bay. Bean shoved the big doors open and cold mist flooded inside, biting through her flight jacket. Jeb had the litter angled to the opening by the time she reached them, and together they eased Ezra from the Bell. He groaned, breath hissing through clenched teeth, but he never complained.

Sloane was already there—gloves on, hair dragged back in a hasty knot, eyes sharp. "Straight to trauma two," she said, voice brisk, as if they hadn't shared the same narrow cabin through the night a week ago. "Status?"

"Ezra Hobbs, age seventy. No known medical problems. Caught in a rockslide hoping to get down the mountain on his RTV." Jax kept a hand on the splint to steady it as they transported over the uneven ground. Another one of the holdouts, stubborn as bedrock, refusing to evacuate even after the road washed out along with half his ridge. Who knew how many more were stranded up there now. "Vitals steady, closed fracture, no neuro deficit. Distal pulses weak."

"Hurts like a bit—devil, Doc," Ezra grunted.

"I'll get you something for that once we're inside on monitors," Sloane said, moving in sync with Jax without looking at her.

She'd thrown a rain slicker on over a plain shirt and jeans, smelled a little like antiseptic and lemon—Gatorade?—and still managed to look beautiful even dripping wet. Jax kept her eyes front and her jaws clenched.

They pushed through the plastic sheeting over the clinic doorway, heat slamming into her like a wall. The triage area hummed—monitors beeped, the ventilator at cot three sighed, Mina murmured instructions to Callie beside a crib across the room.

When Mina shot a questioning look their way, Sloane said, "We're good," and looked at Jax. "Can you run the portable X-ray?"

"Yes." Jax, along with Jeb, who'd followed them in, helped Sloane transfer Ezra to the treatment table. "I'll set up."

"Thank you," Sloane said, still not meeting her eyes.

That distant response, intentional and somehow cold, fired her temper when what she needed was exactly the opposite. Coolheaded rationality. Not the ghost of Sloane's shoulder under her palm that night in the Bell or the soft touch of Sloane's fingers on her neck. She about-turned before she made yet another mistake where Sloane was concerned. This was not a place to get sloppy—where if edges blurred, people died. She knew what Rodriguez would say to that, too. *You don't get to call it* being in control *if it's just fear with a better story.*

Maybe it was fear—the same fear that clawed at her guts while Rodriguez bled beside her. Not that it mattered now. There was work to do, and work was honest. She rolled the portable machine into the trauma cubicle. "Ready for the picture, Doc."

Sloane looked up at her for the first time, her eyes as unfathomable as a fog-shrouded peak. "Thank you, Chief. Let's get this done."

A few minutes later, Sloane put the film up on a portable light box—old school, the computers were too unreliable—and the three of them looked at it.

"Jeb?" Sloane said, ever the teacher. "What do you see?"

Jeb flushed the way he did every time Sloane addressed him. Jax couldn't blame him, since inside she often had the same reaction.

"Ah…" He pointed. "A non-displaced transverse femur fracture, midshaft."

"Stable?"

"Looks like it."

"Why?"

Jeb glanced at Jax, a clear plea for rescue in his eyes.

Jax cut her eyes to the traction splint they'd applied in the field. *Go on, buddy, you know the answer.*

Sloane apparently saw the look and, miracle of miracles, she actually smiled. "Jax?"

"Right now the immobilization and traction is holding everything in place. But he's going to need a rod to stabilize it." She frowned and looked at Sloane. "Transfer?"

Sloane motioned for her to follow. Once out of Ezra's hearing, she said, "What's it like out there? Can you get him to any kind of transport?"

"The window is closing on ground transport getting anywhere close, I think," Jax said. "I'll get Eli on it."

"Then we'll splint him, keep him in traction, and comfortable with pain meds for now," Sloane said.

"Right."

"Please ask Eli to keep me informed."

"Copy," Jax said.

"Thank you."

And that was that. Sloane turned away. Jax read the unspoken *dismissed* and walked outside into the rain. She told herself that was exactly the way she wanted it—everything between them neat and clean and professional. The way it should be—had to be.

Bean found her an hour later, doing her second check when the first had been fine, appearing at her elbow with two paper cups, steam wisping from both.

"Brought you the closest the school canteen has to coffee."

"Tastes like victory already," she said, accepting the cup. "How's the ridge road?"

"Bad. Sheriff took one look and said he's not sending trucks up there again till the water drops. As if it ever will." Bean angled his head at her. "You been sleeping at all?"

"On the clock." She drank. It was awful. She kept drinking. "We have eyes on the dam face yet?"

"State sent a drone. Gave us pretty footage and a wide shrug. Spillway's eating into the base. The concrete's starting to give."

"Well, fuck." Jax blew across the surface of the cup and did not think about Sloane's mouth, or the way Sloane's hand had felt on her throat that morning a lifetime ago, or the pressure in her chest when the radio crackled and it wasn't Sloane's voice answering. "We'll fly a river scan south in twenty. Light and low."

Bean watched her long enough to be annoying. "You going to talk to her?"

"Which her?" Pointless deflection. Bean didn't blink.

"The one you're not looking at."

"We've got a dam to watch and a town to keep from starving," she said mildly. "Talking is optional."

Bean grunted. "Optional till it gets in the way of the job."

"It's not."

"If you say so, Chief."

"Let's go see if we can find somewhere to off-load a guy who needs his femur fixed." She set the cup aside and climbed into the cockpit. Under the familiar dance of slipping on the headset, checking gauges, and flipping switches, the other rhythm she'd been refusing to hear kept time—Sloane's voice in her ear from the Bell's intercom, the exact way it went cool on approach to a scene, how it warmed again when she spoke to an injured man, the precise focus she turned on a broken thing she could fix and the private way she absorbed the responsibility for what she couldn't.

Jax didn't know where to put those thoughts.

They lifted and skated south over the roiling river. She updated Eli as they flew. Debris at the east bend. Cows on a gravel bar that hadn't been a bar three days ago. A barn roof sliding sideways like a hat in a windstorm. On the return leg, she almost contacted Sloane to tell her the flood had cut the field road. No clear drop-off for transport in sight. Almost.

Instead she radioed Eli.

Back on the ground, she saw Sloane from a distance through the open gym doors, sleeves shoved up, hair caught back in a quick knot, gloved hands covered in someone's blood. The involuntary gut clench hit before she could brace. She set her jaw and kept walking.

Rodriguez again—her silent conscience. *What happens when you meet someone worth staying for?* She muttered what she'd said then: *Not my problem.*

Now, cataloging Sloane's habits like they mattered, she could see Rodriguez's smirk.

She meant to button down the Bell and, when Bean left, climb back inside.

She didn't.

Close on to midnight, her steps took her across wet gravel toward the roadhouse because she knew who would be there, even if she refused to admit that was the reason. Light bled through a gap around the warped front door. She stopped on the porch with her hand on the latch and told herself to turn around. She opened the door instead.

❖

Sloane caught herself looking toward the door. Again. That made four times in the last hour. She knew because she'd been counting, which was ridiculous. She had work to do. Charts to review. Supplies to inventory. But her body had developed its own agenda—pulse jumping when boots sounded on the porch, shoulders relaxing only when Jax's voice carried from outside. Like some kind of Pavlovian response she couldn't shut off. She'd watched her parents love Sybil with frightening intensity. Watched that love destroy them when she died. She wouldn't do that. Couldn't. Except denying whatever this was took more energy than she had to spare.

They were heading into the fourth week of this madness, and everyone was bone tired. The school gym—clinic, shelter, rumor mill—smelled like wet wool, the metallic bite of generator exhaust, and despair. Somehow, Jax managed never to be where she was—if she was at the triage tent, Jax was transporting sandbags to the latest washed-out street. If she checked on the displaced families in the community center shelter, Jax was in the Bell. She saw Jax at the daily briefings, but she disappeared like smoke the moment Eli called an end to the meeting.

She really tried not to dwell on the unsettled feeling that plagued her since the night in the Bell. She didn't have time for distractions. That was what she had told herself every morning of the past week as she lined up the day: wound care checks, insulin rationing, oxygen and nebulizers, fevers in the shelter that weren't COVID, weren't influenza, weren't anything she could swab or isolate, just the damp and the crowd and the long week wearing down immune systems. That was what she told Mina when Mina raised an eyebrow at the whiteboard and then at Sloane's face. That was what she told Eli when he asked whether the generators could take another heater and she heard herself answer yes before calculating the amperage because she could not bring herself to say no to a little extra warmth.

Her focus was off, and she knew it. Outwardly she worked with as much concentration as ever, while internally she catalogued the absences. Where Jax was not. When Jax did not come through the clinic door after the Bell landed. When Jax's laughter—rare but powerful—didn't arrow across the grassy lot after Bean said something that probably wasn't even that funny.

She did not look for Jax. When she noticed herself not-looking, she redirected toward a patient, toward a stack of charts, toward a kid with a barky cough, toward anything that wasn't the door. It didn't help. When the Bell lifted, she always knew it. The clamp in her chest was involuntary, her body betraying her by listening for the sound to return and refusing to breathe freely again until the rotor *whup-whup-whup* came back.

Tonight, despite her best intentions, when the footsteps sounded outside on the porch, she refused to hope, but she couldn't help but look. The door opened on a gust of damp night. Jax stepped in, head bare, hair plastered, jacket dark with spray. Jax froze when she saw her, in that still way she had when facing a crisis. Assessing, composed, ready to move.

The air changed, crackling with unreleased electricity.

"Are you avoiding me?" Sloane asked.

No preamble. No softening. She didn't know how else to do this—had never needed to. Had never cared enough to *need* to know.

Jax cursed, a muttered word aimed not at Sloane, it seemed, but at herself.

"Well?" Sloane said, glad her voice didn't shake.

"Yes," Jax said, her mouth twisting into a grimace. "God damn it."

Sloane raised her chin, the honesty hitting like a blast of long-forgotten heat. "Why?"

Jax's jaw worked once, and she took two steps inside, bringing the rain with her. Close enough for the scent of the bloated river and the soap she used to tease Sloane's senses. She held her ground, eyes on Jax's, even when Jax cupped her face with both hands.

"Because of this." Jax's mouth closed over hers, hot and explosive.

The kiss wasn't careful or uncertain. It was all Jax—strident and sure. Powerful. And beneath the power? Tender and waiting. For what, Sloane didn't know and didn't care. She didn't resist. She met Jax halfway and then all the way, clasping the back of Jax's neck, splaying her fingers in the short, wet hair, caressing the warm skin under her palm. Jax's mouth was heat and steadiness and a kind of restraint that made Sloane want to tear it away. She leaned in until Jax took a step back, her shoulders to the closed door, and wrapped her arms around Sloane's waist. Sloane braced her hands on Jax's shoulders, her lower body molding of its own accord to Jax's thighs. Fire swelled within her, stealing her breath.

Sloane broke long enough to breathe and to say the only true thing she had managed all week that wasn't about medications or generators. "Don't avoid me."

"Can't." Jax's forehead touched hers, a small press of warm, soft skin that radiated all the way to Sloane's core. "I tried. It didn't work."

"Good." Sloane trembled, reckless with the heady thrill of choosing something dangerous on purpose. Of wanting someone, finally.

The radio at Eli's comms center blasted to life. "Calling AERIS Ops. Emergency alert. Repeat, emergency alert. Goldman Dam has given way. I say again, the dam has given way."

They both froze, breath suspended, for one impossible second. Jax tense, muscles vibrating beneath Sloane's hands. Sloane, heart pounding, a terrible roaring in her head.

Then the world came back into lethal focus.

Adrenaline surging, Sloane pushed away, still holding Jax's wrist for one more heartbeat. The pulse under her touch beat fast and strong, calming even in chaos. "No matter what, don't avoid me again."

Jax skimmed her cheek with the backs of her fingers. "I won't."

Bean's footsteps thundered like hammer blows as he charged down the stairs, calling, "Chief, I'm with you."

Eli raced to the comms center. "Jax, get the Bell in the air."

"Aye, Command." Jax pulled the door open, her gaze on Sloane. "I'll be back."

"Be careful," Sloane whispered.

And then she was gone, leaving Sloane with an emptiness she recognized and feared more than ever before.

CHAPTER FOURTEEN

Day 1: dam breach

Racing from the roadhouse with Bean, Jax held on to the image of Sloane's face, fierce and determined, for another minute before cold air and the wailing siren blocked out every thought but the action plan. The mechanical howl rising from the roof of the school on the ridge above town cut through the murky air like a blade. Not the cyclical fire tone. The flood tone—one long, ululating, unbroken warning that hit bone deep, a primal scream that they'd advised everyone in hearing range would mean one thing.

Run.

And she did—wind knifing her cheeks, rain needling sideways as she and Bean pounded across the lot. In the distance, the Bell crouched in the floodlit field behind the school like a black insect, blades tied down, gleaming with rain. Jeb veered for the gear shed, shoving up the prefab's roll door and dragging the duffels—swift-water rigs, litters, strop harnesses, throw bags—outside while Bean brought the RTV around, its headlights slicing the mist. She tossed in the gear and piled on for the short run across the field.

Jax's radio barked—Eli, broadcasting across every emergency channel in town. *All units, emergency alert. Goldman Dam has failed. Initiate Flood Plan Delta. Evacuate low-lying areas—evacuees to the shelter site at the community center. Medical transports to Trauma.*

Bean skidded the RTV to a stop by the landing pad. Jeb heaved the gear bags into the cabin while Bean started pulling the tie-downs from the rotors, every movement fast and sure. The floodlights off the gym threw everything into hard contrast—wet asphalt glare, shadows cut like glass, people straggling uphill from the low-lying streets with backpacks, kids on their hips, and pets under their arms.

The sky had that wrong, low bruise it got before a new squall swept in. Floodlight glare flattened everything, just like experience flattened the fear. No time for thought, only action. Jax climbed straight into the cockpit. Switches, master on, fuel, battery, hydraulics—the sequence blurred as muscle memory took over, fast and exact.

Her headset crackled as Eli came back online.

"Jax, listen up—breaches at Mill Creek and Hart's Run. Vehicles in water by the feed store. Road cut east and south. West side is an island. Coulter's Gap is taking water below the switchbacks. The clinic is now trauma central. Sloane and the others are clearing the tents for triage. We need eyes on the damage, pulls on anyone we can reach, and anywhere you can set the Bell down."

Action plan made simple: see it, save them, find ground.

"Copy, Command. We'll start north arc, then swing east. Give me lat-longs or landmarks. We'll improvise landing zones if they exist. If not, we'll go basket."

Voices behind her in the bay. Bean barking a checklist, a familiar tenor responding. She grinned. *Jeb.* Good; they could use him. Bean dropped into the left seat, and Jeb slammed the cabin door, his harness already cinched. Jax spooled the turbines. The Bell growled under her, the vibration crawling up through the pedals into her bones like something alive. The rotors blurred to silver, and she released the brakes.

They rose straight into rain. The school shrank beneath them—clinic blazing with light, the shelter's parking lot higher up the ridge a chaos of headlamps and figures rushing to erect more tents. From this height, the streets below were gone, erased under moving brown water. The town's shape had changed while no one was looking.

Eli again, his voice clipped and impersonal—the way it got when he'd stopped pretending things were manageable. *Sheriff reports propane tanks drifting. Watch your debris field.*

"Copy," Jax said, easing the collective. "Bell One lifting."

The Bell shouldered into the night and found its balance. They skimmed low over rooftops and drowned yards, every landmark half-unrecognizable under floodwater. The siren still keened behind them, fading like a last breath as Coulter's Gap slid beneath them, no longer a town on a ridge but a stubborn island cinched by brown water, the river swollen into a wide, roiling sheet that had erased fields and fences.

Headlamps traced frantic constellations where people fought the flood; taillights bled red along a road that didn't exist anymore.

"Jesus," Jeb breathed on the intercom. "There's nothing down there."

"Eyes up," Bean said. "We start with the living."

"On it," Jeb said, voice tight.

Eli came back, the adrenaline burn gone, replaced by the icy calm Jax recognized. *Two on a roof by Miller's turnoff—white farmhouse, green metal roof. Water up to gutters.*

"Visual on them." Jax nosed lower. The farmhouse was a pale island in a black sea, the yard gone, no driveway, a porch rail just visible under the churn. Foam streaked the current like strips of torn cloth. A propane tank spun in a lazy death roll, hissing through spray, and she marked it unconsciously the way she marked power lines and crosswinds—peril to the unwary. "We don't touch down. Bean, you're on hoist. Jeb, you're my man in the basket."

"Copy," Bean said. "Hoist hot in thirty."

"Ready." Jeb clipped his harness with sharp clicks that cut through the turbine hum.

Jax slid them into a hover, her forearms tightening with the familiar strain. Sweat prickled down her spine despite the cold. Her thighs locked hard on the pedals, calves trembling with the effort to keep the disc steady in the crosswind. Rotor wash blasted the rain into silver needles, stripping shingles and sending the basket swinging like a pendulum. Two people huddled by the chimney, arms around one another, pale faces lifted. Jax took a breath, and the world condensed to a simple objective: Keep the disc clear, hold the hover, keep them alive.

"Line out," Bean said, cable humming free.

The basket swung out, Jeb rode it like he was born to it—knees loose, shoulders square, calm because calm was a thing you could decide to be when the world went to hell.

"Steady," Jax said, mostly to herself, tracking Jeb's descent against the chimney and keeping the tail boom clear of the apple trees, now half-submerged and bucking in the sea of wreckage.

Bean kept the cable centered like he had strings tied to gravity.

"On roof," Jeb reported. "Both stable. I'll send her first."

The woman clambered into the basket, hands white on the rim, skirt plastered to her legs. The gusts slapped Jax's faceplate, the Bell twitching as if the storm wanted to peel her off the air. She leaned back, muscles burning, and kept the disc clear.

"Basket loaded," Jeb said.

"Bringing line," Bean said and drew her up smooth and fast. The basket cleared the roof. Bean caught it at the door and dragged her inside, peeling off the harness while Jeb clipped the man in below.

Jax's pulse leveled as the tension eased to less than critical, and in that sliver of quiet, her control betrayed her. She pictured Sloane somewhere down below, sleeves shoved up, hair held back in a careless tail, voice smooth and steady. Directing traffic, saving lives, while the world came apart. Pride flared under her ribs like a small, steady flame. Fear slipped in next to it.

The worst was yet to come. On the ground didn't mean safe—and she was too far away to be of any help. Sloane was smart, strong, stubborn. But this? This was war with an enemy Sloane had never faced. Jax exhaled hard.

She trusted Sloane.

And got back to work, sliding the Bell a breath to the left to counter sway as Bean brought the man up. The roof gave a long, ugly creak as the water licked higher. Jeb came last, cable swaying in the rotor wash, arms out for balance as he rose.

Jax held them rock-steady until Bean called "Clear," then banked them out, the farmhouse roof swallowed into the dark behind them.

"Eli," she said, "two survivors recovered from Miller's turnoff. We're returning to clinic LZ for drop."

"Copy," Eli said. "Be advised, triage is now at the gym doors. We're at mass-casualty protocol. And Jax—Sheriff Langley reports three more roof calls east of the silos."

"We'll get them," she said.

They dropped low over the school. Floodlights carved an ugly grace note in the mist. The gym doors banged open and a knot of figures moved into the wash—Callie with a litter, Mina calling orders, and Sloane, bareheaded in the rain, face turned upward toward the Bell. Jax saw her clearly for an instant, and the lock on her chest clicked open. Her breath eased for the first time since she'd left her at the roadhouse. Sloane met Jax's gaze for one breath, and Jax's stomach dropped the way it did just before a stall. Heart dropping, breath catching—an instinct older than thought. *Keep her safe.*

"Basket down," Bean said, his voice severing the slight connection.

"Copy." Jax brought them two feet lower and no more, because the wind had gotten ugly and the LZ was a puddled mess.

The woman from the roof looked up at Sloane and started crying the way people did when they finally knew they were safe. Jax couldn't hear the words Sloane spoke, but knew them anyway: *You're safe. I've got you.*

"Clear," Bean said, breaking the spell.

"Lifting," Jax said, and the Bell climbed back into rain.

Every time she lifted away from the gym after delivering an injured evacuee, she caught glimpses of Sloane through the open doors—a flash of scrubs, a quick turn of her head, the precise movements she'd come to recognize even from a hundred feet up. Each sighting sent a jolt through her chest, something between relief and longing she didn't have time to examine. Later, she told herself. Think about Sloane later. But her body didn't wait for permission, already listening for her voice on the radio, already cataloging whether she was safe.

They flew until time dissolved. Sortie after sortie: a man on a tractor cab clinging with both hands while floodwater gnashed at the tires. Two kids on a porch swing that had snapped loose and wedged against a cottonwood. An elderly woman waving a dish towel from a second-story window while the current knocked furniture against the glass. A teen with a dog on the cab of a pickup drifting sideways toward the bridge.

The dog tried to leap for Jeb and nearly took them both into the water. Jeb caught him by the harness and laughed breathlessly into the mic. "Got you, idiot bastard."

"Language," Bean said dryly.

"Talking to myself," Jeb said.

Jax grinned and threaded the Bell down corridors of air where power lines listed like drunk jump ropes and trees skated by in the current like ancient ships. She did not think about sleep or food. She thought about torque limits, disc clearance, wind shear, and how long the hoist motor would tolerate the pace she was demanding.

Words on repeat.

Propane tank, two o'clock.

Seen.

Basket ready.

Send.

The clinic—rechristened Trauma—spread across the field toward the landing site, tents blossoming like lily pads on a pond. Someone, probably Eli, had thrown a makeshift windsock over a bleacher pole. Each time Jax set the basket down in the wash, Sloane was there or just gone, and each time Jax's heart kicked up a notch.

"Medical needs supplies," Eli reported as Jax came in with a volunteer firefighter suffering from hypothermia who'd gotten swept up and nearly swept away trying to extract a stranded motorist out of a truck.

"Get me a list," Jax snapped as Mina and Sarah directed Jeb where to take the firefighter.

"I've got it," Sloane said from behind her.

Jax spun around, half-expecting she'd imagined her voice—conjured it to crack the vise of fear that had been clamped around her for hours, not knowing what was happening back in the Gap. But she hadn't.

There was Sloane again—wet hair, wet lashes, cool, calm expression. Her eyes, though, they were fire as they swept over her. Their gazes caught and the world narrowed. Jax leaned in, pulled by the magnet that was Sloane.

"What do you need?" Jax asked hoarsely, throat raw from hours of radio chatter and everything she hadn't said to her.

"Everything you can get me," Sloane said, handing her a paper. Her hand fisted, knuckles pale, the only crack in her practiced calm. "We're short on blankets, cots, O2, food. God, Jax—everything."

"We'll fly as long as we have fuel," Jax said, "and divert only for critical rescue."

"Life first," Sloane said, her eyes never leaving Jax.

"Always."

Sloane gripped her arm. "You can't fly on fumes, either."

"I'm okay."

"We're looking at a long run here, aren't we," Sloane said flatly.

"Yes," Jax said. Sloane didn't need coddling. She was too strong for that.

"Then I…we…don't need you and your crew burning out."

"I hear you." Jax grimaced. So much more she wanted to say. *I see you. I hear you. I'm not avoiding you anymore.* "How critical is this list?"

"We'll make it another hour," Sloane said.

"Can't promise that, but we'll try," Jax said.

Bean appeared, rain streaming down his face. "Got a bus in a ravine, Chief."

"Copy," Jax said, still fixed on Sloane. "Be careful here. The river's still rising."

"I will," Sloane said. "You too."

For an instant Sloane's attention, fierce and unblinking, bored into Jax, like she could will Jax to come back whole.

"Chief," Bean said quietly in her ear, not a warning, just a truth.

"I know," Jax said, forcing herself to turn away. "I'm flying."

And she did.

Sloane looked out through the open gym doors at the controlled pandemonium in the hastily erected tents where volunteers, masterfully organized into teams by Callie, helped the walking wounded to seats to wait. Callie, who had revealed a startling gift for command—firm but kind, like she'd been waiting her whole life to be useful in chaos—sent anyone with active bleeding or unstable vital signs inside for immediate treatment. Before the words that had changed everything—*the dam has given way*—the gym had been a walk-in clinic. Now it had become a field hospital in under an hour. The bleachers were shoved back against the walls, their lower rails draped with IV bags. Red, yellow, and green duct tape that barely stuck to the damp floor indicated bays for critical, serious, or stable patients. Thankfully they had yet to need a designated morgue area. O2 cylinders stood like silent sentries along the wall beneath the old scoreboard, half of them already tapped low. The hum of the twin generators throbbed through the walls, the reverberations a counterpoint to the *whup-whup-whup* of the Bell's descent.

The first waves had come in shivering and half-drowned, many clinically hypothermic with skin cold and waxy, lips tinged blue, and voices slurred or gone entirely. Sheriff Langley and his lone deputy, who constituted the Gap's law enforcement, brought some in their patrol cars from nearby homes, while others arrived on foot or in the baskets Jax kept dropping from the night sky. River water and mud streaked the gym floor as Callie and Mina pushed stretchers in and Bean or Jeb carried them out for the next run. Every time the Bell landed, Sloane spared a few seconds to look for Jax but rarely saw her.

She told herself Jax was fine. Jax was doing what she'd probably done a hundred times, in battle and in disaster zones—flying into troubled airspace and saving lives. If she hadn't spent that night up on the mountains, grounded by impenetrable weather, she wouldn't have appreciated just how much skill it took for Jax to pilot the Bell while the storm hammered like a vengeful god. She'd learned a great deal that night—about Jax, about herself. Not everything left her comfortable.

She admired Jax's professional ability more than ever, as well as her kindness. But what unsettled her was how fiercely she missed Jax the instant she disappeared into the dark. Things she'd stopped wanting or needing when Sybil died. At least that's what she'd believed until Jax. Now she didn't know what to believe.

She hadn't wanted to need anything, not even kindness, since Sybil. Not until Jax.

"Doctor?" Callie asked, her tone suggesting she'd said it before.

Sloane pushed her hands through her damp hair—was everything here destined to be wet forever?—and focused. "Yes?"

"We're out of sheets and patient gowns."

"Run the blankets through the dryers first. Warm and dry matters more than modesty."

"Sloane," Mina called, stripping wet jeans off a pale, shivering teen. "I need your hands here—he's bradying down."

"Get us whatever you have that's not wet," Sloane told Callie, and hurried to Mina's side. Mina knelt, stethoscope pressed to the boy's chest, while Sloane slid a thermal sheet beneath him and tucked a heat pack into each armpit. "Vitals?"

"Pulse is forty-eight," Mina said. "O2 sat…coming up. Eighty-nine and climbing."

"Good," Sloane said, heart clenching. Good meant alive.

A scream cut across the bay—sharp, raw. Sloane spun. A young woman—mother, sister?—who couldn't be more than seventeen staggered through the doors, faded red sweatpants soaked to the thighs, clutching a baby wrapped in a sodden towel.

"Here," Sloane said, already moving. "What's your name?"

"Mollie."

"Put him down here."

Mollie put the baby down on a treatment table and stripped away the towel. The baby, mottled and gasping, maybe three months of age, blinked under the harsh overhead light. Blue lips, labored respirations. "Mina—warm room air, high flow—and heated towels. Start a line, warm saline."

"On it," Mina said.

Sloane listened to his chest—croupy, raspy respirations—probably bronchitis edging toward pneumonia, and looked up at Mollie. "Has he been sick?"

Mollie nodded, eyes anxious, straggly brown hair dripping

unheeded down her neck. "Just the sniffles, the last few days. Then the roof—parts blew off last week. It got pretty cold inside."

Callie handed Sloane warm towels, and she rubbed the baby dry. Mina taped a nasal cannula in place. The baby boy's chest rose and fell a little faster. The sight hit her low and sharp—the raw will to live crammed into a body no longer than her forearm.

"His lungs are tight." She glanced at Mina. She didn't have time for tests, didn't need them. The rhythm in his chest told her enough. "And draw up ampicillin and cefotaxime. Let's cover him. No telling when we can fly him out."

Twenty minutes later, Sloane listened to his chest again, and her heart rate slowed. "He's moving more air. Lungs are mostly clear. How's his temp?"

"Ninety-six." Mina added softly, almost a prayer, "He'll make it."

"He will." Sloane pushed to her feet. The next wave was coming. "You can sit with him, Mollie. He'll need to stay here a while."

Mollie nodded again, her pinched expression turning to relief. "Thank you, ma'am…I mean, Doctor. I won't be leaving him."

Sloane smiled. "I'm sure you won't."

"Doctor," a volunteer called. "Got a guy you need to see."

"Right there." Sloane hurried off.

The Bell returned minutes later, rotor wash rattling the loose panes. No EMTs were in sight when Jax's crew wrestled a stretcher through the doors—a man gray-faced and soaked, gash across his scalp, pupils sluggish. Sloane grabbed the end of the gurney.

"What do you have?" she asked.

"Closed head injury. Hypothermic. BP seventy over forty," Jax said, holding an O2 mask on the man's face as she pushed with the other arm.

"Any history?" Sloane asked, voice sharper than she meant. Almost everyone she saw got urgent care based on the immediate presentation—troubleshooting at its finest. When the crowd thinned, if it ever did, they'd be able to run some labs, get the X-rays they needed. But first they had to keep everyone alive with minimal staff and rudimentary equipment. A far, far cry from Boston.

The chance someone could die because she missed something ate at her, but second-guessing her decisions was worse. Uncertainty cost lives.

"None." Jax looked at her across the litter frame. For one taut second they might have been alone in the roar—the steady pressure of Jax's expression reaching inside her, at once warm and startling. "Found him wedged in a split-rail fence. Pulse was threadbare. Unresponsive the whole trip back."

Jax's voice, ragged but gentle, stirred her like a hand skimming over her skin—knowing and sure.

"He's lucky you were there," Sloane murmured.

Jax's face was pale, her eyes shadowed. How long had she been out there, flying in conditions that under other circumstances would have kept her grounded? Something hot and tight twisted in Sloane's chest. She couldn't think about the risk—she had to function. But the thought of Jax in that dark sky plagued her. Was this what caring did? Made her ineffectual when she had to be at her sharpest?

She looked away from Jax's searching gaze and pointed to a cot.

"Put him down here." Sloane leaned in and checked his pupils while Jax steadied the backboard he'd been strapped to for transport so it wouldn't slide. Their shoulders brushed. The touch should have slid off like the thousands of others that happened in the close quarters of the ER, but this one registered all the way to the bone. Her body recognized what her mind denied.

"I'll take him," Sloane said, straightening quickly.

"He's lucky *you're* here," Jax said, and the look Jax gave her carried something unspoken and fierce.

Before Sloane could even manage a thank-you, Bean called from the doorway.

"Bus in a ravine, Chief."

"Copy," Jax said, and was gone, back into the night, to the Bell, before Sloane could find her breath to say *Be safe*.

Hours blurred.

The generator faltered twice. The air inside the gym, already humid, turned heavy with sweat and discarded layers of wet clothing. Red tags outnumbered green, and still they came. Sloane floated between bays, dictating meds, directing wound care—doing procedures herself that belonged in the OR in a different world—in-between changing out O2 tanks and calculating how many more patients they could hold before they ran out of space. She stole seconds to watch the door each time the rotors approached. Sometimes Jax stepped through, flight suit half-unzipped, shirt beneath soaked, carrying someone half-dead or pushing a stretcher. And each time she left again before Sloane could say a word.

By 0430 the surge broke, thinned to a trickle. A few new volunteers arrived to give the staff in the triage tents a break. Most of the team inside collapsed onto the far bleachers, covered with blankets that were probably mostly dry. Callie, her head on a mound of towels, snored softly under her slicker. Mina sat with her back to the wall, eyes closed, a cover gown draped over her knees.

Sloane lay flat on a nearby cot, staring up at the shadows quivering on the ceiling. The smell of the river clung to everything—silt, metal, something half-rotten. Her body, empty and wired at the same time, refused to relax. Her mind raced in an endless loop of every face she'd touched, fearing the one she wouldn't reach in time.

She should be sleeping. This was the false quiet she knew only too well. Fleeting, like a teasing kiss that never came.

Instead she lay listening, every muscle straining for the sound of the Bell.

When the night was quiet enough to seduce her into pretending it was safe, her brain betrayed her still. Sybil's face rose out of the dark—the drowned pallor, the slack mouth, the silence where a heartbeat should be.

She jerked upright, heart slamming. Not Sybil. Not tonight.

She pushed off the cot and slipped into the clinic's rear hallway. The utility room they used as a staff lounge still smelled faintly of burnt popcorn and bleach. She started the coffee maker that sat on a wire shelf, its hiss loud as rotor blades, and leaned on the counter with both hands while her pulse climbed down from its frantic ladder.

The door creaked.

"Knew I'd find you here," Mina said.

"Couldn't sleep."

Mina eyed her. "Because you're waiting for the next flood of patients or because you're watching for the Bell?"

Sloane willed the coffee dripping into the pot to hurry. "She hasn't been back in two hours."

"She's not made of glass."

"Neither was Sybil." The words slipped out before she could stop them.

Mina came closer, voice softer. "Jax isn't Sybil."

"I know."

"But it's not Chief Warrant Officer Kincaid you're worried about, is it?" Mina squeezed her, an arm around her waist. "Jax is more than our pilot, isn't she."

Sloane closed her eyes. She wanted to lean into Mina so someone else could carry the pain of remembering and the fear of reliving it, just for a while. But the memory of the night on the mountain was so sharp, and the feelings too new, too raw. The quiet peace of the Bell's cabin at dawn. Jax's breath steady against her cheek. The thrum of Jax's pulse under her hand. The moment the world had tilted.

"I kissed her," she said quietly. "Or almost. She stopped it."

A second passed. "Whoo-ee. I can't say I'm totally surprised. I am—that you made the first move—but there's been something in the air around you two since day one." Mina held her away with both hands on her shoulders and studied her. "And now you can't stop thinking about her."

"I can't stop *listening* for her," Sloane said. "Every time the rotors go quiet, I think maybe she's not coming back."

Mina shook her head, made a little tsking sound as if Sloane had forgotten what was important. "*Believe* that she will. And let that be enough for tonight."

The coffeepot clicked off. The silence stretched, filled with questions.

Faint and far at first, the thrum of rotor blades beat in the dark.

Believe.

How long had it been since she'd believed in anything but her work? Could she even begin to believe in anything—*anyone*—again?

Questions without answers, at least tonight.

Tonight there was only work.

Sloane straightened, squared her shoulders, and took the first mug from the rack. "Grab some coffee. We have incoming."

CHAPTER FIFTEEN

Day 2: post-breach

After thirty straight hours in the gym, Sloane managed a quick break to shower at the roadhouse before the all-hands-available briefing Eli had called. In her room for a quick change of clothes, she scanned Jax's empty bunk and tried to ignore the whispered worries. Where was she now? How dangerous were the conditions out there?

With no answers, she hurried downstairs, drawn by the scent of coffee and the murmur of voices. Eli, the mayor, and Callie were already there, gathered around an aerial projection of a ravaged landscape on one of the big monitors—gullies as wide as four-lane highways carved down the sides of mountains, rivers so swollen beyond their banks they looked like lakes, and islands of rooftops surrounded by miles of muddy water.

Sloane's stomach dropped. She couldn't pick out a single road.

"Where are we in all of that?" she blurted.

Eli looked over his shoulder, then flicked a laser pointer at a spot below the ridgeline, mostly obscured by forest. "Here—luckier than most that the whole town isn't gone, but we've lost a lot of the outlying homes. And all the roads in."

"Marooned," Lynette muttered.

"That's one word for it, Mayor," Eli said drily.

The door opened and Jax, still in a mud-splattered navy-blue flight suit with a tear in one sleeve, came in with Bean and Jeb on a gust of morning air that smelled above all else of dead fish. She took in the group, her gaze landing on Sloane. A smile flickered for an instant, and Sloane's heart turned over. Seeing Jax, unhurt and clear-eyed despite the fatigue lines etched in her face, settled her deep inside as nothing in her memory ever had.

"How are we looking?" Jax asked Eli, stopping next to Sloane. Her hand briefly skimmed Sloane's and disappeared as swiftly, but the warmth lingered.

"Weather service says the system's beginning to shear apart." Eli traced the swollen lines of the rivers, some of which hadn't been there a month ago. "Rain will taper in three to five days. But roads—" He let the word hang. "Bridges are out. Every approach is underwater or washed clean away."

"Yeah. We've been seeing that from the air." Jax unzipped her flight suit and let it fold down around her hips, revealing a tight black tee that hugged her shoulders and chest.

Sloane caught herself staring and looked away.

"So—no resupply," Lynette said, her tone fierce, though her voice was frayed. None of them had likely slept since the dam went.

"Not for a week at least." Eli grimaced. "Maybe two. State says air drops if and when assets free up. That could mean tomorrow. Could mean never, if the capital decides somewhere else screams louder."

"Any word from FEMA?" Jax asked.

"Same story—they're working on deploying to all critical areas." He grunted. "Which means high-density population areas first."

No one spoke.

"Then we assume we're on our own," Sloane finally said. The situation couldn't be clearer, and she'd been in similar ones since the day Sybil died.

Callie made a small sound, almost a laugh. "Like we haven't been all along."

"And we'll keep making it work," Eli said, and clicked off the pointer. "Sloane? Medical report?"

"Overall numbers of new arrivals are slowing, but we'll run out of space soon. We'll need an overflow shelter for those who still need medical oversight but not twenty-four-hour observation."

Eli glanced at Lynette. "Can you round up a team to put up whatever tents we have left?"

She nodded. "We'll get it done today."

"Good, that will work," Sloane said. "I've set up overlapping shifts at the med center." She couldn't think of the space where she had performed an emergency trach a few hours before and had twenty critical inpatients on cots as a *gym* any longer. "Everyone needs time to eat and sleep, or we're going to have accidents."

"Good idea." Eli eyed Jax. "Your crew needs the same."

A muscle in Jax's jaw jumped and Sloane expected her to argue, but Jax just said, "We sleep between callouts. We're good."

Eli studied her, then nodded. "Okay then. We all know what we need to do."

Callie and Lynette left together. Eli called to Bean to give him a hand inventorying their remaining supplies and followed them out. Jeb trailed after them, eating something out of a wrapper like he couldn't remember he was doing it.

Sloane almost smiled. MREs. A month ago she wouldn't have recognized that.

Jax stayed, leaning against the long counter that had once been a lunch area for the workers who'd occupied the rooms upstairs, watching her. Despite her steady expressions, her shoulders sagged like she was bracing even when standing still.

"You need to conserve your strength," Sloane said. It came out more abrupt than she meant. "Use extra caution on these runs."

One of Jax's brows lifted. "Caution?"

"We can't afford to lose you."

Jax's eyes narrowed—not hard, but sharp and searching. "We, or you?"

Heat rose at the back of Sloane's neck. "Jax—"

The radio on Jax's shoulder crackled. Eli's voice: "Bell One, confirm you're ready. Sheriff just called in—multiple stranded on the east flats."

"Copy." Jax pushed off the counter. "I've got to go."

"I know." Sloane grasped her hand. "All of us need you. But… especially me."

That smile again, so fleeting it shouldn't have made her heart race. But it did.

"Good." Jax's lips brushed hers so quickly, so lightly, she might have imagined it.

But she didn't.

Jax strode for the door and didn't look back.

Sloane stood in the empty echo of the lobby, her pulse climbing. She touched her lips where the kiss still lingered. Work. She had work to do.

So did Jax.

She hated how helpless that made her feel.

Jax jogged through the mean and gray, the kind that didn't brighten so much as thin. Sleep was mostly a rumor. Right now, only the next callout mattered. Fuel up. Walk-around. Hydraulics. Rotors. Bean's hand tapping each inspection point like he was reading braille from the Bell's skin. Jeb hauled the sling net to the threshold and buckled in like he'd been born wearing a harness.

Jax dropped into the right seat and took one minute to remember Sloane's appreciative gaze as she'd unzipped her flight suit, and the way Sloane had said *especially me* with her fingers curled on hers, and the way Sloane's breath had hitched when she'd kissed her. She hadn't meant to, even though she'd wanted to the instant she walked into the roadhouse and saw her. But she just couldn't leave again without touching her.

Yeah. That was trouble, and that was all the time she had to think about it.

"Bell set for liftoff," she radioed to Eli.

Eli came back on the open channel. "All units—all non-medical evac now to the high school. Repeat, the baseball diamond is our evac center. Tents going up now. Volunteers to Sarah Hull. Bell One, Langley's got four vehicles stuck along Willow Creek, two with people on the roofs."

"Bell One lifting." Jax eased the collective, nose light, pedals answering with their familiar bite. "We'll start there, then sweep the east flats to the river bend. Call priority pulls."

"Copy," Eli said.

The town fell away, roofs bowed and in places gone under the weight of water. Beyond, the flood spread into a slow, brown churn, chewing through fence lines, trees, and lives. Coulter's Gap sat like an island cupped in the northern face, just as Eli had warned: no roads in, no roads out. Everything they moved, they'd move through the air.

"Wind's cross from the west," Bean murmured, eyes on the trees. "Shear at thirty."

"Seen," Jax said. Seen meant accounted for. Accounted for meant survivable.

The first roof came into view. A pickup bed turned raft, a teenager standing in it with a rope around his waist and a dog tucked under one arm like a squirming, furious football. The water shouldered the makeshift boat against a porch rail and ground it there.

"We start with the kid," Jeb said.

"Strap him to you on the first lift," Jax said.

"That's the plan." Jeb had lost the shake in his voice after the first twenty-four hours out.

Jax held them in hover while Bean fed line. The basket swayed, Jeb rode it down, one hand on the guideline. The wind tried to snatch them. Jax adjusted to counter the gust. Jeb got the safety strap around the kid, snapped the clip to his own harness, and waved for the rise. The dog lunged, teeth flashing at his hand. Jeb hip-checked him into the basket with a muttered "Not today, buddy. Now stay down there. Don't want you going for a swim."

Another rush of water rolled in, the porch rail gave up, and the truck went under. Jax lifted clear and reported in.

"Eli, one teen and one canine on board," Jax called. "Heading for roof two."

"Copy. Clinic LZ crowded—use the far field. Sloane's shifted triage to the first tent."

The name hit like a quick, private spark. Jax let it shimmer but kept her eyes ahead and her focus sharp. When they returned to the Gap with the bay filled with soaked, terrified survivors, the LZ appeared through mist and rotor wash, floodlights flaring white despite it being midday. Volunteers hurried between tents, and everywhere the displaced wandered, many carrying household items in addition to their children and pets and bags of clothes. Jax brought the skids down, Bean swung the cabin door open, and Jeb passed the teen to waiting volunteers, then the howling dog. Which promptly tried to bolt into the rain on some desperate mission. Jeb kept a hand on the harness until the leash clipped.

Sloane arrived. Bareheaded, hair darker with wet, sleeves shoved to her elbows. She moved like a fixed point while the chaos bent around. She looked up as if she could sense the focus from the cockpit, and Jax's world narrowed to only her. She grabbed the end of the basket and helped a volunteer transfer a middle-aged guy with hypothermia and a broken tibia to a litter.

"Basket clear," Bean called a minute later.

"Lifting." Jax giving herself just a second longer with eyes on

Sloane. Sloane lifted a hand as the Bell rose, then turned to direct another volunteer wearing a red armband and was lost in the sea of bodies.

Jax turned east. Two more roof extractions, a minivan tilting into a ditch, a backhoe stuck halfway across a field. The operator had chosen badly and couldn't make the math work to back out. They hauled him from the cab while he cursed himself and cried on the same breath.

"Fuel at three-eighths," Bean warned.

"We'll do one more pass downriver, then set for sling-loads," Jax said.

The river bend told a new story every hour. Now it showed a footbridge that had pivoted off one pin and lodged against a cottonwood. Two elderly individuals waved frantically, marooned on the canted planks like stubborn squirrels.

They got them up, got them under warm blankets, and circled for the next stranded citizens. On the return, the white tents bloomed on the evac hill like pale mushrooms across the baseball diamond. Strings of volunteers moved boxes hand to hand. A tractor idled with its bucket filled with red-coded trash bags from the med center. Jax kissed the skids to the grass, and volunteers hurried to help the stranded and injured to safety.

"Bean, Jeb—drink water," Jax said, already spooling up.

"Bossy," Jeb said, but took the bottle Bean shoved at him.

"Eli," Jax radioed. "We're swinging upriver for a dam pass."

"Copy," Eli said. "State still says sit tight for official assessment."

"We'll bring back something better than official," Jax said.

They followed the river upstream. The gorge was a throat torn raw where the dam had been, the spillway a mangled basin. Water poured through the ruined mouth, a clutch of concrete lay where it had no right to be, and hunks the size of trucks teetered marooned on shelves of new silt.

"The foundation's showing," Jeb said softly, like the dead were listening.

Bean adjusted his harness to lean for a better angle. "Undercut below the old wall. Not going to last long."

Jax took them in a slow orbit, reading the flow the way she read wind on the mountainsides. Direction, power, threat level. And called command. "Eli, this is Bell One. Tailwater's still rising. Scour at the base is bad. The eastern foundation's giving under the new channel."

"How bad?"

"Enough that there's another pulse coming," Jax said. "Anyone in the lower third should evac uphill now."

Silence, then Eli: "Copy. I'll pull the trigger. Jax—good eyes."

She didn't say thanks. She banked them downriver and pointed back toward the people waiting on rooftops and tractors and unlikely islands of dry. The next hours were a juggling act of decisions. A woman whose chest wouldn't rise—Jeb doing compressions while Bean hauled them up and Jax held a hover over a tangle of branches and cable. A farmer with a flail-lacerated forearm. A man with a head lac and unequal pupils—basket and straight to Sloane.

Sloane met the Bell, face pale beneath streaks of sweat, eyes too bright, mouth set. She took a quick look at him, assessing even as Jeb rolled the stretcher, then looked over at Jax in the door of the bay.

"We need O2, blood, and blankets," she called. "Short on morphine and ketamine, too, if you can find us any."

Her voice still did that thing to Jax's chest, the small untying of the knots that she'd never noticed were a constant companion.

"We're running sling-loads from Blue Ridge Regional next," Jax answered. "Water, blankets, O2, meds, blood. Got it."

"How long?"

"Two hours round trip."

Sloane's gaze held hers for a beat longer than necessary. Her hand—clean now, someone else's blood washed off—brushed hair from her face.

"Be careful," she said, quiet as if not for anyone else.

"You too," Jax said, which wasn't what she wanted to say. But then when was it ever.

They sling-loaded. The evac hill turned into something that looked almost organized. More weather moved in at dusk, a wind line darkening the low sky.

"Fuel at a quarter," Bean reported.

"We do one last pull, then we sit down and refuel or we become the problem," Jax said.

"Copy."

One last pull was a kid waving a red towel from a shed roof on the wrong side of a flooded ditch. The current there ran sideways and mean. Jax put the Bell into a hover that made her neck ache. Jeb rode the basket down and hooked the kid by the waist, quick and firm. The shed shifted on its piers. Jax eased up a foot and slid left to keep the disc clear. Bean brought them up slick as a prayer.

"LZ or hill?" Bean asked as the basket cleared the skid.

"LZ," Jax said, already angling them toward the gym. "Sloane will want eyes on him. He's cyanotic."

"You can see that from—never mind," Jeb said. "Of course you can."

Jax set them down in a wash of spray. The door slid. The world tilted into noise and hands and orders. Sloane appeared at the edge of it all like she'd been drawn there by the same vector that brought Jax in. Jeb handed the kid off and Sloane's fingers were on the boy's face immediately, thumb under chin, head tipped back to open his airway.

"He's breathing," she said and flicked her gaze up at Jax. Not a smile. Something smaller and more dangerous. Gratitude. Relief. Want.

Her gaze went through Jax like a wire.

Sloane sat cross-legged on the cold gym floor beside the triage table, a chart still in her lap. She'd stopped typing ten minutes ago. She should have been checking vitals, pushing fluids, confirming meds had been given—something. But the last two days had blurred into a dreamlike collage of exhilarating highs and devastating lows, hollowing her out to the core.

The gym had gone eerily quiet, the way trauma bays sometimes did after a mass-casualty surge burned itself out and left everyone echoing with emptiness. Rows of evacuees curled under blankets with the BRRMC logo along the far wall, the sounds of their breathing rising and falling like a slow tide, the hum of the generator and the occasional cough the only other sounds. She sent Callie back to the roadhouse at midnight with orders to sleep.

She kept listening for the Bell.

It wasn't logical. Jax had been flying sorties for nearly eighteen hours straight. Logic said she'd either refueled and kept going or she was on a short break somewhere out of sight. Logic wasn't helping. Every time the rotors faded, the silence scraped at her nerves.

She stood finally and walked back to the supply room. Coffee seemed the only answer. When she heard footsteps behind her, she said to Mina without turning, "You shouldn't be here."

"Neither should you," Jax said.

Sloane stilled, empty coffee mug in hand, and turned. Jax had left her flight suit somewhere and wore the same black T-shirt and black pants she always wore under it. Her dark hair needed cutting, her usually brilliant blue eyes were dull with fatigue, and her smile was rueful. She was beautiful.

Sloane drew a breath. "I am on night call. *And* I'm not flying a thousand-pound machine through storm shears on no sleep."

Jax's mouth twitched. "Fair."

The silence stretched before Sloane set the cup aside and crossed the room to where Jax leaned against the wall.

"You need to stop for a few hours," she said.

"Can't."

"Jax—"

"If I stop, I'll think. And that won't help anyone."

Sloane heard the unspoken. Thinking meant remembering. Remembering meant pain. A wall cracked inside Sloane's chest, and she reached for Jax's hand without deciding to. She stroked Jax's knuckles, remembering the feel of them against her cheek. "I keep thinking about what would happen if you didn't come back."

Jax's eyes widened, dark and fierce and unbearably tired. "Then stop thinking about that."

"I can't."

Jax's hand turned, caught hers, held.

She'd always been cautious. This screamed reckless. She didn't care.

Jax let out a long, shaky laugh and leaned her head back against the wall. "This is stupid timing."

"The worst." Sloane leaned a little closer until her body just touched Jax. Heat washed over her. Her heart thundered.

"We're still doing it, aren't we," Jax whispered.

Giving her time to say no. Time to be smart. Time to be who she'd always been—apart and alone.

Sloane shifted closer. "Yes."

Jax's breath hitched, and for a heartbeat neither moved, the air sharp between them. Then Jax cupped her jaw, careful as if she might break, and kissed her.

Not urgent. Not frantic. Slow, unguarded, almost reverent, as if she was terrified of scaring her off. Sloane gripped Jax's shoulders, sinking into the softness of her mouth, the quicksilver brush of her tongue along the inside of her lower lip. Parts of her dissolved and came back together as if *she* had changed somehow—as if every barrier she'd built since Sybil had been swept away like the world outside that room.

She tugged down the edge of Jax's tee to kiss the hollow of her throat, reveled at the pulse hammering against her lips. Jax groaned, her fingers digging into Sloane's hips like she was anchoring them both.

"Tell me this isn't just exhaustion clouding your judgment," Jax whispered.

"It isn't." Sloane nipped at her throat, the move unlike anything she'd ever done. And amazingly arousing. "I want…you."

She had no other words, only sensations she couldn't decipher while her head spun.

"Right here." Jax kissed her again—deeper, lingering, more like a promise than a question now—and for the first time in days, Sloane felt warm all the way through.

When Sloane finally pulled back, needing to find her balance on trembling legs, Jax rested her forehead against hers, eyes closed.

"We could break each other," Jax murmured.

"No," Sloane said, voice steadier than she felt. "We won't."

The radio on Jax's belt crackled before she could say anything else.

Eli's voice: "Bell One, reports of SOS from ranger unit twelve. Officer down."

Jax exhaled, her breath ragged. "I've got—"

"To go. I know." Sloane stepped back, her palm on Jax's chest, over her heart. "Can you radio me when you get back?"

Jax's mouth softened. "Copy."

When the door swung shut behind her, the quiet she left behind felt sharper, and more unkind, than before.

Chapter Sixteen

Day 5, dawn
The water holds

The gym had fallen into the restless quiet that came after the storm passed but before anyone dared believe it was over. Sloane moved between the rows of cots, checking vitals on autopilot—pulse, capillary refill, breath sounds—while her mind tracked a different rhythm altogether. The Bell's rotors had gone silent forty-seven minutes ago. She knew because she'd counted the minutes out herself, then counted them again when her chest wouldn't unclench.

The last sortie had been a supply run to the families still stranded on the north ridge—insulin, antibiotics, and clean water for people who'd been cut off for days. Standard mission. Routine, even. No reason for the hollow ache that had taken up residence under her ribs or the way her hands wanted to shake every time she reached for a chart.

"Doctor?"

Callie waited with a worried expression, a BP cuff dangling from her hand. "The gentleman in bed twelve is asking about his wife again."

"Right." Sloane blinked. The two from the roof Jax had brought in…yesterday? So many they had begun to blur. She pictured the man now—early seventies, thinning gray hair, a big man who had once carried more muscle, diminished now by fear and helplessness. His wife—petite, a decade younger, frail from lifelong arthritis. "Tell him she's stable. The hypothermia was severe, but she's responding well to warming protocols."

"I told him." Callie's voice was gentle. "Twenty minutes ago."

Heat climbed Sloane's throat. She was losing focus, and in a place like this, that could cost lives. "Thank you. I'll speak with him myself."

She crossed to the last cot in the row, across from the one where his wife lay breathing shallowly as she slept. Sloane glanced quickly at the clipboard hooked on the IV pole beside him and conjured up a calm tone she didn't feel. "Mr. Mercer, your wife is doing much better today. Her labs and temp are normal. She's just exhausted, so letting her sleep is the best thing we can do. How about you? Have you eaten?"

He grimaced. "Can't say I have any appetite."

Sloane rested her hand on his where it lay on top of the gray wool blanket. "I understand. I need you to keep your strength up, if you can, so you can help look after your wife when she's a little stronger. We'll need to move you both to the evac center up the hill and—"

"Why didn't somebody say?" He raised up on his elbow, cast a glance across the narrow aisle toward his wife. "Sure, I can do that."

"Good. Soup sound okay?"

He nodded. "Thanks, Doc."

Sloane smiled. "I'll have someone bring it. Try not to worry."

He nodded again, but he had to know as well as her the words were meaningless. Caring meant worrying. Worrying and fear. Did she really want that in her life? *Could* she bear it?

Outside, dawn pressed thin and gray against the windows. She signaled a volunteer to bring a food tray for Mr. Mercer and stopped to check an IV line on a woman with a broken wrist when the familiar sound finally came—rotor blades growing louder by the second as the Bell approached the landing zone.

Her shoulders dropped, releasing tension she was so used to she didn't notice until it was gone. The relief was so acute it left her a little dizzy.

"That's our girl," Mina said behind her.

Sloane didn't trust her voice just then and hurried to the open doorway to watch the Bell off-load. The helicopter landed in a sheet of muddy spray. The doors slid open, but only Bean emerged, jogging across the field with a med kit in one hand and an expression she'd never seen on his face before. Worry mixed with urgency.

Sloane watched the Bell, waiting.

No Jax.

Sloane's throat clamped shut as if a hand squeezed around it, but she forced herself to move. Grabbing a med kit out of habit, she hurried to reach him halfway, and pushed the words out through the panic. "What is it? Where is she?"

"Took a branch to the windscreen last leg," he said, flat and tight. "Windscreen held, but Jax took a hit from the glareshield during the rebound. She's got a laceration across her forehead and probably a mild concussion. Refused to let me fly her back."

"Refused—" Sloane bit off the rest of the sentence, struggling for the professional composure that was usually automatic. Apparently not when the situation was much more personal and infinitely more frightening. What registered was the picture Bean's words painted. Jax alone in that cockpit, blood on her face, refusing help. A sharp bolt of fear stabbed through her, fierce enough to steal her breath, and she hated that Bean could see it. Hated even more that it was the truth. "Where is she now?"

"Still in the Bell, doing post-flight checks like nothing happened." Bean shook his head. "You know how she is."

Oh, she *did* know. Jax would work until she collapsed before admitting she needed help. Sloane had seen it over and over. Exceptional pilot. Stubborn and driven. Terrible patient. She reined in her temper. Don't shoot the messenger. "I'll handle it."

Crossing the field took a year, every step accompanied by yet another mental image of the hundred ways a helicopter could go down, taking its pilot with it. Debris strike. Engine failure. Wind shear. Her lungs burned as she sprinted, fear curling hot around her ribs. Each step was a struggle against the relentless current, pulling her down—pulling her beneath the surface.

No. Sloane slowed as she approached the Bell, drew a deep breath. Not drowning. Not lost. Needed here. Work to do.

The panic slid away beneath the surface.

She found Jax where Bean had said, bent into the engine compartment with a flashlight, one hand braced on the canopy. A rivulet of dried blood ran from hairline to jaw, a replica of the twisting dark ribbons of floodwater she'd seen every morning on Eli's screen. The way the light wavered, then steadied told Sloane more than Jax would likely admit. Dizziness? Blurred vision.

Anger warred with concern.

"You should be in the med center." It came out sharper than she meant. Fear did that—stripped her of control. She hated that almost as much as she hated that ribbon of blood on Jax's neck.

Jax looked up, flashlight beam wavering slightly again before she steadied it. "Just finishing up. Five more minutes."

"Now." She didn't care how it sounded. She was beyond diplomacy. "That's not a request."

Something in her tone must have gotten through, because Jax set down the flashlight and straightened slowly, one hand briefly touching the side of the aircraft for balance.

"It's not that bad," Jax said.

The faint slur confirmed what Bean had predicted. Probable concussion.

Sloane stepped close—close enough that the heat coming off Jax's body through her flight suit and the few inches of air between them registered on her skin. A laceration ran along Jax's temple, ugly but not too deep, surrounded by the beginning of what would be spectacular bruising. "What hit you?"

"Branch tried. Came out of nowhere." Jax pulled the grin she used to ease other people's concerns and missed. "Windscreen held. Built Ford tough."

"This is a Bell."

"Built Bell tough." Jax's mouth twitched, still with that damnable grin.

Sloane smiled, too. Damn Jax. Even bleeding, even concussed, Jax had a way of settling her fears. The realization of how much she'd come to need that humor, that steadiness, hit hard. Almost as frightening as the picture of how much worse the accident could have been.

She could have lost her.

Sloane slammed the door on the quicksilver flash of pain. She recognized the agony. Knew it could paralyze her. And right now? Jax was her responsibility. Her patient. She had no room for the personal here—maybe never had.

"Sit," Sloane said, guiding her to the open door. "I need to take care of this."

Amazingly, Jax complied, settling on the threshold, legs dangling over the side. Her willingness to be examined was a sure sign she wasn't herself. Ignoring the churning worry in her middle, Sloane opened the med kit and snapped on gloves, hyperaware of every small thing—the steady thread of Jax's breath, the way she went still for Sloane in a way she didn't go still for anyone else. The trust exposed by that small tell made Sloane's heart ache.

"It's favorable as these things go," Sloane muttered, gently irrigating the laceration with a pulse of saline from a syringe and noting the wince Jax tried to hide. She'd treated dozens of head wounds that week, but her hands had never felt so clumsy. She told herself it was the adrenaline—but she knew better. "Down to muscle but linear. Should come together well."

Once the wound was free of debris, she injected the local and loaded up the sutures. "I can close this here—save you waiting at the med center."

"Hell, yes," Jax muttered. "I've got callouts to run."

"Uh-huh," Sloane said, in no mood to argue. They'd cross that bridge when she got the wound closed. "How's your vision?"

"Fine now. Had a little blurriness for a minute or two right after the head bounce."

"Nausea?"

"Nah, I'm good."

That answer came a little too fast.

"Headache?" Sloane reached for the 5–0 suture. Her fingers trembled slightly. Damn it.

"Yeah. Not bad, though." Jax quieted for a beat. "Sloane?"

"Mmm?" Sloane placed the first suture, willing her hands to steady. They did.

"You okay?"

"Fine." The first brought the edges together cleanly. Better.

"Better?" Jax echoed, as if reading her mind.

"Than what?" Sloane placed a second, then a third. The way Jax asked it shook her. Softly, intimately, as if Sloane's feelings mattered more than the wound in her head. Beyond ridiculous. Unprofessional, dangerous. And yet her pulse beat faster than she wanted to admit.

"Than when you were first stressing about me taking a little shot to the head."

Sloane leaned back, met her gaze. "There's nothing *little* about a traumatic head injury, Chief." She scowled. "And I wasn't stressing. I was evaluating." She held up her hand. "How many fingers?"

"Three." Jax blew out a breath. "Sloane, I'm okay."

"Seeing as I'm the doctor here, you don't get to decide that." She sounded annoyed and knew it. Fear did that—and she couldn't let it. She finished the closure, reinforced it with Steri-Strips that wouldn't interfere with Jax's flight helmet. Normal. As if her world hadn't tilted on its axis when she thought she might have lost Jax before ever really having her.

"There," she said, peeling off her gloves. "You'll need monitoring for the next twenty-four hours. Concussion protocol. And no flying until I clear you."

Jax rolled her shoulders, as if signifying the irritating delay was over and she wanted to get back to business. "I'll be fine in the bunkhouse."

"No." The refusal was immediate, instinctive. "You're not staying alone tonight."

Jax really looked at her then and must have seen what she'd been hiding, how tightly she held the threads of her composure. Jax grasped her wrist, tugged her just a step closer. Sloane ended up between her spread thighs, looking down into eyes the color of a sky she hadn't seen for weeks. Brilliant, beautifully blue.

"Hey," Jax said. "I'm good, babe. I wouldn't lie to you."

That touch, that soft *babe,* undid her. All the control she'd maintained through the endless hours of not knowing, day after day, night after night, cracked just like the dam under pressure.

"I thought you weren't coming back," she whispered, the words scraping her throat raw. "When Bean came across that field without you, the look on his face, I thought—"

She couldn't finish the sentence. Couldn't voice the terror that had consumed her in that moment, the vivid flash of memory—another person she'd failed to save, another hand slipping through her fingers.

"I'll have to kick his ass for scaring you," Jax said lightly, teasingly, stroking her thumb over the top of Sloane's hand. "I'm here. I'm okay."

"You could have been killed." The words came out in a rush, all the worry and anger and desperate relief she'd been holding back. "That debris could have come through the windscreen, could have knocked you unconscious, could have—"

"But it didn't." Jax stood carefully, swayed for a microsecond, and steadied. She clasped Sloane's shoulders, her face so close the silver flecks in her irises glittered. The bruise on her forehead was already spreading. "I came back, like I said I would. I'm just a little banged up. No harm, no foul."

"You're impossible," Sloane muttered, letting herself lean against her, just for a minute.

Jax's arms came around her immediately, one hand settling at the small of her back, the other stroking her hair. "I've got you. I'm not going anywhere."

"It shook me, that fear," Sloane confessed. "And I don't know what to do about it."

"I know."

Sloane looked up at the neat white line of Steri-Strips, the kindness—even sympathy—in Jax's gaze. At the woman who already commanded too much of her heart. "Do you?"

"I know what I feel when I'm up there and I don't know what's happening to you down here," Jax murmured. "Scares me, too."

Sloane glanced down the hill, saw the volunteers arriving, the town stirring, grasped the sanity of the known. "I need to get down to the med center."

"I know." Jax still held her, fingers gently stroking her nape, heart beating against hers. "I'm not going anywhere."

Sloane didn't argue, despite the untruth. Jax would leave. So would she. When the town recovered. When the job was done.

But that was a problem for later.

For another sliver in time, though, she let the woman she was very much afraid she was falling in love with hold her.

Jax sat on the edge of the cot in the clinic's makeshift staff area, submitting to Sloane's neurological checks with what she hoped was good grace. Every few hours, Sloane appeared to test her reflexes, check her pupils, and ask the same series of questions designed to assess cognitive function.

"What year is it?" Sloane asked, shining a penlight in her eyes.

"2026."

"Where are we?"

"Coulter's Gap, North Carolina. Population depending on who you ask." The small joke earned her the ghost of a smile, which made the persistent headache almost worth it.

"Follow my light."

Jax tracked the penlight left, right, up, down. The headache sat behind her eyes like fog. Dizziness nipped at her if she turned too fast. And new data point.

Sloane's presence changed the room's air pressure. Made objects clearer, sensations sharper. None of that unnerved her half as much as the warmth of Sloane's hand steadying her chin. And from the way

Sloane's gaze lingered an instant longer than necessary, maybe she wasn't the only one unnerved.

Apparently satisfied, Sloane clicked off the light and made a note on the chart. "Any nausea since the last check?"

"Not for a while." Jax studied the lines of tension around Sloane's eyes. The careful way she held herself. Sloane was either very tired or very stressed. Maybe she thought she was doing a good job of hiding it, but then most people missed the storm beneath her always controlled surface. "You know, I've had hard bumps on the head before. Military medicine wasn't this attentive."

"Military medicine would ground you for a week," Sloane muttered. "We don't have that luxury."

"No," Jax said softly. Luxury wasn't a thing they'd had much of.

The quiet that opened between them stretched into all they hadn't said. People still depended on them—strangers, friends. Supply runs needed to be made. Medicines delivered. Water rescues executed despite the risks.

Jax wanted to say something that would make Sloane laugh, something that would take away the strain at the corner of her mouth. Instead, she only said, "Headache's better. Vision's clearing."

Mostly true.

"Good." Sloane made another note. Didn't look up. "No flying for twenty-four hours."

"Sloane—"

Sloane raised a brow, finally meeting her gaze.

Jax nearly flinched. "Doc—"

"Non-negotiable. Bean can run supplies. Evacs can wait."

Jax's instinct was to argue, but training won out. Sloane's voice carried authority that Jax respected. This was Sloane's command.

And looking closer—at the worry Sloane was trying so hard to hide? Jax swallowed the protests. "Okay."

Sloane blinked, clearly having expected more resistance. "Okay?"

"Twenty-four hours. But then I'm back in the air," Jax added, already chafing at the expected inactivity.

"We'll see how you're feeling tomorrow."

"Sloane." Jax caught her hand before she could turn away. "I know what this is about."

"It's about proper medical care for a head injury."

"No, it's you being scared." No extra weight. Just truth. "It's this morning when Bean came in without me, when you thought I wasn't coming back."

Sloane went very still. "I was concerned about a team member. That's all."

"Is it?"

The question hung between them while emotions flickered across Sloane's face. For a second the mask slipped, and what lived beneath—denial, fear, something deeper and more complicated than Jax could decipher—shook her more than the hit to her head had.

Sloane finally said, "Twenty-four hours, Chief. Now, I have patients to check on."

But she didn't pull her hand away.

"I know." Jax's thumb traced over Sloane's knuckles, a small comfort for her more than Sloane maybe. "Go. I'll be here when you get back."

"You'd better be." The words slipped out before Sloane seemed to realize she'd said them, raw and honest in a way that made Jax's chest tight. Sloane had given something away she hadn't meant to, and Jax wanted to wrap her arms around her and swear she'd always be back.

But *forever* was not even a word she recognized.

"Count on it," was the best she could manage—but she meant it in ways that had nothing to do with a head injury and everything to do with the woman whose hand was still warm in hers.

CHAPTER SEVENTEEN

Day 7, late evening
Deeper

At dawn, Sloane cleared Jax to fly. It had been that or tie her to a bedpost—and since that was neither feasible, seeing there were no bedposts to be had, nor possible, considering Jax's barely restrained temper fueled by a night of inactivity, she relented.

"I'm telling Bean you don't fly back-to-back callouts without food and a half hour out of the cockpit."

Jax's brows furrowed, storm in her eyes. "Can't promise."

"Bean will."

"That's jumping chain of command."

"Not *my* command." Sloane grabbed Jax's arm and yanked her—gently—into the storeroom. "I don't have time to argue. Neither do you. I don't need you to be a hero. I need you to be standing when this is all over."

Jax scrubbed her face with a hand. "I hear you."

"Is that a yes?"

"Copy."

Sloane hesitated for less than a heartbeat, grasped her shoulders, and kissed her, swiftly but firmly. "Thank you."

Jax looked stunned. "That's a first."

"What do you mean?"

"First time you've kissed me first."

"First time I've kissed anyone first. I have to go."

Jax caught her hand. "Hard to believe that, but I'm feeling damn lucky."

Sloane stepped toward the closed door. If she didn't get back out there, she'd stay. Just…stay. And kiss her again. "I'll see you later."

"You will."

The rest of the morning—just a steady flow of walk-ins and a young woman with pneumonia—lulled her into a false sense of relief. Then three cases arrived at the main shelter that could have been simple food poisoning or stress-related digestive issues. By midday, she had fifteen cases of severe dehydration, diarrhea, and high fever.

"Mina," she called, signaling her over where they wouldn't be heard, "we have a big problem. This might be simple dysentery, which will be bad enough in the crowded conditions we've got out there, but if this is cholera, we're going to lose people."

"Quarantine tents?"

"Do we even have any left?"

Mina sighed. She'd lost weight—all of them had—but her energy and her optimism never flagged. "Eli will know. He'll magic up something."

Eli called Lynette, who organized anyone in town with room to take in as many healthy displaced people currently in tent shelters as they could. Volunteers helped move uninfected patients to the secondary hospital units, and they turned the gym into an isolation unit.

"If and until Jax can get samples to a lab, we treat symptoms first," Sloane said. "Push fluids, as much as we can, and monitor urine and GI output. Antibiotics if it looks like conditions are worsening."

"I'll tell Callie to get a count on our IV bags. It will be tight," Mina said.

"Then Eli needs to find us more. We're not in the damn outback here—wherever that is," Sloane muttered.

"We are now," Mina said and hurried off.

Sloane spent the afternoon managing IV fluids, electrolyte replacement, and the delicate balance of keeping people hydrated without overwhelming their systems. Every case required constant monitoring, frequent lab draws with their limited testing capability, and the kind of hypervigilance that left her feeling scraped raw.

"Last bag's running," Mina reported, checking the IV on an elderly man who'd been their most critical case. "Urine output's improving."

"Good." Sloane made a note on his chart, then rubbed her eyes with the heel of her hand. The glaring overhead lights had been giving her a headache for hours. "How many are we down to still needing IV support?"

"Eight. The others are stable on oral rehydration."

"No new cases up on the hill?"

"Sarah says no. She's been passing out hand wipes and lecturing everyone on infection precautions."

It was progress, but precarious progress. One setback, one patient who didn't respond to treatment, and they could be looking at their first fatalities not directly related to the flood itself.

Sloane radioed Eli. "We're out of everything. Another rush like today and I'll lose people. Fix this, Eli."

Eli's voice, even over the radio, was his usual calm. "Guard just called. Their drop's delayed. Weather on the flats."

Sloane bit her lip to keep the panic at bay. Later, she'd let herself scream, at least inside. "What about Jax?"

What she wanted to ask was *Where is Jax? Why hasn't she been back?*

"She's out doing what she does. Don't worry."

"Get me supplies, Eli." Sloane wanted to throw the damn radio, but clipped it back on her scrub pants.

"Trouble?" Mina said.

Sloane shook her head, not trusting her voice. She went back to work. Always work. But now, part of her listened. And counted the minutes.

The Bell came in like a promise fulfilled. Late afternoon, when rotors finally cut through, the sound landed inside Sloane like a warm hand closing over hers. Her lungs remembered how to fill, and she took a long, slow breath on her way to the door.

The skids settled into gravel. Jeb and Bean were out first, wrestling a sling pallet toward the sawhorses that marked the LZ. Boxes stenciled BLUE RIDGE REGIONAL spilled into view. Oxygen concentrator filters. Blankets. Cases of IV fluids banded in plastic that gleamed like salvation.

Her fear retreated. Still, she waited.

Jax, the white line of Steri-Strips visible even at a distance, jumped out, T-shirt clinging to her chest and shoulders. She stopped, gaze tracking to Sloane immediately, as if she'd known exactly where she'd be in the chaos. Sloane's heart rattled in a way that would have worried her if she hadn't known why. Jax. Jax, safe and sound and righting her world.

Jax jogged down to her. "What do you need first?"

"Fluids," Sloane said automatically, but what she meant was *you*.

"Fluids. Then OR packets. If they gave you antibiotics, I want them last—we'll inventory them when needed."

"Copy." Jax's lips pressed into a hard line. "How bad?"

"Bad enough. Too early still to tell if it's a limited outbreak. We're washing hands like it's religion. But if we don't keep ahead of the dehydration—"

"You will." Jax touched one finger to Sloane's cheek as she turned back toward the Bell. "You will."

Jax, Bean, and Jeb ferried boxes into the gym. Sloane wanted to watch Jax's every movement, just to assure herself she was still there. She didn't. She brushed past her once in the doorway, and the heat of that moment carried her through the next hour.

"Blue Ridge says more tomorrow," Jax said as she set a case of saline onto a table Mina had turned into a supply altar. "Weather permitting."

"Weather doesn't ask," Sloane said, too weary to hide the bitterness.

"No," Jax said softly. "It doesn't."

They stood too close for a beat, the kind of pause no one notices in the middle of a battle. The pulse in Jax's throat ticked faster. Jax touched Sloane's elbow—one second, two—and was gone back into the wash.

The afternoon wore on into evening. Sloane cataloged the new supplies and directed volunteers where to store them, made rounds on the patients in the two long rows of cots, adjusted IV rates, checked temps. When no volunteers were nearby, she changed sweat-dampened sheets and held plastic straws to the lips of those who could not lift a cup. She kept moving because stopping would let the reel in her head start: Jax in wind shear with a half-busted chin bubble. Jax's face bloodied and bruised. Jax walking away because the town asked. Jax coming back because she said she would.

She caught herself listening and pretended she wasn't.

Callie appeared at Sloane's elbow with a sandwich that looked like it had been assembled from whatever remained in the disaster supplies. "You need to eat something. And you need to sleep."

"I'm fine."

"You're running on fumes," Mina said, joining Callie in what was obviously a coordinated intervention. "When's the last time you ate a full meal?"

Sloane couldn't remember. Sometime yesterday, maybe. The days had blurred together into an endless cycle of crisis management and recovery. "I'll get something later. The patients need—"

"The patients need you functional," a familiar voice said from behind her. "Not collapsing from exhaustion."

Sloane turned to find Jax standing in the gym entrance, flight jacket slung over her shoulder, hair damp from the evening drizzle that had been falling since afternoon. She looked tired, too, they all did, but the intensity in her eyes when she looked at Sloane—as if she was the only person in the crowded room—made Sloane's pulse quicken despite her exhaustion.

"I'm not collapsing," Sloane said.

"Yet." Jax's tone was mild, but her expression serious. "When's the last time you stepped outside this building?"

"I don't need—"

"Humor me." Jax stepped close enough that her presence felt like a physical force. "Walk with me. Fifteen minutes of fresh air."

Sloane looked around the clinic—at the patients who were stable, at Mina and Callie who were perfectly capable of handling things for a short while, at the charts and monitors and endless demands that would still be there when she returned. Her body answered yes before her head considered the consequences.

"Fifteen minutes," she said finally.

The evening air was cool and clean after the recycled atmosphere of the clinic. Sloane breathed deeply, some of the tension leaving her shoulders as they walked away from the building.

"Better?" Jax asked.

"Maybe." Sloane glanced sideways at her. "How long have you been planning this intervention?"

"Since the last run when Mina might have mentioned you hadn't taken a break since dawn."

Sloane sighed. "I love her, but—"

"She loves you, too," Jax cut in, one hand on the small of her back. "Let her. Let—"

Sloane glanced at her. "Let?"

Jax sighed. "Let someone care."

"Not so easy to do."

"I know." Jax stroked the length of her back. "Just accept you matter."

Sloane nodded silently. *As long as I matter to you.*

The Bell sat on the landing zone, quiet and still in the dim light.

Jax led her to a supply crate that had been repurposed as seating, and they sat side by side, looking out over the flooded valley. Jax reached for the radio at her hip and turned the volume down a click. Not off. Just enough to make the world less loud.

"Thanks," Sloane murmured. "For being here."

"Nowhere else I'd rather be." Jax reached inside the Bell, handed her a bottle of water. Her knuckles brushed Sloane's hand. "Drink."

"You're bossy." Sloane tried for a bite and failed. She tucked a strand of hair behind Jax's ear, careful of the edge of the laceration, and lingered a fraction too long at the angle of Jax's jaw. Jax's eyes went dark, pupils widening the way they did when they were alone and the air between them thickened with want.

"Later," Sloane said, surprising herself, but she had to say something to keep herself from acting on everything else.

"Later," Jax murmured, but her gaze dropped to Sloane's mouth and back up.

Sloane had to lean away to resist the pull. She sipped the water, lukewarm and perfect. She took three swallows, then three more. Jax watched her like it mattered more than anything else they'd done all day.

"How are the supplies doing?" Jax asked.

"Not enough if the Guard can't drop by morning."

"They will," Jax said. "And if they don't, Blue Ridge will come through for us. And if they won't, I'll make them."

Sloane snorted. "You're very persuasive."

"I'm very stubborn." Jax turned, leaned back on her elbows like the world belonged to her.

"I've noticed." Sloane faced her fully. "When things get hard, you just push back harder."

Jax shrugged. "Don't care for the alternatives."

"How are you holding up?" Sloane asked. The question was completely inadequate for everything they'd all been through, but she didn't know how else to ask.

"I'm okay." Jax was quiet for a moment. "Tired. Ready for things to get back to normal, whatever that means anymore."

"I don't think I remember what normal feels like."

"No," Jax agreed. "This one's been…intense."

There was something in her voice that made Sloane look at her more closely. "What is it?"

"Nothing. Just thinking." Jax picked up a small stone and tossed it. "About what comes after all this."

The words hit Sloane with unexpected shock. She'd been so focused on the immediate crisis that she hadn't thought about the inevitable end of their mission. But of course it would end. Jax would return to whatever assignment came next, and she would go back to Boston, to the ER and her carefully ordered life.

The life that suddenly seemed impossibly empty.

"How long do we have?" she asked.

"Not long. Maybe a week, depending on how quickly regular infrastructure comes back online."

Sloane nodded, keeping her expression neutral even as something inside her cracked. "That's good. People need to get back to their lives."

"Yeah." Jax's voice seemed carefully neutral, too. "People need to get back to their lives."

The weight of unspoken things settled between them. Finally, Jax stood and offered her hand.

"Come on. I want to show you something." She gestured for Sloane to climb into the bell. "Basic maintenance check. I could use an extra pair of hands."

Despite the odd request—Bean usually handled maintenance with Jax, and Sloane's mechanical knowledge was limited to what she'd absorbed through osmosis—she followed Jax into the aircraft's interior.

"What exactly am I helping with?" she asked, curious despite her exhaustion.

"Here." Jax handed her a flashlight and positioned her next to the medical equipment bay. "Hold this steady while I check the mounting brackets."

The task was simple enough. Sloane held the light steady, as directed, pressing against Jax to focus the light where Jax needed it. She'd never noticed before how the confined space of the Bell seemed to amplify every small sound—Jax's breathing, the rustle of fabric as she moved, the quiet clicks of equipment being checked and secured.

"This mount's been loose since yesterday," Jax said, her shoulder brushing Sloane's as she tightened a bracket. "Should have caught it earlier."

"Everything looks secure to me," Sloane observed, though she wasn't really looking at the equipment anymore. She was watching Jax's hands, the sure way she handled the tools, the precision in each small movement. Small movements like the gentle brush of knuckles against her cheek.

"Mmm." Jax finished with the bracket and straightened, suddenly even nearer, so near Sloane could count the flecks of silver in her eyes. "How's that light?"

"Fine," Sloane managed, though her voice came out slightly breathless.

Jax reached up to adjust the light's angle, her fingers covering Sloane's on the flashlight handle. The contact sent warmth racing up Sloane's arm and settling beneath her breastbone.

"Jax," she said quietly.

"Yeah?"

"Are we actually checking equipment, or…"

Jax smiled, her hand still covering Sloane's. "The equipment needed checking."

"And now?"

"Now it's checked."

The flashlight beam wavered as Sloane's hand trembled slightly. She'd been steady all day through medical crises and life-or-death decisions, but this, this simple touch in the dim interior of the aircraft, was undoing her.

"We should go back inside," she said, but made no move to leave.

"Probably." Jax traced small circles over Sloane's knuckles with her thumb. Her eyes had gone dark.

"The med center—"

"Is being handled by two very competent medical professionals who practically pushed you out the door."

Sloane let out a shaky laugh. "They did, didn't they?"

"Conspiracy," Jax said solemnly. "I may have been involved in the planning stages."

"May have been?"

"Definitely was." Jax cupped Sloane's face, fingertips resting on her cheek. "You've been taking care of everyone else. Someone needs to take care of you."

The tenderness in her voice, in her touch, swept away Sloane's last tether of restraint. She longed for more…of what, she couldn't put into words. So many sensations triggered by Jax's touch—heat, tenderness, arousal. She leaned into the contact, her eyes fluttering closed.

"I don't know how to do this," she whispered.

"Do what?"

"This. Us. Whatever this is." Sloane opened her eyes, found Jax's. "I haven't...it's been a long time since I've let anyone close."

"No lovers?"

Sloane laughed, the sound carrying no humor. "No one I would describe as such. And not for a very long time."

"You have a huge heart," Jax murmured, never taking her eyes from Sloane's. She leaned closer, and Sloane's back touched the cool frame of the Bell. Jax's body, firm and radiating heat, pressed into hers. "You deserve to be cared about."

Sloane caught her breath and dropped the flashlight. The beam cut across the floor at their feet like a line daring her to cross. But then she already had. She slid her arms around Jax's waist. "I haven't wanted anyone to."

"Since Sybil?"

The question was gentle, but it hit like a blade—slicing to the heart of her fears. Sloane nodded, not trusting her voice.

"That's a long time to be alone."

"It was safer."

"Maybe. But safe isn't always living, is it?"

The question hung in the air. If she answered, she'd risk the life she'd built around work and solitude, around maintaining a careful distance from everyone. She could run from the question, but then she'd have to run from Jax. And she wasn't strong enough to walk away from everything Jax made her feel.

"No," she said finally. "It wasn't living."

Jax slipped a hand behind her head, spread her fingers in Sloane's hair. "Then maybe it's time to try something different."

This time, when Jax leaned in to kiss her, Sloane didn't think about consequences or complications or all the reasons this was dangerous. She just kissed her back, pouring years of loneliness and want into the connection between them. The kiss deepened, grew more urgent, until they were both breathing hard and the flashlight had rolled away, forgotten on the floor of the Bell. Sloane fisted the material of Jax's shirt, pulling her closer.

"I never knew anyone could feel so good." Sloane struggled for the words to say all she felt. Words she'd never used, never needed to say before. "You make me *feel* things I've never felt."

"I love touching you," Jax murmured, her mouth on Sloane's neck. "I want to touch you everywhere."

"Yes," Sloane gasped. "I...I want you to. I want to touch you."

Jax groaned, pulled away. "Not here."

"No," Sloane agreed, but didn't let go. "I can't leave the clinic."

"You're allowed to sleep now and then. Radio Mina, tell her to call you if she needs you."

Sloane hesitated. Could she steal a few hours? Should she? For the first time in her life, duty warred with desire.

Jax waited, her hands resting gently on Sloane's waist.

Her choice.

"Mina," she said into the radio clipped to her scrubs.

"Here," Mina replied.

"I'm going to grab some sleep. Call me if you need me."

"We're all good here," Mina said. "Go."

Sloane clicked off and met Jax's eyes. "We should go."

Wordlessly, Jax took her hand and led her to the utility vehicle next to the equipment shed at the edge of the LZ. Sloane climbed in, Jax started it up and grasped her hand. Sloane clung to the warmth and refused to question. The trip took moments.

The main room at the roadhouse was empty—Eli was likely in the auxiliary comms center in the shelter where Lynette and Sarah rotated taking calls from distressed families in the outlying reaches. Still, they climbed the stairs as quietly as possible, Sloane hyperaware of every creaking board. In their shared room, Sloane paused just inside the door, facing Jax in the dim light from the single window, suddenly uncertain.

"I don't know what to do now," she said on a brief laugh.

"Good thing I do," Jax said.

CHAPTER EIGHTEEN

Day 9, after midnight
Post-breach

When the door latch clicked behind them, Jax's chest loosened for the first time in—hell, how many days? The constant radio chatter, the endless stream of injured, Bean's worried looks when he thought she wasn't watching—all of it fell away. Now there was just silence. Just them.

Just Sloane.

Then Sloane stood by the window, evening light outlining her body through those thin scrubs. Jax's mouth went dry. Exhaustion should've killed her sex drive days ago, but looking at Sloane now? Heat pooled low in her belly, urgent and demanding.

"I can't believe we're actually here." Sloane's voice carried that edge Jax knew meant she was fighting nerves. "Alone."

"Just tell me, are you sure?"

"I'm sure about wanting this," Sloane said carefully. "And in case you're worried, I'm not a virgin. Just…not practiced."

"Babe," Jax said, easing closer, judging each step for acceptance, ready to back off if Sloane wavered. "The last thing I care about is that. I've wanted this since the night we spent in the Bell—before that, seeing as you got my attention the first time I saw you. That was chemistry—this is something different."

"What?" Sloane asked, her voice tight. "What is this?"

"This," Jax murmured, cupping Sloane's face in both hands, "is me being crazy about you."

Sloane caught the front of her shirt and hauled her in. No warning, just need. Sloane's mouth on hers. The taste of rain. Heat streaking through her. Sloane pressed closer, body melding from breasts down to thigh. Jax's pulse jumped like an engine shifting into high gear. Sloane pushed a hand between them, fumbled with her shirt, yanked it from her pants. Cool air slid across her sweat-slicked skin. She shivered.

Sloane pressed a palm, hot and questing, to her middle.

Fire to ice.

"*Fuck.*"

"What?' Sloane gasped. "No?"

"Fuck, *yes*," Jax said through gritted teeth. She'd never in her life lost control, and she was already close. "Clothes first. I want to see you. Touch you."

"Oh, right," Sloane muttered, backing away. She grabbed the hem of her scrub shirt and stripped it off, tossing it toward the footlocker that sat at the end of the bunk. Careless and unconcerned. Certainty in every movement.

Jax's heart stopped. Just a filmy tank underneath the OR cotton, clinging to the swell of her breasts, firm and hard-nippled. The long sweep of her abdomen, the flare of her hips, scrub pants riding low, a strip of skin bared above the top. Strong, elegant. Beauty made flesh.

"Don't look away," Sloane murmured and untied her scrub pants. A demand, not a plea.

"Aye," Jax managed, head buzzing with need and astonishment. When had she lost all control of what was happening? Had she ever really *been* in control? Since she'd walked into the briefing that first day and seen her, Sloane had centered her awareness. Lying in the bunk above her listening to her breath, piloting the Bell and stealing glimpses of her working over a patient in the bay, unloading wounded on the LZ as Sloane snapped orders. In the quiet, in the chaos, Sloane was always in her thoughts.

Now, as Sloane let the pants fall, revealing long, lean thighs and a triangle of silk between them, she commanded every fiber of Jax's body, too.

"You're stunning," Jax said, only then aware she was still completely clothed. She kicked off her boots, jerked down the zipper on her pants, and pushed everything down. Before she cleared the pile on the floor, Sloane's hands found the bottom of her shirt, fingertips skimming across bare skin beneath. Electricity raced through Jax's nervous system. She gasped, the sound torn from somewhere deep. Sloane tugged, and Jax raised her arms. The tee came up and was gone.

Cool air again, raising gooseflesh. She needed an ice bath, about to combust.

Sloane looked at her, unapologetic and intent, and Jax had to lock her knees. She'd never liked standing still for inspection, but this—this felt like giving, not being taken. Sloane's gaze moving over her breasts, down her torso, halting at the junction of her thighs—as potent as a touch. Her core tightened. Heat flooded her depths.

"You're staring," Jax said, sounding like someone she didn't recognize. Someone who *needed.*

"Yes," Sloane said, frank and totally sure. "Problem?"

"No."

"Good. Get used to it. In case *you* never noticed, I've been staring for a long time."

"Can't say I mind." She probably *sounded* like she was still in control, but inside? She was coming apart. "Although you're the gorgeous one."

Sloane smiled into the next kiss, and God, that look—pleased, as if she'd never been told she was beautiful before. Wanting to be the one, the *only* one, to make Sloane smile that way, Jax drew her close. Close enough to see the pulse jumping at Sloane's throat.

She ached to touch, but the moment felt precious. Fragile. A once in a lifetime first time.

"Been wanting this for a while." Jax swallowed. "Tell me what you need. We can go as slow as you need." The words scraped her throat raw. When had she become someone who wanted instead of just taking what was offered? The words cost her. Every nerve ending screamed for speed, to explore skin and bone. With her hands. Her mouth, her heart. "Or as fast. Whatever you want."

"What I want"—Sloane's voice dropped, husky and urgent in a way that made Jax's knees weak—"is to stop thinking about everything and feel. Just feel. Can you help me with that?"

Jax shuddered. The confession—so unapologetic, so *Sloane*—hit like shrapnel, hot and sharp, lodging somewhere vital. "I want to make you feel everything."

Sloane skimmed off her tank. Dropped it on the floor. Her eyes never left Jax. "I might spontaneously combust if you don't soon."

Jax's brain nearly exploded, but she forced herself to take each step. No mistakes. No retreat. She rested both hands on Sloane's hips, slipping her fingertips beneath the thin ribbon of silk where skin waited, warm and real. "Yes?"

"Yes," Sloane answered.

Jax drew the last barrier between them away and took in the wonder of her, savoring each revelation. The elegant line of her collarbones. The soft curve of her breasts. The way she trembled under her touch like a wire pulled taut. When Sloane stood before her in nothing but evening light, a barricade inside Jax's chest cracked open. Let in air she hadn't known she needed.

"You're incredible." Jax kissed her, and the world narrowed to only Sloane—her mouth, soft and demanding, her hands fisting in Jax's hair with desperate strength. The small sound she made against Jax's mouth nearly buckled her knees. The rush of sensation carried her beyond physical attraction. Beyond want. Into territory that scared her more than enemy fire.

Nearly paralyzed with urgency, Jax hesitated.

"More." Sloane broke away just long enough to breathe the word against her lips. "I need more."

Jax answered by kissing her deeper, tangling her fingers in silk-soft hair while skimming a hand down Sloane's spine. Sloane arched into her touch, her fervor making Jax's pulse hammer against her ribs.

"You're so responsive." Jax pressed kisses to Sloane's neck. Clean and sweet, undercut with a haze of heat. "So fucking beautiful."

"I want to touch you." Sloane's hands grew bolder, skating down Jax's chest and tracing the curve of her breasts. "I want to touch every part of you. God, you feel amazing."

The words—so different from Sloane's usual careful control—made Jax pull back to meet her eyes. Her breath fled. Desire mixed with determination, vulnerability wrapped in steel-strong will. Her heart stuttered, missed a beat, hammered back to life.

"Sloane." Jax could barely breathe. "I'm in real trouble here."

"You're perfect." Fascination chased across Sloane's features as she traced Jax's lower abdomen with her fingertips as if she was cataloging every muscle, every scar for later study. "So strong, so beautiful."

Jax caught her hands before they could reduce her to begging. "Fast or slow, baby? You call it."

Sloane blushed but didn't look away. "I've never wanted anyone the way I want you. I don't want to go slow."

"Show me."

Sloane kissed her, hard and hungry. She explored her mouth with the same intensity she used in everything—deliberate and thorough. Devastating.

After what felt like forever, Sloane pulled away and Jax, fuzzy-headed, muttered, "What's wrong?"

"I don't want to wait any longer."

Jax grinned, the fog clearing, blasted into crystal clarity by the volcano rising inside her. "Come here, then."

Jax pulled her toward the narrow bed, and Sloane followed, anything but passive. Sloane dropped onto the mattress with desperate grace, pushed Jax back, and straddled her hips. Arms braced against Jax's chest, she looked down, her hair teasing Jax's face—a goddess in moonlight.

Caught by surprise, Jax muttered a faint curse.

Sloane grinned. "Tell me if I push too hard."

"You'll know," Jax said, voice low. "Besides, I'm not complaining."

"No?" Sloane leaned over her and kissed her, a thoroughly commanding, claiming kiss. "Good."

A strand of pale blond hair swept over Jax's cheek. She tucked it behind Sloane's ear and trailed her fingertips along the curve of Sloane's jaw. When her thumb brushed Sloane's lower lip, Sloane gently bit down, her eyes fixed on Jax's.

"Fuck," Jax breathed, heat arrowing to her core.

"You said that before," Sloane murmured, the tip of her tongue touching the spot she'd just nibbled. "I assume that's good?"

"Amazing," Jax whispered. Why had she never guessed this fierce fire was hiding behind that icy calm? Too late to wonder. Beyond turning back. "I'm just happy I know now."

"What?"

"You're the sexiest woman I've ever encountered."

Sloane laughed, still watching, only now she moved, gentle undulations of her hips over Jax's lower abdomen that sent rockets bursting inside her head.

A pulse hammered in Sloane's throat. Her hands trembled against Jax's chest. "I love the way you make me feel."

So open, so damn unafraid.

Jax's heart clenched. She rolled them, not to take control but to make time. Time to explore, absorb, imprint every moment that might never come again.

"Don't make me wait too long," Sloane gasped.

"I won't," Jax promised, her mouth at Sloane's throat. She kissed the pulse jumping beneath the smooth skin, ran her teeth over the curve of her collarbone. "Tell me what you need. What you like."

"You. Everywhere." Sloane grasped her hand. "Touch me before I lose my mind."

"You won't." Jax kissed the hollow of her throat and Sloane shuddered. When she took a nipple into her mouth and sucked slow, then harder, one hand cupped around her, Sloane moaned. The sound shot through her, tearing away the last shred of clarity.

"I want you," Jax ground out through clenched jaws. She wanted to go on forever, to build the pressure and watch Sloane ride it until she came undone. But Sloane's hand at the back of Jax's neck trembled, betraying an urgency that scorched her soul. "I want you so much it's killing me."

"Now, then," Sloane breathed, harsh at the edges. Her hips arched upward, seeking contact. "God, now."

Jax slid lower, kisses marking her path, dropping promises she meant to keep. Palms on Sloane's thighs, she slid between them and looked up, needing to see her. She watched Sloane's face as she traced and teased her—the way her breath caught, the flush spreading across her chest, the little sounds she made when Jax found the rhythm that made her grip the sheet in her fists. When she found the place, the pressure, that made Sloane cry out, she nearly lost hold of her restraint. With her head thrown back, back arched, lost in sensation, Sloane was more beautiful than anything Jax had ever seen.

Jax pressed gently, found heat, slick and unmistakable. Sloane's hips jerked. The sound she made hit Jax hard enough to steal her breath. She stroked slowly. Testing. Learning. Sloane's hand slid into Jax's hair and held. Not hard. Just there. Jax kept the rhythm steady until Sloane's thighs trembled, then pressed deeper, angled, found the spot that made Sloane tighten around her.

Sloane moaned. "There. Jax—there."

Jax eased onto her knees, pushed deeper, gentle at first, then not. Watching, following. And Sloane climbed—heat flushing her chest, arms taut, eyes blind. Sloane's climax hit in a long, hard shudder, her whole body bowed, a wordless cry that pierced Jax's soul. Jax held steady and rode it with her, kept moving until the last ripple eased away. Withdrawing slowly, Jax caressed Sloane's hip and leaned over to kiss her breast. Sloane caught her face and pulled her up, kissed her.

"You're so beautiful like this," Jax murmured.

"Don't go anywhere," Sloane whispered. "I need a minute."

"Not a chance." Jax's body hummed at a pitch that wasn't going to come down anytime soon, but she'd wait as long as Sloane needed.

"We're not done yet." Sloane surprised her again, turning them quickly, one hand sliding over Jax's ribs and down the center of her body.

"Affirmative," Jax gasped.

Sloane laughed and cupped a hand between her thighs, the slow press making Jax's muscles jump. She bit back another curse. Sloane's hand slid lower, confident now, like she'd learned the controls and was ready to fly. She touched Jax, sure and certain, and Jax made a sound she'd be embarrassed about anywhere else. *With* anyone else. But not here. Not now. Her hips moved with Sloane's hand with a will of their own.

"You're shaking," Sloane murmured.

"You're doing that," Jax managed. "Don't stop."

"Not planning to."

Sloane's fingers moved, faster, and Jax gripped the post to the upper bunk. Not long now—please, soon. Sloane set a pace calculated to destroy—firm, even, relentless. Jax forgot how to breathe, control gone. Not caring. Just…reaching. Needing.

"More," Jax gasped. "Harder."

Sloane gave her what she needed, every stroke sure and strong. The crest hit—so fast it punched a small cry out of her, streaking through her in a wave that made her legs shake and her vision spark and Sloane's name become a benediction.

Sloane slowed when Jax did and stilled when Jax finally let go of the post and slumped back with a long sigh. "Mission accomplished. And then some."

When she opened her eyes, Sloane grinned down at her.

"That was…" Sloane struggled for breath, for words. "I had no idea it could feel like that. Could *be* like that."

"Neither did I," Jax said. Truth, and damn scary. Time to think about that later. She held out her arm, the need to hold Sloane as urgent as the need that had driven her a minute before. "Come here."

Sloane curled against Jax's side, head on her shoulder, one leg thrown over her thighs in unconscious possession that made Jax's chest clench tight. She dragged the quilt up and around them, ridiculously happy to tuck Sloane in with her. She pressed her face to Sloane's hair and breathed her in—sweet and clear, like cedar warmed by sun.

"Can I say that I had no idea sex could be so…exhilarating," Sloane said, her breath warm against Jax's skin. "I loved touching you. I love the way you feel. The way you make me feel."

"More than sex," Jax said, swallowing hard before she could say anything else.

"I noticed." Sloane's laugh was a breath that held a question she didn't ask. She tipped her head back, met Jax's eyes, serious again. "I don't want this to change anything."

Jax put a finger to her mouth. "It won't."

Not a lie, even if for her everything had already changed.

Relief entered Sloane's face like light through cloud. "Okay."

Unsure how to read that, Jax pulled her closer. "You should try to sleep."

"I should check on the clinic." Sloane made no move toward her radio.

"Mina has it handled." Jax pressed a kiss to the top of her head. "You're allowed to rest. She'll find you if she needs you."

"I haven't felt this relaxed in…I can't remember how long."

"Good." She traced lazy patterns on Sloane's bare back. Memorizing the texture of her skin, the way she fit against her side like she belonged there. "You deserve to be taken care of now and then."

"Is that what this was? Taking care of me?"

"Among other things." Jax tilted her chin up. "Do you mind?"

Sloane went quiet, her eyes distant. "No. I wasn't thinking about what came next or what I should be doing. I was just…here. With you."

Warmth unfurled in Jax's chest. "I'm here with you. Close your eyes."

Sloane did, and Jax did the same, more relaxed than she could ever remember being. Her last thought was ridiculous and simple. *Mine.* Not possession. Just belonging. Hers to come back to, again and again, until they ran out of sky. Before she could even process what that might mean, Sloane's radio crackled to life, cutting through the intimate quiet like a blade.

Mina's voice, urgent but strong. "Sloane, you there? We've got a situation."

Sloane jerked upright, the quilt sliding away as she reached for the radio. "I'm here, Mina. What have you got?"

"Not sure—might be bad. Langley just radioed—he's bringing in a girl, unresponsive. Sounded like they're doing CPR on the rig."

"I'm coming." Sloane slid from the bunk, already reaching for clothes.

"I'll get the RTV," Jax said, pulling on her pants. "Just—"

Her radio crackled to life. Eli's voice. "Bell One—you copy."

"Roger." She grabbed her flight jacket.

"Family up on Pine Ridge calling for medical help. Infant in distress—fever, trouble breathing—mother sounding weak."

"Five minutes to liftoff," Jax said. "Bean?"

"Hasn't called in yet. Jax—we're under heavy cloud cover, high wind alert. No fly zone."

Jax cursed, halfway to the door. Sloane waited, listening, her expression searching. "Can we get there on the ground?"

"Doubtful."

"Then we fly." Jax clicked off the radio and grabbed Sloane's hand. "Come on. Let's get you to the clinic."

As they raced down the stairs, Sloane said, "You'll wait for clearance from Eli?"

Jax gritted her teeth. "For a while."

"Jax—you can't—"

"Been here before—trust me on this." Jax jumped into the RTV, started it up. Sloane piled in, and Jax tore off for the clinic. Two minutes later, she turned to Sloane. "Go. I'll see you later."

Sloane touched her face. "Don't be a hero."

Jax grinned, looking at Sloane. Desire banked, not gone. "Not my style."

Sloane looked as if she wanted to say more but the flashing lights of Langley's cruiser crested the ridge below the clinic, tires slewing in the muck and loose gravel. "I've got to go."

Sloane jumped out and Jax watched her run to the door before swinging the RTV uphill and heading for the Bell. The steady thrum of the rotors signaled Bean had arrived.

Her shoulder tingled where Sloane had rested her head, heat moving through her despite the cold night air. She'd taken a path she'd never meant to travel, and now there was no going back. Not for her. The thought probably should have been terrifying. Maybe in the morning, it would be. For now? She had a job to do, and she'd never felt so damn good.

Chapter Nineteen

Day 9, deep night

The doors burst open at 3:27 a.m., letting in cold air and the sound of rain hammering the old cinderblock walls. Outside, a truck's red and blue lights stuttered like a pulse about to fail. Sheriff Langley and a deputy, muddy uniforms plastered to their skin, a backboard between them, barreled inside. A third woman in a yellow slicker with a CFD patch on the arm kept pace, performing chest compressions on the victim.

"Johnboat capsized in the overflow channel," Langley shouted as they rushed in. "Four of them. Got them all out. This one was under longest."

A girl, blond hair falling in wet ropes around a gray, waxy face. Twelve, maybe fourteen. Sloane's chest cinched tight, and for one blinding second, fear swallowed her.

Sybil.

Drowned.

No. Not Sybil. Another girl. A girl who needed help.

"How long was she under?" Sloane asked. Her voice came out steady despite the roaring in her ears. Her mind cleared, the cold white light above her head snapping the scene into sharp focus.

"Ten minutes down," the deputy at the end of the stretcher panted, voice hoarse. "We started compressions in the truck."

Ten to twelve minutes submerged. The odds constricted Sloane's throat, but she shoved the knowledge aside. Numbers didn't save lives. Action did.

"Treatment one. Mina! Crash cart."

"Here," Mina called.

"Where are the rest?" Sloane said, guiding them into the cubicle.

"Truck," Langley panted as he and the deputies slid the backboard onto the table.

"Callie," Sloane said, "get the others inside. Take them into the back. Check for hypothermia."

"Yes, ma'am." Callie ran for the door.

"I've got the warming blanket," Mina said, already sliding it under the unresponsive girl.

Sloane turned to the firefighter doing compressions.

"Switch with me," she ordered, already positioning her hands over the girl's sternum. Bracing her shoulders, hands locked, she started the first thirty. The chest gave beneath her palm—cartilage yielding, not yet broken. "Mina, clear the airway. A hundred percent O2."

Her own voice startled her—too calm, too steady, a stranger's. Figures moved behind her, a woman's voice cried out. She shut everything out, the rhythm drumming through her forearms, up through her shoulders, into her chest becoming her whole world. The girl's chest dipped under her palms, ribs flexing with each thrust.

"Airway's clear," Mina called, the sound of a suction catheter breaking the silence.

Thirty compressions.

"Bag her," Sloane snapped, easing back. She looked at the girl's face beneath the mask—white, bloodless.

Not Sybil.

The chest rose twice. Oxygen in.

Back to compressions.

Callie appeared at her side. Started an IV. Hooked up EKG leads.

The flatline mocked her.

Her shoulders burned. Sweat broke across her forehead despite the cool air. The girl's face blurred. Became Sybil's face. Became every moment Sloane had reached for her and missed, had tried and failed, had chosen herself over someone else.

Her hand slipping. Water closing over blond hair. The terrible silence after.

Another thirty compressions.

"Bag her. Callie—push an amp of epi."

Mina squeezed the Ambu bag, forcing oxygen down the airway passages. The chest rose—barely. Once. Twice.

Nothing on the monitor.

Thirty compressions. Two breaths.

"Three minutes," Mina murmured. "Switch?"

"No. Temp?" Sloane asked of no one, beginning the next round. One, two, three…

"Eighty-seven," Callie replied. "Hanging another warm saline."

Beneath her hands, the sternum gave a sharp crack—the sound like kindling snapping. The brittle pop ricocheted through her. Rib or cartilage—didn't matter. She didn't stop. Couldn't stop. The only way to save her was to keep the blood flowing.

Sloane's breath rasped in her chest.

Let go. You have to let go. Choose yourself.

"Asystole," Mina said quietly.

"I can see that." Push. Push. Push. Her arms screamed. Sweat trickled into her eyes, blurred her vision. "Callie—repeat the epi."

Sloane kept compressing, counting in her head, watching the monitor for any flicker of hope. Her vision narrowed to the space between her hands and the girl's sternum.

"Clear." Mina pushed the medication.

Sloane paused, watched the monitor. The line stayed flat.

Back to compressions. Her arms shook now, muscles screaming. More medication. More desperate breathing into lungs that wouldn't inflate properly because water had gotten there first.

Still no pulse. The skin beneath her hands remained cold, waxen. Sloane swallowed bile. *Come on. Come back.*

Sybil's laughter spooled out of memory, bright and unbroken. A summer dock, wet footprints slapping boards. Then the scream. Then the silence. She pressed harder, harder, as if she could press the memory back into the past.

"Thirty compressions. Breaths…" Sloane blinked sweat from her eyes.

"Eight minutes." Mina's voice was steady.

"Temp ninety," Callie said.

"Here," Langley said from somewhere far away, "let me take over."

"No," Sloane gasped. Her arms quivered. She shifted her weight, found leverage, kept pressing. Thirty. Bag two. Thirty. Bag Two. Her chest ached in rhythm, like she was trading her heartbeat for the girl's.

"Ten minutes," Mina said.

"Get the paddles." Anything, anything now to give her a chance.

Mina dialed up the defibrillator. "Ready."

Sloane stepped back. Shook her arms to restart the blood flow.

"Clear," Mina called, and discharged the electric current.

Flatline.

"Again," Sloane ordered.

"Clear," Mina said. Another electric shock.

The heart remained still.

Sloane clenched her jaw, restarted compressions, driving down with every ounce of strength she had. *Come on, Syb, come on.*

"Sloane." Mina's voice, gentle but immovable. "Sloane, switch."

"No. I can—"

"You can't—you'll injure yourself. Let Langley."

She couldn't feel her hands. "All right."

The sheriff slipped his hand beneath hers.

"Time?"

"Sixteen minutes."

Langley, jaw set, pumped with metronomic relentlessness.

Thirty, two, thirty, two, forcing blood and oxygen to a heart that didn't beat, a brain that had gone still. Sloane shuddered, caught her breath, looked at the girl fully for the first time in almost twenty minutes. Lips gray. Skin the cool translucency of the newly dead.

If she let go, Sybil would be gone. Her laughter would vanish again. The silence would rush back in.

"Sloane." Mina's voice, steady and calm.

No pulse. Pupils fixed. All her dreams and hopes, gone.

Langley's breathing grew labored.

"Twenty-five minutes."

"Temp?" Sloane shot back. If she was still cold, they had a chance.

"Ninety-seven point five."

A glance at the silent monitor.

Flatline.

Thirty minutes.

Sloane straightened. Squared her shoulders. "Sheriff, stop."

Took a breath. "Time of death three fifty-seven a.m."

Calm. Clinical. As if she was reporting on a stranger's failure instead of her own.

Langley made a choking sound and turned away. The firefighter brushed tears from her face.

"The family—" Callie murmured.

"Yes," Sloane said. "I'll be right there."

She stripped off her gloves, washed her hands with methodical care. The water ran cold over her skin, but she couldn't feel it. Couldn't feel anything except the weight of failure pressing down on her chest.

She found the parents huddled side by side under coarse gray wool blankets in the curtained area they used for quick naps. A boy, less than ten, slept the sleep of exhaustion on a nearby cot under another blanket. The mother's eyes, huge and dark, met Sloane's.

"I'm so sorry," Sloane said, the words like stones in her mouth, cold and heavy. "We weren't able to bring her back."

The father broke, burying his face in his hands, his chest heaving with silent sobs.

The mother straightened, tears overflowing her wounded eyes. "Thank you for trying. Thank you for being here—for us."

The gratitude cut like a blade. *I failed. I failed. I let her die just like I let Sybil die.*

Sloane's heart hammered like she had been the one dragged from the water, gasping for air that would not come. She forced words out, brittle and useless. "When you're ready, you can see her. Callie will help you." She paused. "I'm so sorry."

The words were hollow, useless.

She signaled to Callie to take care of them and stumbled to the locker room to change her sweat-soaked scrub shirt. Automatically, without thought. A ghost with hollow eyes and damp hair plastered to her face looked back from the mirror. She turned away, fists clenched, water dripping to the floor.

The grief, the anger, would come later. No time now for blame or sorrow.

Her radio crackled, Eli's voice cutting through the white noise in her head. "Ops to med center. Ops to Dr. Marshall. Do you copy?"

Sloane splashed water on her face, wiped it with a rough paper towel, clicked the receive button. "Sloane here."

"Emergency call from Pine Ridge—opening a channel to Jax," Eli said.

Sloane's stomach heaved, and she fought down nausea. Jax? An emergency? The image of a helicopter spiraling out of control flashed through her mind. Shaking with adrenaline, she shuttered her mind to the possibility.

Static, then Jax's voice, faint but unmistakable.

"Two patients in distress—twenty-year-old female, temp one-oh-three-point two, hypoxic, likely pneumonia. Male child—eighteen months. Temp one-oh-three-point eight, stridor, retractions, drooling. Ribs retracting."

"Jax," Sloane cut in, her blood turning to ice picturing a cherry-red epiglottis bulging like a thumb into the narrowest airway in the body. The swollen tissue could close off the passageway completely in minutes. If she was right, the child would suffocate, gasping for air that couldn't get past the obstruction. "How's his color?"

"He's blue. We're masking with straight O2."

"Bring them both in, now." No hesitation. No room for doubt. "Keep the child upright, as calm as you can. Mother on an IV. Start a loading dose of ceftriaxone for her."

"Negative," Eli cut in immediately. "Weather is zero-zero your location. Fog down to the treeline. Gusts thirty. Bell is grounded. Repeat, grounded."

Sloane's fingers tightened around the handset until the plastic creaked. If they attempted intubation in the field and failed, the boy would die. "Eli, this is a medical emergency—time matters."

"Regional medevac is on hold," Eli repeated flatly. "I've got State advising stand fast until ceiling lifts. Ground transport—"

"We don't have time for a ground extraction," Sloane snapped. A half room away, the parents of the drowned girl hovered in a silent knot beside the treatment table, their hands clasped, the mother slowly stroking the girl's hair.

No more, damn it, no more losses tonight.

"Jax," she said, "how hard is the child working to breathe?"

"Intercostal and suprasternal retractions," Jax answered. No rush. No panic. Just that clean pilot's report, the same cadence she used to call bearings in turbulence. "He's tiring, Sloane."

"Eli," Sloane said, "we'll lose him if we wait. If Jax—"

"Negative." Eli's voice carried a warning. "Visibility is under a quarter mile, ceiling at four hundred feet with heavy precip. Wind shear warnings across the entire valley. I cannot authorize flight."

The world tilted. Sloane gripped the radio, her knuckles white. Behind her, parents wept over the body of a child she'd failed to save. And somewhere up on Pine Ridge, another child was dying, his airway closing minute by minute.

Sloane's pulse hammered. "If you wait, the child dies."

"And if Jax flies, they all die," Eli shot back.

For a split second, Sloane's throat closed so tight she couldn't swallow. She saw it: gray hull split among black pines, rotor blades twisted like broken wings, rain puckering the fuel sheen in the mud. Jax's helmet cracked, her eyes empty. She pressed the radio against her sternum until its hard edge bit bone. "I understand."

She took a deep breath, her blood running cold. "Jax, start ampicillin and a dose of dexamethasone. If he worsens, you'll need to get an airway in him."

"And if he needs a trach?" Jax, still calm, still steady, didn't say *if we can't intubate him.* She didn't need to. She was far too experienced not to know the risks.

"We'll deal with it if and when."

Silence on the radio. Long enough that Sloane heard her pulse hammering in her ears, rain battering the roof and quiet sobs the only other sounds. She rubbed her fingers on her scrub pants, erasing the feel of the drowned girl's skin. Closed her eyes against the image of Sybil's hair fanning out in the water as she sank. Remembered Jax's arms around her, warm and strong, when they'd awakened. Fear flared so bright it felt like flight, every muscle in her body screaming to move, act, to *win* this battle.

"I don't like those odds," Jax said.

"This is not negotiable," Eli said.

Jax's voice came again, less radio and more Jax—closer somehow, intimate in Sloane's ear. "Out here, I call the shots."

Sloane's chest squeezed so tight she couldn't breathe. She stared at the radio, knowing what it might cost. Rodriguez had bled out calling Jax's name. Would Jax risk them all not to fail again? "Jax, you need to be sure."

"If I sit pretty," Jax said, avoiding an answer, "I'll hear him choke out while I'm safe on the deck. I'm not built for that."

"Four lives against one," Sloane finally said. Her chest ached, her heart hurt. Her soul died a little. "Don't risk—"

Jax came back, voice hardened with decision. "I can thread the valley low, stay under the ceiling, use the ridges for reference. It's going to be tight, but I can make it."

"Jax—" Eli started.

"Bell One spooling up now. ETA to LZ eighteen minutes."

"I'll prep the bay," Sloane said, surprised at how calm she sounded. "We'll be ready the second you hit the pad. Keep him quiet."

It came out cold, harsher than she meant.

"Roger that." Jax's voice softened. "Sloane?"

Sloane didn't answer right away. If she let anything in, all the fear would become a flood. "Go. Fly safe."

Static rustled. "Affirmative."

Sloane stood frozen. The parents' sobs faded into white noise. The radio chatter became distant static. She could have told Jax no. Could have lied, said they had more time. She'd made a choice, and if she was wrong?

Sloane trembled. She wasn't strong enough to lose her.

Jax's voice: *I'm not built for that.*

"I'm not built to lose you," she whispered.

Mina appeared at her elbow, saying something she couldn't hear through the roaring in her ears. The girl's body lay just feet away, proof that sometimes trying wasn't enough. And somewhere above the mountains, Jax flew into impossible conditions to save a child who might die anyway.

Love equals loss. I should have known better.

The minutes crawled. Sloane moved through preparations on autopilot—crash airway kit, pediatric intubation supplies, warming blankets for a child whose body temperature might be dropping with hypoxia. Her hands shook as she checked equipment. Her mind played endless scenarios of helicopter failure. Wind shear. Disorientation in zero visibility. Uncontrolled descent into rocky terrain. The list scrolled through her consciousness, each possibility more terrible than the last.

"Sloane." Mina's hand on her arm. "She'll be okay. Jax is the best pilot I've ever seen. She knows what she's doing."

Sloane nodded because she couldn't speak. Because agreeing was easier than admitting she'd been complicit in sending someone she cared for to potential death, all because she couldn't accept that sometimes children died no matter what she did.

Not just someone she cared for. Someone she loved.

She stared at the tiny endotracheal tube in her hands. Was that even possible? How could she let herself love, knowing the cost?

Sloane watched the doorway the way she'd watch a wound for bleeding, waiting for the first slick hint of disaster. The whispered rustle of rain on the roof changed pitch with each gust, sometimes a soft hiss, sometimes a rush, as if the storm inhaled and exhaled over them. Every shift ratcheted up the tension in her shoulders.

She made another pointless circuit: oxygen tank valves checked, sat probe ready with pediatric wrap, pediatric Ambu bag connected to

02, the smallest laryngoscope blades placed and then placed again. Not for control, for speed.

The tightness behind her eyes was just fatigue.

Pretty little lies.

The minutes elongated. Time lost edges. She tried to listen only to what she could control. She tracked her breath in and out, counted to four on the inhale, six on the exhale, the way she had taught patients in panic. Her chest refused to loosen. She stopped counting.

Then a faint thrum threaded the air, so low she thought she had invented it. The noise built slowly until it lived inside her bones, a low roll that gathered in her chest and refused to leave. Twenty-six minutes after takeoff—eight minutes longer than the estimated flight time—the radio crackled.

"Bell One to Ops. Two minutes out. Mother's stable on 02. Kid's barely moving air."

The relief hit so hard Sloane's knees buckled. She gripped the crash cart. *She's alive. This time, she's alive.*

This time. What about the next flight? What about all the endless situations where Jax would *always* choose to risk everything?

Sloane exhaled for the first time in minutes and realized her hands were numb. She flexed her fingers, forced them back to life. And waited.

The doors flung inward and the storm came with them in a rush of cold and wet and relief. Bean pushed a gurney with a woman—small, pale, face covered by a mask—sitting with a toddler across her lap, eyes closed, skin blue-tinged, each breath behind the tiny mask a harsh rasp.

"Straight through," Sloane called, already pulling the airway cart closer to the bed. "He's priority. Callie, take Mom."

Jax didn't flinch at the order.

Sloane's gaze caught on Jax for half a heartbeat—rain-soaked, exhausted, triumphant—before she focused on the small face beneath the oxygen mask. He was flushed with the sheen of fever. Skin hot to touch. Retractions cut deep between his ribs with every labored breath. She lifted him up, passed him to Mina. "Keep him upright."

"Brilliant flying, Chief," Bean said.

"Just doing the job." Jax's voice carried exhaustion and satisfaction and the easy confidence of someone who'd beaten impossible odds.

"What's his name? Anyone know?" Sloane asked without looking up.

"Caleb," Bean replied.

"Hi, Caleb." She risked a quick peek in his mouth. Epiglottitis, as suspected. The swollen tissue had nearly closed his airway completely. Minutes more and he would have suffocated. But she could manage this. She could save this one.

"Sloane?" Jax's voice from behind her. Close enough that Sloane could smell rain on her flight suit, could feel the warmth radiating from her body. "He going to be okay?"

"I have work to do," Sloane said without turning. She adjusted the oxygen flow, checked the child's pulse ox. Anything to avoid turning, to avoid seeing Jax's face. Her voice sounded distant, clinical, someone else's. If she let herself feel, the drowned girl's slack face would be back under her hands, ribs breaking, minutes lost. And over it all, the pounding terror of Jax in the air, the Bell vanishing into fog. She could still feel the silence on the comms like it lived inside her soul. "Your job is done, Chief."

"Copy," Jax said finally, her voice gone flat. Professional. Empty of everything that had been there hours ago when they'd lain tangled together in the dark.

A chasm opened in Sloane's heart as Jax walked away, her boots clicking on the tiles. But she didn't turn. Didn't call her back. Just kept working because work was safe and work meant she didn't have to face what she'd almost lost.

What she couldn't afford to lose.

To Mina: "Epi nebulizer."

"On it," Mina said.

Minutes stretched. The boy's breaths grew longer, less sharp. The stridor dulled. Two minutes. Three. The rasping eased a notch. Five minutes. The 02 sat crept up. Not normal but better. Relief tried to uncoil, and Sloane strangled it where it started. *You don't get to feel yet.*

Mina met Sloane's eyes, nodding once. "He's holding."

"Good. Give him some liquid Tylenol and schedule his next dose of antibiotics and dex." Sloane stripped off her gloves, dropped them in the bin. "I'll go check Mom. Call me if anything changes."

Hours later, when both patients were stable and the storm had broken into fitful rain, Sloane retreated to the supply room. Just for a minute. To gather her armor. The adrenaline had drained, leaving only a tremor in her hands and the echo of ribs cracking under her palms. Outside, the storm was easing, but inside the same flood remained—fear, grief, the impossible need to breathe in a world where breathing meant feeling.

The drowned girl haunted her—blond hair lifting with each compression, blue lips, the terrible stillness after. Sybil's face overlaying hers until past and present merged, until Sloane couldn't untangle which failure hurt more.

And Jax. Flying into conditions that could have killed her. Flying because every life—every other life but her own—mattered. Proving with every dangerous choice that loving her meant accepting any flight could be the last.

I can't do this. I can't watch someone I love die.

She'd survived Sybil's death by building walls. She'd survive this the same way.

Better to let Jax walk away, while she still had the strength. Better to retreat where feelings couldn't touch her. Better to be alone than to love someone who might walk out the door at any moment and never return.

The vow forged itself again, cold iron around her heart.

Love equals loss. I can't do this. Never again.

She scrubbed her face with the back of her hand and forced herself upright. The next day would come, as they all did, and she'd be ready. She'd make sure of it.

Even if it meant her heart would break, she'd still survive.

Even if it meant choosing survival over living.

Surviving was something she knew how to do.

And love—love was a luxury she couldn't afford.

Not ever.

Chapter Twenty

Day 10
Clear skies

Dawn didn't so much arrive as bleed in, a bruised light seeping in through the rain-streaked window. Jax rolled out from under the blanket and shook the stiffness from her shoulders. The roadhouse was quiet at oh-four-hundred. Eli was likely downstairs at the comms station, where he often napped in his chair. Bean was…somewhere. Probably with Sarah. Good for him—at least he wouldn't question why Jax was bunking in his room rather than her own. A quick shower and, with luck, she could slip out without running into anyone.

Like Eli.

Her stomach twisted. The lie tasted bitter.

Not Eli. Sloane.

She didn't want to see Sloane—hadn't been able to face spending even a few hours in the same room with her, not when the cold look in her eyes cut all the way through. Not after the careful blankness in her voice when she'd said *Your job is done, Chief.* Like Jax was just another crew member. Like hours before they hadn't been wrapped up in each other, skin on skin, whispering things that had felt like promises.

Her luck held, and twenty minutes later she pushed the gym door open. The place smelled different at dawn—less antiseptic, more human. Sweat and coffee and the particular mustiness that came from too many bodies in too small a space for too many days. She stood in the doorway while her eyes adjusted to the dim interior where a handful of patients still slept on cots arranged in neat rows.

Mina looked up from where she was adjusting an IV line on an elderly woman, her face showing the particular exhaustion that came from pulling a double shift. "Chief. Didn't expect to see you this early."

"Couldn't sleep." Her voice felt rough, like the storm had left grit in her throat. "How's Caleb?"

"He's stable." Mina gestured toward the nearest bay where the baby, his face covered by the blow-by mask, lay sleeping in his mother's lap, his face nestled to her shoulder, his breathing audible but no longer labored. "Airway's clear, fever's down. Another day or two of antibiotics and he'll be good as new."

Jax nodded, not trusting herself to speak. A win, then. The odds in their favor once again. The flight from Pine Ridge had been tight—tighter than she'd admitted over the radio. Wind shear that had nearly put them into the ridge, visibility so poor she'd been flying by instruments and instinct, praying the terrain mapping was accurate. But the kid was alive. That counted for everything.

"You look like hell," Mina observed quietly.

"Thanks."

"I mean it. When's the last time you slept more than two hours at a stretch?"

Jax shrugged. "Where's Sloane?"

The question came out before she could stop it.

Mina's expression shifted, became assessing. "Finally convinced her to get some rest an hour ago. She refused to leave until Lynette took the parents of the drowned girl to a shelter house."

The drowned girl?

Jax narrowed her eyes. "Is that the emergency Eli called her for last night?"

Mina raised a brow. "Mm-hmm. Right about the time you left for Pine Ridge."

Jax flushed. Mina was too sharp not to pick up that she and Sloane were together when Sloane got the call. Nothing to do about that—not that she needed or wanted it to be a secret.

"The girl didn't make it?"

Mina's eyes filled with sorrow for an instant. "The girl arrived in full arrest. Had been down too long. She was already gone."

Sloane lost a girl. A drowned girl. Jax's throat clamped tight. No way that didn't tear Sloane up inside. God damn it. She hadn't been there for her.

"How's she doing?" she asked carefully.

Mina's look turned sharp. "You should ask her yourself."

"I don't think she wants to talk to me."

"You know why?" Mina set down the clipboard she'd been holding, crossed her arms. Unflappable, solid in a crisis, always-positive-Mina looked hugely pissed.

Jax's stomach tightened. "I wasn't—"

"Fifteen-year-old girl. Blond hair. Not much older than Sloane's sister was when she drowned." Mina's voice stayed level, clinical, but her eyes held fury. "Sloane did CPR for thirty minutes straight. Broke the girl's ribs trying to bring her back. Came close to breaking herself."

Fuck. Jax's head pounded. Blond hair. Sybil's age. Sloane's hands on a dead girl's chest, compression after compression, trying to save someone who was already gone. She couldn't give up, though, could she? She'd built a life saving people—had saved countless numbers the past few weeks. But that was never enough. And to lose a girl just like her sister…

"I wasn't here," Jax muttered.

Mina jerked a hand dismissively. "*That* is not on you. No one could have changed what Sloane felt just then." Softer now, "Believe me, I tried."

"But then what? She iced me. Like we were strangers." Jax pushed a hand through her hair. "Because I flew Caleb and his mom back?"

"Because you could have died," Mina said, as if she was correcting a clueless student.

The pieces clicked together with sickening clarity. Sloane standing beside a drowned girl who looked like her dead sister, while Jax insisted on flying against Eli's orders, into a storm no one was supposed to fly in.

"It's the job," Jax said, hearing how weak that sounded even as she said it. She wanted to rage. Wanted to shout at Sloane that pushing people away didn't keep them safe—it just made *you* alone. But anger wouldn't help. Anger was easy, and Sloane deserved better than easy.

"She was terrified," Jax said quietly. Not a question.

"She stood by the radio for twenty-six minutes, listening for your voice. I've never seen her look like that. Like she was waiting for the world to end." Mina shrugged, as if the answer was obvious. "Then you walked in and she did what she always does—work. She also did what she does when she's bleeding inside—she put up a wall."

Jax clenched her fists. *I'm an idiot.*

She'd known the flight was risky, had made the calculation that the kid's life was worth the danger. But she hadn't thought about what it would cost Sloane to wait. Hadn't connected the dots about how Sloane would feel watching someone she cared about fly into potential death. And she'd let Sloane push her away. Had stayed away like a damn coward. Pride, maybe. Or worse, fear.

Almost to herself: "So she pushes me back so I can't be a thing she loses."

"And maybe pushes herself somewhere she can't get hurt," Mina said.

"She thinks loving me means watching me die," she said, the words tasting like ash.

"Does it?" Mina's question carried no judgment, just honest curiosity.

"I don't know." Jax met her eyes. "I fly rescue. That's what I do. Sometimes the conditions are shit and I fly anyway because someone will die if I don't. I can't promise her I'll always come back."

"Then what can you promise her?"

The question hung in the dim gym. What could she promise that wouldn't be a lie? "I don't know."

Mina nodded, no judgment in her eyes. "Then that's your answer—at the least the one you need to find."

"I don't like being shut out," she said. There. The truth. Why should she take a chance on opening up when Sloane might just walk away? Like everyone else in her life had done.

"I don't see you as a quitter, Chief." Mina's voice stayed gentle. "You'll have to decide what matters, the job or the woman."

"That's not fair."

"No one ever said love was fair." Mina picked up her tablet again. "I need to make rounds. Don't wait too long to decide."

Jax nodded, her chest too tight to breathe properly. She heard Eli's voice—*Bell grounded*—and heard her own answer—*Out here, I call the shots*. She could admit the cost of that truth.

Talk to Sloane. And say what? *I love you but I might die doing my job, so let's just see how that goes*?

Mina was right. Silence wouldn't fix this. Distance wouldn't bridge the gap Sloane was building between them, brick by careful brick.

"I won't let her push me off the pad and pretend that's safer," she said, more to herself than Mina. "That's not how we land this."

Mina shifted the tablets to her other arm. "You want coaching or you got it?"

"I've got it," Jax said.

She didn't. Not really. But she had stubbornness and a mission, and both had gotten her out of worse weather. "When she wakes up, I'll try again. Not at her. With her."

Mina's mouth eased. "There's the pilot I trust."

"Thanks…for this." She'd survived enemy fire and mechanical failures and weather that should have killed her. She could survive a difficult conversation with a woman who was terrified of loving her. And she would not let fear—hers or Sloane's—be the thing that decided where they landed next.

She hoped.

❖

Sloane woke from uneasy half-sleep to the crackle of the radio. For a moment she didn't know where she was, only that her hands ached and her forearms buzzed as if she were still doing compressions. Then the smell—coffee gone old in the pot and pine cleaner—brought the room into focus. The roadhouse.

The sheets on the bunk above hers, still tucked in military-tight the way Jax always left them, confirmed she was alone.

She hadn't seen Jax since she'd sent her away. That was also the point.

Weary, nearly numb, she rolled over and grabbed the radio off the floor.

Eli's voice cut through the static. "All available, briefing in five."

Groaning, Sloane stumbled down the hall. The shower ran cold but she didn't care, let the water wash away sweat and the particular exhaustion that came from too many hours on her feet. She dressed in clean scrubs—her last pair—and went downstairs to find coffee.

Eli was in his usual place in front of the comms array, but his posture was different. Relaxed instead of coiled for crisis.

"Trouble?" she asked automatically.

He grinned, the expression so surprising Sloane halted mid-step. "What?"

"FEMA is coming."

The words took a moment to penetrate. FEMA. Federal Emergency Management Agency. Which meant official disaster response, which meant infrastructure support, which meant—

"We're done?" Her voice came out flat.

"Transition for a day or two, but basically yeah—we're wrapping up."

She should feel relief. Pride, maybe. They'd accomplished what they'd come to do—provided emergency medical care in impossible conditions, saved lives that would have been lost without intervention.

Instead, a hollow ache filled her.

People straggled in over the next few minutes—Bean looking rumpled, Callie her usual energetic self, Mina moving with the careful fatigue of someone who'd worked through the night. And lastly, Jax, appearing in the doorway in a crisp, clean flight suit despite the early hour, her expression professionally neutral, her gaze sliding past Sloane without hesitating.

She should feel relieved—again—and yet, for the second time in as many minutes, only the dull throb of disappointment registered. Her chest constricted, and she looked away first, focusing on Eli.

"FEMA liaison is inbound. They'll be here by mid-morning to start takeover operations if their birds thread the passes." Eli's grin widened. "Well done, team. We survived another one, and so did a hell of a lot of people who wouldn't have without us."

A round of exhausted applause sounded.

"Sloane," Eli said, "we'll need updated evac priority ASAP."

Sloane nodded, focusing on the details of the work to come. Work, always work, came first. And for her, brought sanity. FEMA would bring their own medical team, their own logistics support. The gym would be converted to a proper field hospital. Critical patients would be transferred to appropriate facilities. The Bell would fly its last supply runs and patient transports.

"We're looking at forty-eight hours before full turnover," Eli concluded. "Let's make them count."

FEMA is coming. The thought was both relief and threat. Relief: ventilators, drugs, evacuation transport, fresh bodies who weren't running on fumes. Threat: strangers with clipboards who hadn't spent time with these patients in the dark.

The end of the greatest challenge in her career. The end of something else she didn't want to examine now. She walked the half mile down to the gym because setting a brisk pace in the misty air distracted her from thinking. Even the town looked different under a sky too clean for the damage below it, as if readying for a new beginning.

Inside the gym, the tempo had shifted. Less frantic, more purposeful.

"Morning," Callie said, sorting names into columns on a whiteboard with a marker: *hold/stable, watch, move when able*. Mina moved bay to bay checking vitals, explaining with a smile what was about to happen. "Hard to believe it's all so easy. Yesterday seems like forever ago."

"Yes," Sloane said flatly. Yesterday was another world ago. "Caleb?" Work. Keep the focus.

"Sleeping with his mom," Callie said. "Stridor's gone. Dex is doing its thing."

"Good." Sloane dragged the word from somewhere beneath her ribs that stung and crossed to the board, steadying herself with the cap of a dry-erase marker in her fingers. "Priorities?"

Callie slid her a list. "Two cardiac with unstable rhythms—"

"Beecher and Townes," Sloane said.

Callie blushed. "Yes. Um…" She glanced at the list. "Hoffman, with the second-trimester bleed. She stabilized overnight but needs observation and probably extended bedrest."

Sloane only half listened. She knew the history of every patient in their makeshift hospital, but Callie needed the training. "Frankel?"

"Oh, yes," Callie said quickly. "His temp is better but the latest white count is up. We're out of vanco, too."

"He goes early, then. Possible sepsis. If FEMA can land, those all go first. If they can't, Jax and Bean can start doing short hops out of the valley to the nearest FEMA ground command."

Callie blinked. "Um, I should let her know that?"

"Yes." Sloane walked away to start the drug inventory.

Jax. Just saying the name burned through her—heat and despair braided together.

"Medical," Eli's voice came over her radio, "you copy?"

"Sloane here," she said automatically.

"FEMA bird is calling the pass marginal. Not committing yet. Jax and Bean are prepping anyway. They'll lift if the window opens."

"We'll prepare the first four for transport," Sloane said, and her voice didn't crack, so that was something.

The day unspooled in a blur of activity that left no room for thought. Jax and Bean ferried short hops south and back when a window opened: the septic man first, then the bleeding mother with her partner's hand rigid around hers like the grip itself could stop loss, then the patients with probable myocardial infarcts.

Every time Sloane heard the Bell return, something unknotted a little and then retied itself, as if letting down even for a second would invite the next disaster.

The afternoon wore on. Seeing last-minute cases: the man who'd minimized his chest pain until he couldn't, the teenager with a splinted forearm that looked straight but wasn't, the young girl with rule appendicitis who turned out to be pregnant. Patient assessments and discharge planning, coordinating with incoming FEMA personnel, inventorying remaining supplies.

The specter of the girl in bay one, the time 03:57 carved into her bones.

Every time the rotors spooled, she automatically started the minute count, caught herself, and ruthlessly dragged her mind back to the work before her. She would not listen, would not wonder where Jax was, what she was doing. What she was feeling—if she felt anything at all.

Then Jax's voice would sound on the open channel, coordinating a run with Eli, reporting a successful drop-off, updating the weather conditions. Sloane's breath would catch, her chest tighten, and inside longing would blossom.

Time after time Sloane pushed the ache deeper. She had done this. She had pushed her away. That was what she'd wanted.

Except it wasn't. What she wanted was impossible—Jax safe and close, the risk eliminated, love without the shadow of loss. But that wasn't how the world worked. Loving someone who flew rescue meant accepting that any mission could be the last. Meant living with constant low-level terror that the next radio call would bring news of a crash.

And she couldn't do it. Couldn't survive that kind of fear.

Better to end it now. Better to—

"Sloane." Mina's voice cut through her spiraling thoughts. "Got a minute?"

Sloane nodded and followed her into the supply room, the space cramped with boxes waiting to be carted out to ground transport. Mina closed the door, crossed her arms, and fixed Sloane with a look that promised no mercy.

"What are you doing?"

"Working. Same as you."

"Bullshit. You're avoiding Jax like she's got something contagious."

Sloane's jaw tightened. "This isn't the time."

"You're almost out of time."

The words hit like a slap. Sloane stepped back, anger flaring hot in her chest. "You don't know—"

"Not everything, no. But I know you're scared. I know that girl yesterday looked like Sybil and it broke something open in you." Mina's voice gentled slightly. "I know watching Jax fly into that storm terrified you."

"Then you understand why I can't—"

"I understand why you're scared. I don't understand why you're giving up."

"I'm not giving up. I'm being realistic." Sloane clenched her hands. "Jax flies rescue. That's who she is. I can't ask her to change that, and I can't live with the constant fear that she won't come back."

"So instead you choose to lose her?" Mina shook her head. "That's not being realistic. That's just a different kind of drowning."

The metaphor landed with surgical precision. Sloane's throat closed, tears threatening for the first time since the girl had died under her hands. Since she'd lost her.

"I can't stand to have someone else I love die," she whispered.

Mina sighed. "Well, that's a start?"

"What?' Sloane mumbled, rubbing her forehead as if that would ease the pounding inside her skull.

"You just admitted what matters the most." Mina shrugged. "You've never been a coward, Sloane."

"But I am," Sloane whispered.

Mina hugged her. "Bullshit. You're not."

Sloane laughed shakily and gave herself one minute to rest her forehead on Mina's shoulder. "God, this is so hard."

"Mmm. Yeah. That's called living." Mina held her away with both hands on her shoulder. "My money is on you, baby."

"I don't even know what I'm supposed to do," Sloane muttered.

"Live. Every minute, as fully as you can."

"You make it sound simple."

"It's not simple. It's the hardest thing in the world." Mina's voice softened. "But, Sloane, you deserve to be loved. You deserve to let yourself love someone without punishing yourself for it. Sybil's death wasn't your fault. And Jax's choices aren't your responsibility."

"I don't know if I can do that," she admitted.

"Then figure it out. Because Jax deserves better than being pushed away because you're scared. So do you."

Mina left her alone in the supply room, surrounded by orderly shelves and the illusion of control. Sloane sank onto a storage crate, her head in her hands, and let herself feel the full weight of what she'd done. She'd spent twenty years believing that if she just tried hard enough, was good enough, she could prevent loss.

But she couldn't. The drowned girl had proven that. All her skill, all her desperate effort, and the girl had died anyway. Then she'd pushed away someone who made her feel alive for the first time in her life.

The coward's choice, Mina had called it. And she was right.

But that didn't mean she was strong enough to make the brave choice.

By nightfall, FEMA's white vehicles dotted the field, and strangers moved through the med bays that had once been hers to command. Sloane finished rounds with the lead FEMA physician, a National Guard captain who moved much the way Jax did—self-assured, clear-eyed, unwavering. The confidence, the competence, made Sloane recall the first time she'd seen Jax, and pain lanced through her so swiftly she almost stumbled.

Was that what the future would hold? Instead of the fear of loss, the pain of it?

Too wired to sleep, too tired to eat, she lingered on the roadhouse porch, watching the last light fade behind the mountains. The storm had cleared, leaving behind air so clean it hurt to breathe. On the hill behind her, the Bell sat empty—Jax and Bean had returned from the last flight of the day hours ago. She hadn't seen Jax when she'd returned.

She should go inside. Should eat something, sleep, prepare for tomorrow's continued transition. Instead, wrapped in a borrowed jacket, she watched the river below, still roiling but finally receding, and let herself feel the ache of loss.

The door behind her opened and footsteps scuffed on the planks. She knew the gait before the shape took form.

Jax stopped, not too close, the warmth of her a step away, the faint scent of motor oil and clean wet air rising off her.

"We need to talk," Jax said, voice quiet but carrying an edge that made Sloane's pulse jump.

Sloane didn't turn.

Run or stay?

Risk or safety?

Win or lose?

Chapter Twenty-one

Day 11, after midnight

A chill traveled through the porch boards and up through the soles of Sloane's boots. Below, the river, high and silt-brown, curled back on itself where boulders broke the flow before rushing on as if hoping to escape. Part of her longed for escape, too. Away from this place that had worn her defenses thin, body and soul. But Jax's presence behind her was a physical thing, patient and solid and electrifying. The constant she'd come to count on. Search for. Need.

Her pulse kicked against her throat. She'd been listening for Jax's footsteps all evening, dreading and wanting this confrontation. She turned slowly. Jax stood in jeans and a dark blue button-up shirt, backlit by the interior lights. Her expression was unreadable, but the set of her shoulders radiated a sense of determination that vibrated in the air between them.

"Jax, we'll both be going our separate ways, tomorrow or the next day." Sloane grasped the porch post, steadying her tattered resolve. "Can't we just move on?"

The words tasted like ash. Splinters bit into her palm, the sting a pale echo of what burned inside.

"No." Jax stepped close enough that even the semidark couldn't cloak the weariness in her eyes. "You don't get to decide alone. You don't get to push me away without at least a conversation."

Sloane's throat closed. She'd known this was coming. Had dreaded it and wanted it—pretty much exactly what Jax instilled in her every time she saw her. Desire and retreat.

"I'm not good at this," she said finally.

"Talking?"

"Not just talking…any of it."

"Then I'll start," Jax said, her voice low but steady. "I know about the girl who drowned. I know how hard you tried to bring her back."

"Mina told you." Sloane sighed, not even angry. Mina knew her, had never pushed her all the years she'd shut herself away from others. And more importantly, Mina loved her. "People die."

"Yes, they do." Jax lifted a hand as if to touch her, then let it fall. "I know you were afraid I would be next when I flew back from Pine Ridge."

Sloane lifted her chin. "And I had every right to be afraid. Fear keeps people alive."

"Sometimes," Jax said. "Sometimes it just keeps them alone—banks built high until the river rises and breaks them apart."

Sloane didn't flinch, but the strike landed. She wrapped her arms around her middle, holding back the anger and the pain. "She was only a little older than Sybil." Her voice cracked. "Blond hair floating every time I…just like—" She stopped, swallowed hard. "I can still see her. See both of them. Their faces blur together until I don't know which memory is which, which failure hurts more. I lost them both."

"That must have been hell for you—losing *anyone*, but like that?" Jax shook her head. "If I could bring her back to you, I would."

Sloane's throat tightened. At the bottom of the slope, a branch spun in the current, drawn down, released, drawn down again. No escape from the inevitable power of the relentless water. "You can't bring them back. Not the ones already gone." She looked back at Jax. "You can only not lose another."

"Is that what last night was?" Jax asked. "You don't want to lose me, so you just want me gone?"

Sloane closed her eyes. The honesty in the question hurt more than any accusation. "It was me trying to avoid the kind of pain I already *know* will destroy me." She opened her eyes. The river rushed on, no time for grief. "You flew when *everyone*, including Eli—whose judgment you trust—warned you not to. God, *ordered* you not to."

"You're angry about that," Jax said quietly.

"Angry?" Sloane's voice rose and she didn't care. Heat flooded her chest, her face. She was past pretending she didn't feel what she felt. "I was—I am—*furious* with you. I stood by that radio for twenty-six minutes thinking you were going to die because you insisted on flying into that storm. Because *you* couldn't accept that you aren't invincible."

"I *flew* because I couldn't live with not trying," Jax said. "That's how I'm wired."

"I know that. I also know you could have died, and you'll risk that again one day."

"I need you to understand something." Jax moved closer. "I'm not Sybil. I'm not drowning. And I don't want to die."

Sloane caught her breath. "I can't watch you fly into situations that might kill you and just pretend I'm okay with it."

"I'm not asking you to pretend." Jax's voice gentled. "I'm asking you to trust me. To trust that I know what I'm doing, that I'm as invested in coming home as you are in having me come home."

"What if that's not enough?" The question came out broken. "What if you're as good as you think you are and you still die? What if I lose you anyway?"

"Then you lose me." Jax reached for her hand, held it despite Sloane's instinct to pull away. "How is that any different from what you're doing right now? You're pushing me away."

"At least this way I'm in control of it."

"Are you?" Jax's thumb traced circles over her knuckles. "Because from where I'm standing, fear is in control. Not you."

The truth of it struck deep. Sloane tried to pull her hand back, but Jax held firm, forcing the words to live between them. When her life had shattered, she'd built walls and called them shelter. They *had* sheltered her—until they didn't.

"I have a right to be afraid," she said softly. "It's about what happens to me if…"

She couldn't finish, refused to be haunted by the images.

"When I was in Afghanistan," Jax said, her voice barely audible over the water, "we had a pilot. Guy named Martinez. Best stick I ever flew with. He could thread a needle in a sandstorm."

Sloane waited. The cold air bit at her cheeks. Jax's hand tightened fractionally on hers.

"He died on a milk run. Supply drop, clear skies, routine as hell. Mechanical failure no one could have predicted." Jax's jaw worked. "I was supposed to fly that mission. He took it because I'd been up for thirty-six hours straight, and he told me to get some sleep. He didn't make it back."

Sloane's chest tightened. She squeezed Jax's hand, unable to find words for what that image did to her—of Jax, young and watching her friends die. "I'm so sorry."

"I spent a year thinking I should have died instead of him. That if I'd just flown one more mission, if I'd been less tired, if I'd checked the bird one more time…" Jax stopped. "But that's not how it works. There's no magic number of checks that keeps you alive. No amount of skill that makes you invincible. You do the job, you accept the risk, and you come home when you can."

"How do you live with that?" Sloane asked. "How do you get in the cockpit knowing you might not come back?"

"Because someone has to." Jax turned to face her fully. The moonlight turned her face to sculpted marble. Cool, beautiful, timeless. "And because the alternative—not flying, not helping people who need it? That would kill me slower but just as sure."

"If you don't come back," Sloane said, "I don't know if I can survive that."

"You survived the worst thing already," Jax said softly. "And you made a life where other people survive, *live*, because of you."

"That's work," Sloane said. "This is…" She searched for a word that could describe the magnitude. "This is the part of my life that isn't protected by professional distance. This is…all of me."

Jax sucked in a breath. This time she didn't stop when she reached out to cradle her face. "You want a promise I can't make. I can't swear I'll always come back." She skimmed her thumb along Sloane's jaw. "But I can swear I won't lie to you about risk. I can swear I won't take stupid chances to prove anything to myself. And I can swear I won't walk away because loving you scares me."

Sloane half laughed. "Does it?"

"Terrifies me."

"Why?"

Jax sighed. "I'm afraid I'm not enough to make you believe I'm…we're…worth the risk. Afraid that you'll choose safety over us, and I'll lose you without ever really having you."

"You have me," Sloane whispered, grasping Jax's hand. Warmth flooded into her, reaching places she hadn't realized were cold. "The other night we had each other."

"And that was incredible. *You* were incredible." Jax squeezed her hand. "But I want more than one night. More than one week. I want whatever lies ahead for us…for however long we have."

Sloane looked at their joined hands. Jax's calloused and strong, hers still trembling. She'd spent twenty years running from this moment. Twenty years choosing safety over connection, control over vulnerability. And where had it gotten her? A half-life of work and loneliness, relationships that ended before they were even born, a carefully ordered existence that grew more hollow each year.

"I don't know how to do this," she admitted. "I don't know how to care about someone without trying to control every variable that might hurt them."

"Time for a new plan. In the ER, you control every variable that you can," Jax said. "With me, you trust what you can't."

Sloane shook her head, unable to hold back a small incredulous laugh. "That sounds like a terrible plan."

"It's the one I have," Jax said. "And I'm asking you to try it with me." She leaned forward. Kissed her gently. "Be the one who keeps people alive and be the one who loves someone who flies into fire."

Sloane's heart filled in places she'd never before realized had bled with emptiness. She wrapped her arm around Jax's waist. She needed space to breathe, but not from Jax. "Walk with me?"

"Anywhere."

The muddy path along the river grabbed at Sloane's boots, little stones sliding away as she walked. Jax still held her hand, steadying but not leading her. The river flattened into a long, even tongue of water that reflected the sky. A kingfisher chattered somewhere up ahead. The roadhouse lights faded behind them until only the moon lit their way, silver on black water. They walked in silence for several more minutes, their boots crunching on stones, their breath visible in the cold air.

Jax stopped where the riverbank flattened into a narrow strip of stone. She didn't let go of Sloane's hand. "Say it—tell me what scares you most."

"I'm a doctor," Sloane said. "I'm supposed to save people. That's what I do. That's who I am. And I couldn't save Sybil, and I couldn't save that girl yesterday, and if something happens to you?" She pressed her palms against her eyes. "That's a failure that will destroy me."

"That's not how it works." Jax's voice was firm now. "You didn't fail Sybil. You were twelve. And that girl yesterday? Mina said she was already gone when she arrived. You gave her every chance. That's not failure. That's just…" She paused. "That's just loss. And loss isn't your fault."

"It feels like my fault."

"I know." Jax wrapped an arm around her shoulder—the same move she'd made in the Bell that night up on the mountain. Comforting, strong, gentle. "But, Sloane, you can't save everyone. No one can. Not you, not me, not anyone. And trying to prevent every possible loss by shutting people out? That's just dying slowly."

Sloane gripped the back of Jax's shirt. The river rushed past, dark and endless.

"What if I can't do it?" she whispered. "What if every time you fly, I fall apart?"

"Then you fall apart." Jax's voice was matter-of-fact. "And then you put yourself back together. And we keep going."

"That's not fair to you."

"Let me decide what's fair to me." Jax kissed her temple. "I'm not asking you to be perfect. I'm not asking you to never be scared. I'm just asking you not to run."

Sloane took a shaky breath. "I love you. The feeling is so big, so powerful, it scares me more than losing Sybil, more than that girl yesterday. Because this—" Her voice broke. "This I chose. This I walked into knowing the risk."

Jax's breath caught, her whole body going still. Her free hand came up to cup Sloane's face, fingertips brushing through her hair. "I love *you*." Each word deliberate. "Even when you're being stubborn about it. Even when you're scared. Even when you try to push me away."

Despite everything, Sloane laughed. "I'm going to be terrified every time you fly. I'm going to struggle with this. I'm not going to magically stop being scared."

"I don't need you to stop being scared." Jax leaned in, pressed her forehead to Sloane's. "I just need you to stay. Can you do that?"

Could she? Could she stand in the fear instead of running from it? Could she love someone without the guarantee they'd survive? Looking at Jax's face in the moonlight, feeling the warmth of her despite the cold air, Sloane made her choice.

"Yes," she said.

"Then that's enough." Jax pulled her close, wrapped her in an embrace that felt like coming home.

"The whole truth, then." Sloane framed her face, met her searching gaze. "I love you. And whatever comes, I won't stop loving you. I won't punish you for doing work you're made for, and I won't let fear control me—control us. If I need you to come home to me, I will say that aloud, and I will trust you to hear me."

Jax pulled her close, kissed her with a tenderness that made

Sloane's throat tight. The kiss tasted of promise and moonlight and the cold river air. "I will, Sloane. I will always hear you."

The river rushed past, the night settling around them like a benediction. In the circle of Jax's arms, Sloane relinquished her doubts and surrendered to the need for her. The careful control she'd maintained for twenty years finally released her. Desire for Jax filled all the hollow places she'd protected for so long. A passion, a need, she welcomed now, without fear.

"I am never going to get enough of you," Jax murmured against her temple.

"I'll be there." Sloane threaded her arms around Jax's waist. "FEMA takes over tomorrow. Then what?"

"I fly for a living." Jax's voice was careful now, measured. "I can live anywhere."

Sloane's heart kicked hard against her ribs. She knew Jax's rhythm like the rhythm of the rotors spooling up. Knew Jax never lifted off without a course firmly set.

"Flight plan?"

Jax lifted her chin. Kissed her lightly. "Waiting to file it."

"Then I want you to live with me." The words hung in the cold air between them. Sloane's heart hammered so hard she thought Jax must be able to hear it. She'd never asked anyone to share her space, her life. Had never wanted to until now.

Jax's breath caught. An endless moment passed before she rested her forehead on Sloane's. "Okay. Okay, *yes*."

Sloane laughed. "Just like that?"

"Just exactly like that. You…" Jax closed her eyes briefly, and when she opened them her eyes shimmered. "You make me want more than I ever dreamed possible. You make me want a home."

Sloane pictured it with sudden, vivid clarity: boots by the door—no, on the mat where they belonged; two mugs on the counter each morning; a flight kit hanging on a hook by the door; the sound of rotors only sometimes meaning goodbye, more often meaning welcome home. The image didn't scare her. It looked like the future she'd stopped believing she could have. "We can do that. Together."

Jax's smile came slowly, bright enough to rival the moon overhead. "Yeah?"

"Yeah." Sloane sealed the vow with another kiss, deeper this time, pouring everything she couldn't say into the connection between them.

When they broke apart, both breathing hard, she rested her cheek on Jax's shoulder. "Tomorrow we start a new mission, one that will take us a lifetime or more."

Jax rested her chin on the top of Sloane's head. "Copy that."

Morning mist lifted off the river in slow curls, the current carrying sunlight instead of debris. Ahead, the first clear day waited—unfinished, uncertain, and theirs to make of what they chose. The river ran on, still high but no longer threatening. The banks held. The water, for now, had found its course. And so had they.

Chapter Twenty-two

Boston
Six months later

Sloane woke in the dark, her internal clock marking the time before she opened her eyes. Four forty-seven a.m. Jax's flight briefing was at seven. She'd need to leave in just over an hour. Shifting closer, she pressed against the warmth of Jax's body, splaying her palm across the firm plane of her stomach. She ought to be used to the ripple of muscle, the softness of silky skin, after touching her hundreds of times in the last months, but every caress brought a rush of breathless wonder and renewed anticipation.

Jax's breathing changed, the subtle shift from sleep to waking that Jax often tried to hide so as not to wake her. It never worked—when Jax was anywhere near, she knew it.

"I'm awake," Sloane said quietly.

Jax turned her head, finding Sloane's eyes in the pre-dawn darkness. "Hey."

"Morning." Sloane traced the line of Jax's jaw with her fingertips, absorbing the softness of her skin, and skimmed the small scar above her eyebrow. She smiled at the way Jax's pulse jumped when she dipped lower and rested her hand on Jax's chest. "What time do you need to leave?"

"Hour and change." Jax's hand covered hers, stilling her exploration. "Sloane—"

"I know." Sloane heard the unspoken questions. Was she okay? Would this morning be like the early ones when watching Jax leave tormented her with fears of disaster and loss? "I'm good. I promise."

And she was. The fear was still there—would probably always be there, a low hum of anxiety whenever Jax flew into danger. But it didn't paralyze her anymore. Didn't make her want to hold on so tight that neither of them could breathe.

She leaned in, kissed Jax with deliberate intent. Not goodbye, not yet. Just *here, now, us*.

Jax responded immediately, rolling them so Sloane was beneath her, their bodies fitting together with the practiced ease of six months' learning each other's rhythms and desires. "You're sure?"

"I'm sure." Sloane pulled Jax's tank top over her head and mapped the familiar yet endlessly fascinating landscape—the strong lines of her shoulders, the scar tissue on her ribs from an old injury, the way her muscles tensed and released under Sloane's touch. "I want you. I want this."

Making love in the pre-dawn quiet couldn't be more different than those desperate times in Coulter's Gap. Less frantic, more certain—but never less exciting. Beneath the rising tide of need, Sloane embraced everything—the weight of Jax above her, the heat of skin on skin, the building pleasure that made thought impossible and necessary all at once.

When she came apart, Jax's name on her lips, the lightness of being echoed the breathless moment when the Bell lifted away and left the earth behind, soaring into endless sky. And as sharp and indelible as the moment in a trauma when everything narrowed to the essential—breath, heartbeat, and the singular focus of living.

This was freedom—the moment of *her* choosing to be fully present, fully vulnerable, fully *here* with someone who might leave but would always come back.

Afterward, they lay tangled together, Sloane's head on Jax's shoulder, listening to her heartbeat slow. The room lightened gradually, gray to pearl to the first hints of gold.

"I love you," Sloane said. The words came easily now, without the accompanying terror that they'd once carried.

"I'm so glad." Jax pressed a kiss to her temple. "God, I love you."

When the alarm on Jax's phone finally broke the spell, Jax tensed slightly—the shift into mission mode, the gathering of focus that happened whenever she prepared to fly. Sloane eased away just enough to say *I know you have to go, but don't forget where you belong.*

"Shower?" Jax asked.

"I'll make coffee while you're in there." Sloane sat up, reached for her robe. "You want breakfast or just coffee?"

"Just coffee. I'll eat at the briefing."

Sloane padded to the kitchen, the familiar routine soothing in its ordinariness. Ground the beans, filled the reservoir, pressed start. While the coffee brewed, she leaned against the counter and looked around their apartment—*their* apartment, not just hers with Jax's things added.

Jax's flight jacket hung by the door. Her boots lined up neatly on the mat. The bookshelf held a mix of Sloane's mystery novels and Jax's history books. Two coffee mugs on the counter, one that said *World's Okayest Doctor* that Jax had given her as a joke.

Evidence of a shared life. Evidence of choosing each other every single day.

The shower shut off. Sloane poured two mugs of coffee, carried them to the couch, and waited. Jax emerged in her flight suit, hair damp, moving with the efficient grace of someone who'd done this a thousand times.

"You know what you said once?" Sloane asked as Jax sat beside her. "About the joy you found in flying?"

Jax accepted the coffee, took a sip. "Yeah?"

"You said it was the purest thing you knew. Being at altitude, everything falling away except the aircraft and the sky and the mission." Sloane set down her mug, turned to face Jax fully. "I didn't understand it then. But I think I do now."

"Is that good?" Jax's expression was soft, open in the way it only was with Sloane.

"Yeah." Sloane took Jax's free hand, threaded their fingers together. "Because that's what loving you feels like. Everything else falls away and there's just this," she gestured between them, "this connection that makes everything else make sense."

Jax's eyes went bright. She set down her coffee, cupped Sloane's face in both hands. "You're killing me here."

"Sorry." Sloane wasn't sorry at all. "I just wanted you to know. Before you go."

"I'm coming back." Jax's voice was fierce. "I'm always coming back."

"I know." And she did know it, deep in her bones where fear used to live. "I'm not afraid anymore. Or rather"—she corrected herself, because honesty mattered—"I'm still a little afraid every time you leave. But it doesn't control me. You leaving doesn't feel like losing you. It feels like you doing what you were made to do. And that makes me proud."

Jax's thumb traced her cheekbone. "Sloane, I love you. Every time I leave, a part of me is thinking about coming home. Home—a place I never thought I'd have, so I stopped dreaming of it. Until you."

Sloane kissed her. "I spent twenty years believing that love meant loss. That caring about someone gave them the power to destroy me. But you taught me something different."

"What's that?"

"That love isn't about preventing loss. It's about choosing connection despite the risk." The words felt true in a way that nothing else ever had. "So I'm telling you to go. To fly into those variable winds and dicey terrain. To do the work that makes you feel alive. And I'll be here when you get back."

Jax stood, pulled Sloane up with her, held her close for a long moment. Sloane breathed her in—soap and coffee and the particular scent that was just Jax—and let herself feel the fullness of it. The love, the trust, the bone-deep certainty that this was real.

"I'll be home soon," Jax murmured against her hair. "Two weeks, maybe three."

"I know." Sloane crossed to the door, stood close. "I'll be here."

"I know you will." Jax cupped her face, kissed her slowly. Memorizing. Promising. "I love you."

"I love you, too." Sloane's hands fisted in Jax's jacket. "Fly safely, baby."

"Always." Jax kissed her once more, then opened the door. She stepped into the hallway, turned back one more time. They held each other's gaze for a long moment, everything that needed saying already said.

Sloane stood in the doorway, watched her as she headed to the stairs, waited for her footsteps to fade as she disappeared into the stairwell.

Then Sloane stepped back and closed the door.

Inside, Sloane moved through the apartment—*their* apartment—and headed for the shower. She had her own shift starting in two hours—twelve hours at Boston Mercy, twelve hours of trauma and triage and the particular satisfaction of bringing order to chaos.

Her life. Not half a life spent waiting, not an existence built around avoiding pain. A real life—full and complicated and sometimes scary.

A life that included loving someone who flew into danger, trusting them to be careful, believing they'd come home.

Until then, she had her own work to do. Her own lives to save. Her own days to fill with purpose and meaning.

A life to live.

And someone worth coming home to, who was worth waiting for—because coming home to each other was a choice they both made.

Every single day.

About the Author

In addition to editing over twenty LGBTQIA+ anthologies, Radclyffe has written over seventy romance and romantic intrigue novels, including a paranormal romance series, The Midnight Hunters, as L.L. Raand.

She is a three-time Lambda Literary Award winner in romance and erotica and received the Dr. James Duggins Outstanding Mid-Career Novelist Award from the Lambda Literary Foundation. A member of the Saints and Sinners Literary Hall of Fame, she is also an RWA/FF&P Prism Award winner for *Secrets in the Stone*, an RWA FTHRW Lories and RWA HODRW winner for *Firestorm*, an RWA Bean Pot winner for *Crossroads*, an RWA Laurel Wreath winner for *Blood Hunt*, a Book Buyers Best award winner for *Price of Honor* and *Secret Hearts*, and a 2023 Golden Crown Literary Award winner for *Perfect Rivalry*. The first book in the Red Sky Ranch romance series, *Fire in the Sky*, was a 2024 GCLS romance award winner. She is also a featured author in the 2015 documentary film *Love Between the Covers*, from Blueberry Hill Productions. In 2019 she was recognized as a "Trailblazer of Romance" by the Romance Writers of America. She was named a Woman of the Year by *The Advocate* (2021), included in the Out100 (2022), and was selected for *Curve*'s Power List (2025).

In 2004 she founded Bold Strokes Books, one of the world's largest independent LGBTQ publishing companies, and is the current president and publisher.

Find her at facebook.com/Radclyffe.BSB and follow her on Twitter @RadclyffeBSB.

Books Available From Bold Strokes Books

Experts Only by Kel McCord. Torn between comforting solitude and the irresistible pull of connection, Michelle and Cas begin to wonder if the life they thought they wanted is enough. (978-1-63679-945-2)

Never Say Die by Meredith Doench. Detective Rory Scott's personal and professional lives converge as she races against time to find the connection between two crimes and bring a killer to justice. (979-8-90035-051-6)

Swept Away by Radclyffe. When ER physician Sloane Marshall is called in as a last-minute replacement for a federal outreach mission in the remote mountain town of Coulter's Gap, she doesn't expect to fall in love with a sharp-edged helicopter pilot. (979-8-90035-050-9)

When Hearts Collide by Renee Roman. A car accident isn't a likely way to meet the love of your life, but when Harlen's and Annie's hearts collide, they may not have a choice. (978-1-63679-923-0)

Yes, Honey by Claudia Parr. Four sexy couples break stereotypes about committed sex to explore lust and love when the honeymoon is over. (978-1-63679-992-6)

The Moon to Me by Ana Hartnett. Sometimes it takes traveling thousands of miles to discover what's been yours all along. (978-1-63679-918-6)

Royal Rush: 75 Days to Fall in Love by Lissandra Rowe. When a royal matchmaking scheme leads to a chance encounter with Isabella Acosta-Ramon, a slow burn sparks that neither can deny. (978-1-63679-965-0)

To Love Violets for Their Thorns by Rachel Sullivan. Forced to face the heartbreak they never quite got over, Elly and Sonia must decide: breathe fresh life into an old love or try again with someone new? (978-1-63679-928-5)

Virtually Perfect by Melissa Sky. If your AI flirts better, listens harder, and never ghosts you…does that count as love? (979-8-90035-005-9)

Brooke Takes Queen by Alaina Erdell. Brooke Staley faces personal and professional upheaval when Elizabeth Bettancourt, the emotionally scarred new owner of the resort she works for, considers selling. (978-1-63679-886-8)

Coda by Anna Gram. Parker is intriguing, magnetic, impossible to ignore—and completely wrong for Hannah. But sometimes love's melody refuses to end. (978-1-63679-926-1)

The Debutante Dilemma by Jane Walsh. Two debutantes are engaged to wealthy and titled brothers…but discover they only have eyes for each other. (978-1-63679-896-7)

The Love Book by Gun Brooke. When literary agent Rowan Cross receives an anonymous manuscript that deeply resonates with her, Verity realizes she has accidentally sent her own manuscript, complete with her very real feelings for her boss! (978-1-63679-850-9)

Secrets Under the Junipers by Suzie Clarke. Who killed Hallie Lynn Peeples? Cecilia McConnel needs to know. Bitsy Hanover holds the key. Can love uncover secrets? (978-1-63679-845-5)

Traveling Toward Forever by Erin Dutton. When almost-strangers take a road trip through America's national parks, love may be the final destination. (978-1-63679-894-3)

Beautiful Things by Emma L McGeown. A warmhearted romance of missed chances, undeniable chemistry, and a stubborn love that maybe, just maybe, can find its way back. (978-1-63679-934-6)

The Great Popcorn Romance by Georgia Beers. Opposites attract, and Riley Shaw stands no chance of resisting Hannah Kramer's magnetic pull. But opposites know just how to drive each other crazy… (978-1-63679-910-0)

Love Takes a Village by Karis Walsh. As Lena Preiss struggles to manage a busy restaurant in the Bavarian Christmas village of Leavenworth, Washington, chocolatier Devin Meyer brings an unexpected richness into her life, along with her delicious desserts. (978-1-63679-902-5)

Secrets of the Heart by Jenny Frame. When a beautiful stranger starts asking questions about Nikki Sharkey, head of an infamous crime syndicate, Nikki will stop at nothing to protect her daughter Isla. (978-1-63679-653-6)

www.ingramcontent.com/pod-product-compliance
Lightning Source LLC
LaVergne TN
LVHW090601110826
845146LV00001B/215
* 9 7 9 8 9 0 0 3 5 0 5 0 9 *